I0595819

the
Ebony
Queen

The Ebony Queen

A Medieval Romantasy

ABBY LANE

A REIGN OF BLOOD & MAGIC

BOOK TWO

Published 2016, 2020 by Abby Lane
(abby-lane.com)

ISBN: 978-1-7770699-1-9 (Print edition)
ISBN: 978-1-7770699-2-6 (Kindle eBook)
ISBN: 978-1-7770699-3-3 (Other Digital edition)

Design and cover art by J. Caleb Designs
Copyediting by Karen Crosby, Editarians
Proofreading by Ted Williams

For Pat Hynes
For his inspiration,
For believing in an author's story,
For supporting me even before a pen
scribed words into sentences.

Pat, I've thought of you often while writing
The Ebony Queen.
I hope you enjoy this second book in the Odin Saga.
Thank you for your support and encouragement!

Acknowledgments

To my readers, family, and colleagues, thank you for supporting my writing career. I especially thank my husband, Wayne, who assists me and supports me in every thing I do.

I am grateful for my adult children and their partners: Carrie and William, Shawn, and Alicia and Trevor. I love the joy, puppies, a new bunny, and even the noise they bring to my life.

I appreciate my mom, Inez, who shares every one of my Facebook posts! I wish my friends would, too. 😊

No book is published without assistance and advice. I thank my author colleagues, Katie O'Connor and Brenda Sinclair, for their thoughts and suggestions. I thank my champion copyeditor, Karen Crosby, and my line editor, Ted Williams, for polishing my words.

A huge shout out to J. Caleb Design for a kick ass cover, which I adore. The cover image of Her Majesty Cynara in the forest represents a cunning witch in the best way possible.

And thank you—for buying my book! You have supported my author goals, and I hope you enjoy reading book two of A Reign of Blood and Magic.

Chapter One

QUEEN MOTHER CYNARA

The sun dipped beneath the horizon of an anxious kingdom, a kingdom where medieval corridors and peasant quarries were shadowed with a concerned people, fretting about the marked consequences that had befallen them since the death of King Rickard. What future harm might come to pass during the miserable days ahead, and what could a secret alliance do to solve the difficult matter of *the Ebony Queen*, if anything?

Autumn had arrived. The preceding months had reaped persistent chaos: Princess Scarlett was dead, *the people presumed*; Princesses Ruby and Rose were missing from the castle; King Lowell was a puppet to his mother's commands. Every bad omen, it was said, began in one wicked place and ended there, too.

The Queen Mother Cynara…

It made no difference to her what the kingdom believed. She had determined to rise above malicious women and their whisperings since a bitter experience as a servant. If fateful schemes came to her now, years later, cutting words and curt dismissals were to blame. *Queen Cynara evil?* Bah! It wasn't malevolent sin flowing through her arteries, her mind cleaved intelligence, her heart no more than a motor to drive her purpose, to seed plans of supreme magic. There was nothing wrong with using magic.

While she suspected spying, no one in the kingdom was wise enough to predict her desire for further power. 'The learned' believed that artistic talent, such as invocation spells, were unattainable. Yet, she trusted that black curses, bewitching spells, and well-crafted plagues were a means to further her ambition.

Cynara had delved deeper than most witches and wizards had dared to go; by seeking the vilest spirits who had been condemned to the Netherworld, thus sinking into nether lands of self-consciousness and depravity. She meditated until demons had been written into her spells, spells that would set her world downside right. *What was wrong with discovery?* Discovery seeded ambition and power could not be gained without taking risks.

If the dark ages were about to dawn, *as the people say*, Cynara embraced the night and the evil she had become. She strode toward her goals with a sleek determination.

Deep inside the king's forest, beyond the hollow glen, she waited in the vale, eager, *listening*, sitting on the earth's reconstructed floor. A black cape fell from her shoulders and extended away from the length of her petite form like a fan-shaped tail, its silk settling on the ground. Seated inside a three-ringed circle, Cynara waited for Daemonis, the satanic devil.

She stretched her arms wide, her fingers reaching for an apparition she had envisioned in her third eye; her fingers extended, not raised to the setting sun, but palms downward to where the earth rumbled, bled and sorrowed, as she sought the one who could cause greater harm and contract her revenge.

Daemonis—

"Come to me, assist me," she said, chanting. "Visit me inside the circle."

Cynara didn't know whether the lord of the damned would grant her request. Neither did she trust a fallen angel to assist a woman who had not fallen herself. But her greed was rewarded when the wind moaned and caliginous vapors swept in from the sea, howling through the trees and blowing her hood from her head. She searched the forest, trying to see from whence he came, but only the sight of flying dirt and scurrying leaves met her investigation, but then her ears were pierced by a screaming whistle that only a fallen angel would cry.

Eager to see him, she reclined against the ground and prostrated her arms and legs outward, extending her limbs toward the quadrants of a three-ringed circle she had enclosed herself inside, her forehead pressed against the ground, her breathing controlled, inhaling and exhaling in a measured way while smelling the pungent scent of earth beneath her nose.

"Attend me. Come to me, Daemonis," she said, whispering, chanting in humming tones, sometimes singing, mumbling an unspoken language of the gods.

Consequor mea...

A fiery wind caressed her back and a clutch of slithering coils attempted to snatch her from the ground. She closed her eyes and her hair flew wildly about her face. *His* fingers pressed against her side and grasped her buttocks. A grating voice penetrated her eardrums from somewhere within the gust.

"Here I am, the fallen angel you cry for. The lord of the damned you wish to overpower. *Again. Ego paeniteo huc,* I am here. What do you want?"

Cynara attempted to rise, but a burning sensation held her immobile and enveloped the contours of her feminine figure, forcing her to merge with the topsoil. She shuddered, sinking. "Let me rise, and I will tell you."

"You don't want to rise, Queenie, or see the one you greedily cry for. You seek to sink further into the ground. You think by doing so that everything you want will come to you. You will not see me, or garner my full attention, until you share why you lured me inside this vale, and why I should listen to a word spoken from your mouth."

Impatience rankled Cynara, but she had expected his testing, having experienced it before. She didn't attempt to rise, but she did desire to manipulate his power for her own benefit, so she pressed her lower back against his strength and found him strong and wanting.

"I desire the gifts that only a god could give me. I desire a partner who will satisfy this strength."

A hand, an embrace of the wind, wafted about her silken-clad figure. She closed her eyes, intrigued by the heated contact that caressed her back, his fingertips, momentarily stroking the contours of her face.

"I've entertained your desires before, but why should I satisfy you now? I can obtain human souls much younger than yourself, slipping inside a varied lap of sexual sin."

"I have more experience than the cattle you're accustomed to fetching inside your den with a staff." Cynara snickered, licking her lips. "I'm not a lamb, nor a sheep to follow the flock to slaughter. I carve my own destiny. I have risen to the height of queen. I aim to rise higher."

She felt his respiration against her neck, a warmth that stressed his authority, gave credence to his power, and affected her awareness. His hands slid across her calves, his fingertips massaged her legs and caressed her thighs, his length pressed against her buttocks and settled more firmly atop her feminine shape. Cynara understood this attempt at dominance.

"You didn't rise to your societal stoop alone," he crowed, licking her neck. "I remember your attributes; I remember them well." He breathed hot air against her neck, his whisper scorching the soft tissues. "Even so, I didn't say I wouldn't want you, or that you had not captured my interest. A devil would be remiss to ignore a woman who holds such fine and evil attributes."

Cynara attempted to shift her position.

"Oh no," he crooned. "Please don't move, Queenie. I enjoy a pliant woman, a woman who is open to evil doings. But are you willing to do everything required to have your desires fulfilled? What will *you* sacrifice to fall deeper into sin?"

Considering the question, Cynara closed her eyes, enjoying the painful heat he inflicted on her figure. She felt his hand stroking the delicate tissue of her right breast, then slowly meandering along the length of her right arm, prodding with his fingertips, reaching for the fingers that lay compliant but were still touching the edge of the circle.

"Everything," she whispered. "The promise of my soul, if necessary."

He snickered. "You don't have a soul. You gave up your heart years ago to feed your own self-worth."

Cynara knew his remark was true. She remembered lying beside him, desiring the build-up of heat emanating from his body, the strength, authority and supremacy, even the subsequent orgasm. Having seen his evil presence as a powerful force, once she'd touched such influence, she had wanted the ability for her own.

"Despite our past, I'm willing; I'm ready."

He laughed, a cry that threatened to burst her eardrums. "I see what you want. Greed and gluttony flow through your mind like the blood circulating through your veins." He pressed his lips to her earlobe, clasped her fingers and enclosed them within his fist. "But I'll never relinquish my powers, not even to you. One man has already become a victim to your deviance, but you cannot impair an angel who has already fallen."

"Daemonis—" Cynara argued with him, "I don't want your powers. I desire only to use your supremacy, to achieve my goals."

"A goal named Scarlett? You want to harm the princess Scarlett. No more than a slip of a girl, what did the woman do to earn your hatred?"

"Does one have to act to earn disfavor? I need a lioness's

cub out of the way, weakened so she can never threaten the seat my son sits on. It's the roar of nature."

"Your quest has nothing to do with *Panthera Leo*. You stole the throne from the princess," he said, guffawing. "The only being that threatens the current chair of state, as I see it, is you, Queenie."

The remark caused her to anger. Nicknames were no more than an unwelcome epitaph borrowed from the grave, and she wasn't prepared to sink that far. She fought his grip, twisting beneath him, but he was stronger than her and brought the back of her hand to his forehead. "Let go of me," Cynara screamed, raging. "If you won't help me—"

"I didn't say I wouldn't help you," he said, kissing her hand. "But I don't extend ability or influence without gaining a fee in return, and more often than not, a remuneration of greater value."

Cynara slumped to the ground, sinking further.

"What must I sacrifice to gain your assistance?"

"To have a life, you must be willing to give a life."

Cynara had to see his face, and although he held her hand, she turned in his grasp. He permitted her to move, permitted her to shift until she stared into his black eyes. A handsome man, Daemonis exuded power in a dark and sinister way, but maybe she saw what she wanted to see. When she felt his power, her eyes brightened with interest. "What must I give?"

His lips rose upward into a grin; his hips settled against her erogenous zone. "A child."

Cynara's eyes rose upward in speculation. "I'm beyond the age of childbearing."

"Queenie," he purred, kissing her forehead. "The spawn need not be delivered from your loins."

"Who then, will carry this child?" she asked, wincing.

He splayed her on her back. She arched her neck backward, giving him full access to her flesh. The pleasure, *oh,* the pleasure, she hadn't experienced such sensuality since... The sensations weakened her.

"I won't tell you. You must agree, not knowing."

"What are you up to? Why would I agree to such a scheme without knowing the entire cost?"

"Because the payment serves my purposes well. If we are successful with your plan, I may rise from the fallen, and that notion intrigues me. Do we have a deal?"

"How do you know what I want?"

"I know what you hunger for. I see the power you seek." He licked her lips, and she shivered. "My patience has worn thin. Agree to my demands, to my fee, or let the power you seek slip away."

Cynara thought about the agreement. What choice did she have? No other option existed but to partner with the devil to achieve her goals, and damn the fallen angel, he knew as much.

"We do," Cynara replied. "We have a pact."

He let her rise to her feet, but a look in his eyes made her wary. "I require one precondition."

"What would that be?" Cynara demanded, her cheeks reddening.

"Your name written on my blood contract."

Cynara smirked, but the humor did not reach her eyes. Though as long as the deal was struck, she wouldn't burden herself with the consequences. What did she care about a babe not yet born? Some seeds spoiled.

"I will give you a child, but I need one gift in return. Call it a sign of good faith."

A brush of wind paired with her hand.

"I respect you, Cynara Musadora. You are perfectly made. An evil fortress and profane to the core, but be warned, *be careful;* the edge of the circle you reach for could become your undoing and your destiny. Balance, Queenie. Evil winds require equilibrium, or disaster ensues."

Slicing her wrist, Cynara dabbed her finger in the red blood and signed the devil's contract, not heeding his warning or bothering to read the fine print. The deal was done.

PLEASED AND OPTIMISTIC for her future, Cynara reined her chestnut mare along the beaten earth of the trail, loitering in the king's forest, and in no hurry to return to the castle. Dead leaves crunched beneath the horse's feet.

Looking upward, she reflected absent-mindedly on the gray crevices of a large, full-white moon while visions of malice and victory caused her hand to clench into a fist. Absorbed in her hateful schemes, she nearly missed the frightened whimper of the pawn. But when Maisie came to a halt on the trail, her ears raised and alert, Cynara listened, too.

"Ah," she said, reflecting. The thrumming pulse of fear hid within the shadows, crunching amid the leaves. And then, a human brushstroke rubbed against an oak. A stranger waited, watching from somewhere within the bracken. *Had someone followed her? But who would be so bold?*

"Who goes there?" she called out, searching beyond tall grasses and ferns, eyeing the bramble and tall oaken trees, scouring the night shadows to pinpoint where the beating heart hid.

Cynara decided to try her new gift and moved her hand in a circular motion. When a slight breeze dispelled from her fingertips, she smiled with satisfaction. Her stellar wind infused the air, disturbing particles, as the draft swept through the trees.

"Come out!" she cackled, searching. "You're already found."

But she wasn't surprised when the rodent didn't respond. The nature of the small at heart was to hide in their getaway spot, hoping. She shook her head, understanding, having once been a trivial sapling, too.

She jumped down from the horse and walked toward the fluttering thrum. Unafraid, she raised her hand in front of her, reaching toward the heartbeat, which was surely an enemy's. She tested her strength a little more, urging the wind to strengthen into a gust. She wondered what drafts she could throw if she were angry. She tested that, too, considering her enemies, permitting anger to flow through her veins, and then, furrowing her brow, she pulled her arm back and thrust the wind forward. It funneled through the trees, causing them to bend, causing her little mouse to scurry from its hiding place and scramble through the bracken.

Cynara rushed forward, pursuing, reaching toward a young, ordinary man. Though he was well muscled, the spy was soon wrapped in an invisible grip. Throwing him to the ground, she stalked closer until she stood above him, staring downward.

Cowering, the pawn raised his hands to protect his face. "Who are you?" she said, scrutinizing the pest. "Do you spy on me?"

"Your Majesty, my queen. I won't tell a soul," he said, visibly trembling. "For the sake of my wife and my children, don't hurt me."

Cynara laughed, considering the fear etched on his face. "It's too late to care about your family," she replied, stepping closer, unaffected by sympathy or empathy. Hardened, Cynara saw that his hand shielded his face as if she might strike him.

Insensitive, she snickered. "I don't know how you found this place, but I won't permit you to share my secrets, what you may have seen or heard. As for your children, it's you who should be fretting. No one can know; not even my son."

She sensed his fear; he nearly soiled his pants with the trepidation. "Finding you here was an accident." He croaked. "I was taking a walk."

"And a lengthy exercise, you've undertaken." Cynara challenged him, her tone curt. "How dare you lie to me. Do others know of your meddling here? Who sent you? Who begged you to spy on the queen?"

"No one," he responded, almost too fast. "I assure you, 'tis only I, a peasant, hungry in the forest, seeking a stag to feed my family."

"You have no weapons."

"I dropped them when I tried to escape your notice."

Cynara paced forward until she stood so close to him that she could see his eyes shifting back and forth. "You lie once, I take your tongue. Twice, you lose your arm. Thrice, your life hangs in the balance. I'm warning you. What traitor sent you to spy on a queen?"

He did not respond. Without touching his skin, she squeezed his throat. "Tell me."

He stared at her, his face turning blue. "I. Will. Not."

Cynara released the pressure and he fell backward in relief. "It doesn't matter. Whoever sent you to spy on me has failed. We will return to the castle. I'd have you tortured to get to the truth, but you might spill the details of my visit in the forest. Ah, we can't have that. So, I'll awaken the guards when we return, and have you placed in a cell. The price is high for hunting a stag in the king's forest, and higher still for taking the animal's life."

"I didn't. I haven't!"

She waved her hands as if manipulating an enchantress's wand. "Oh, but you have. And with blood dressing your peasant clothes, everyone will believe it's true."

Clearly shocked, he stared at her in astonishment as crimson red soaked and spread across his tunic.

Cynara then threw a widow's curse and wrapped the interloper within the strands. Returning to Maisie, she brought the mare to where the culprit lay, fretting on the ground. She retrieved a length of hemp from her saddlebag, tied it around his ankles, and then secured the rope to the saddle horn. The tough fibers of her curse flexed and wobbled in his forlorn attempt to free himself.

She dismissed his actions. He was wasting precious

energy. No benefit could be gained from his struggle as he'd find no escape. She climbed aboard her mare, soon prompting the horse to walk.

Satisfied the pawn could not harm her, and that a *spell* had silenced his tongue, she dragged him behind the horse and made her way back to the castle.

Chapter Two

KING LOWELL

On a bitterly cold day, lacking warmth and human compassion, the kingdom of Velez faced the queen mother's treachery. The people prayed a god might intervene to deliver them from her madness, thereby preventing Wodensday from dawning, but their prayers went unanswered and the morning dawned anyway, as mornings always do, although graver than expected.

A thick white haze crept in from the sea, smoking the lower hills and denying a shaft of sunlight from penetrating the eastern horizon. Perhaps the god of war didn't understand the situation, as he had not done his part to grace the land with protective magic.

King Lowell didn't welcome pagan gods and had ignored the Privy Council's warning. Preparing himself for a sentence that must be carried out, he stood in front of a golden reflecting glass, appraising his shoddy appearance. A strained forehead, grizzled cheeks, and tense worry lines darkened the hollows beneath his steel blue eyes. He searched for the likeness of his father in the reflecting glass, considering the blue of his own eyes while remembering the emerald green of the former king. His father's visage had begun to slip away, blurring with the passage of time, but the man's opinions still carried weight.

If the choice were yours to make, Father, would you have decreed the same punishment?

Lowell supposed it didn't matter what a former king may have reasoned; he was dead, helpless to support the actions of the new king either way. The opinions of his royal parentage or his king's men—or anyone else's, for that matter—shouldn't concern him. He alone must face his reservations and live with the consequences.

Still, the deed he must bear witness to brought him no joy. He did not smile as he withdrew from the mercuric glass. *Good humor would not find him smiling on this sickening day.*

He walked to the bureau and reached for a pair of tan leather gloves, which lay haphazardly on its wooden surface. Slapping them once across his arm, he strode across the space to a large wooden door. Kennard of the bedchamber waited for his approach, wearing an equally dire expression that Lowell had worked hard to weal against his tanned skin. The servant opened the door like a well-trained soldier. Obedient, he did not talk to his sire unless instructed to do so.

Lowell passed beneath the threshold with his head held high, his booted feet striking a drum chord against the stones, which to him echoed the coming act. No more could he play the boy; the boy-king now marched forward as a man while contemplating the hunt. He hurried through the gallery's corridor, giving no notice to the door warden, Roydan Risley, while passing.

I can do it. I can pull the crossbow taut and let the arrow fly.

The pending decree held no different drama than the official signing of a royal order. He promised himself, he would see this nasty business accomplished, and by his own hand. *Who was he trying to convince?* He must prove his merit as a man and as a king, to everyone, to the people, but especially to his privy councillors.

Finding the entrance to the turret, down the stairs he strode, his booted feet tapping on the stones in a well-spent rhythm while making his way to the bottom. A female servant yielded to him on the landing, her head lowered, her hands clasped on top of her rounded belly. He made no comment, gazing past the space where she stood as if her simple stance, with her eyesight cast to the stones, meant nothing at all. The chambermaid didn't acknowledge her king, as was expected, though she saw him pass, and would go to his chambers after his departure to attend his royal apartment. Her toils would be for naught, for after his labor, *after her labor*, he would ruin her exercise with a messy reappearance.

Blood. There would be blood.

Normally at this morning hour, he proceeded to the great hall to break his fast, but the fire vents were cold with no logs burning in the hearth to prepare a meal. The previous evening, he had commanded that no man or woman would dine until the hunt had concluded. Frankly, he couldn't stomach the slightest form of sustenance right now, not when regret twisted in his gut like a knife.

Although he could hear a mixture of laboring sounds while nearing the outer courtyard, it was apparent the hounds had been assembled. The eager howl of yowling and yapping dogs, readying for the chase, bruised his hearing. He was prepared, too, though little glory would be found in the chase. Even so, a king didn't shrink from responsibility, whether he liked the labor or not. A boy-king must prove his worth as a man and as a sovereign to his people.

He hoped a son's actions made a dead father proud. His mother for a surety was much pleased with him. *How could the deprivation of life make anyone rejoice?*

When he strode into the courtyard the royal courtiers were waiting, their expressions were grim and scrutinizing as he passed them by, as if their opinions judged his footpath. The grand master of the hunt, Boyce Burleigh, sat on a massive black steed, staring at the ground. The master of the horse, Keldan Ashburn, stood beside a sleek chocolate mare, pretending to study her flank. Henryk Thayer, a large, burly man, glowered at him with an accusatory expression, but Lowell couldn't concern himself with the thoughts of a war bear. Disregarding the large defender, he slipped his hands inside leather gloves and approached his squire, John Willard, and then accepted the reins of Drakones from the young squire's hands, mounting the beast in one fluid leap upward.

He didn't rush to converse with his king's men while settling in the saddle. Instead, he assessed each man in turn, preferring to wield a stern mien, while Drakones shifted on his feet, prancing beneath him, skittish and anxious to run. He held tight to the reins, considering.

Some of the king's men judged Lowell as a boy-king, as

yet too young to rule aptly. He sensed their admonitions by the way they stared at him, measuring his character for a period longer than was discreet. He heard the sarcastic sputter, their voices riddled with sarcasm. He sensed their disapproval through physical movements of heads shaking, eyes rolling, and frustrated sighs.

It was up to him to teach them proper manners. It was time to demonstrate his abilities, physical and otherwise, to these bastards. He would show them the man King Lowell had become, and the stern values he and others must live by. He'd strike the iron if he had to, if only to prove his worth and make his judgments known to all. To everyone.

He took a moment to intimidate the councillors, staring at each of them in an assertive manner before giving thought to speech. Of course, the men knew he was the son of a witch, so they were cautious in their behavior, but he preferred their fear to rise from 'Lowell the King' without the threat of a woman's name bandying about their heads.

"Sir Boyce," Lowell rumbled, clearing his throat. "Has the fox been released?"

Astride his horse, Boyce glanced at the ground. "The fox has been loosed from his cage," he growled, before meeting the king's expression more fully. "A full two hours ago, as you commanded, Your Majesty."

Lowell shifted in the saddle. "And did you wound the fox, as the fox wounded my royal stag?"

"We can end the pretense. The thief has been injured, Sire, stabbed in the ribcage with a queenly knife, but not so much that he could not run, just as you instructed."

"Very good," Lowell said, ignoring the impertinence. He

pivoted on his saddle, holding tight to the pommel with one hand and the reins with the other, openly glaring at the master of the horse. "And what of the horses and the hounds, Sir Keldan, are the animals fit for the chase? Are the dogs hungry for their bounty?"

Keldan's stance emanated confidence. Although he wore a grim visage, an expression presenting no differently than the rest of the king's men, he didn't retreat from the questioning and met a king's bearing with a mien that suggested he disapproved of this business. Lowell was partial to the man, given he was of similar age; even so, he'd been cautious about appearing too friendly.

"The horses have been fed, given water, and are steady on their feet. The dogs have not partaken of their usual chow, as per your instructions, Sire."

Lowell nodded in understanding, then searched for his squire.

"John, pass me my crossbow and quiver."

The lad responded, gathering the quiver and arrows first, and then passing them into the king's outstretched hands. Once the quiver was safely slung on his back, John passed the crossbow to him, too.

Henryk Thayer possessed the cunning of a commanding officer. His distaste stewed for this nasty business, waxed bitter in his angry expression, and echoed in his forbearance. "Do you think to use that weapon, Sire?"

Lowell leveled the crossbow in the constable's direction. "I think to partake in the hunt, Henryk. I won't tolerate disrespect from anyone, including my commander at arms."

He urged Drakones into a slight trot and reined the horse

toward the gate, then gave Henryk a steely glare before passing by him.

"Blow the horn, Nevin," King Lowell called to the intendant of the civil list, who sat awkwardly on a russet mare, perhaps unaccustomed to sitting a horse. "Blow your horn, long and often during the hunt," Lowell reiterated. "Give the people of Velez notice that the penalty phase has begun."

He searched for Boyce, daring him to disobey the order, while Keldan finally climbed aboard his horse. The horn sounded, carrying across the landscape. "Give the dogs the blood scent and then release them to their chase," Lowell commanded.

He struck the reins against Drakones' neck and the magnificent steed sprang into a canter, springing toward the front gateway. The dogs ran ahead of them, yowling and yapping.

"Away with us, my councillors, my king's men."

The gates opened and the riders passed under the portcullis. Lowell listened to the sound of hooves striking against wooden planks as they trotted over the drawbridge, horses and men following the path of the hounds, leading them beyond the castle.

A crowd of peasants had formed on the farthest bank at the opposite end of the bridge. They parted, forming a long human line. The dogs came nearer to them, but soon raced past the people and into the fields beyond.

Nevin Islip blew the horn again and the mournful wail echoed the riders' flight as the councillors trotted past their king, soon passing the people lining either side of the pathway, forming a trail all the riders were forced to pass through.

Lowell didn't rush Drakones forward. He moved among his people slowly, scrutinizing the crowd of onlookers standing on either side of him with the same serious expression he had lorded over his men. He not only wanted the highest peerages to understand his rulings, but also simple men, women, and children.

A peasant woman stepped before him with a young babe nestled in her arms. She searched his sight with piteous alarm while the babe bawled. He didn't have the compassion to look away.

"Please, Your Majesty," she appealed, her face a swollen ruin, rushing in the path of his horse. "Please, don't do this, this wrongdoing…"

He stared beyond her grief and maneuvered his horse to circumvent her petite figure, slinging the crossbow to his back, pressing his knees against the horse's flanks, he urged the equine to run. The response was immediate. The stallion charged forward, leaving the woman and her worries behind. Lowell soon caught up with the hunters. Together, they raced across the field in the wake of baying dogs, who, he could tell, held the blood scent, deep in their nostrils.

Nevin Islip blew the horn again.

Chapter Three

PRINCESS RUBY

A bolt of lightning discharged a current of energy, briefly illuminating the mountain pass. Thunder followed the light and boomed violently, clapping against the upper ridge. Ruby cried out in fright while reining in her skittish mare. She held the reins tightly while the horse pranced and was soon able to bring the equine under her control, before twisting on its back to study a new light trail. Lightning zigzagged across the wintry landscape while she reflected on threats that were similarly ominous if not more so than a natural phenomenon.

When will this nightmare be over? When would she be safe?

A man and woman had risked their lives while riding through the pass and their travels had been laden with difficulty. *What would happen next? What harm waited for them around the bend?* Somehow, she knew an ensuing incident longed to announce itself, and as if in response to her thoughts, a grating din tolled nearby. She searched for the rhythm, a sound and silence that insinuated the forward movement of fear. She held her breath, *waiting*, and her fears were realized when ice fractured high above her head. Peering skyward, dumbfounded, she screamed—sighting a large, sandstone boulder shifting—

Helpless, Ruby watched the massive shelf of blue-gray rock. When it broke free, the noise, more so than the falling rock, caused her mare to dance away from the danger. The boulder rolled and bounced down the mountainside, followed by a deluge of rock, shale, ice and snow. Ruby, too shocked to react, reached for her heart. Time held no meaning; adrenaline and heat suffused her body, her mind. She watched the boulder rolling, breaking into pieces and continuing its journey to land far below on the valley floor, her mouth forming the shape of an O.

"Oh my," she gasped, releasing a sigh. "We've escaped another danger. When will this infernal madness be over?"

Garrett pivoted on his gelding and reined in beside her. He reached for her reins and pulled her mare closer to him, urging her horse away from the slide to probable safety. She witnessed the concern in his patient stare, but was not prepared to admit that while her protector chaperoned her to safety, he could not safeguard her from harm.

"Rubessa," Garrett exclaimed, as rocks and debris continued to fall, "that was close. Are you all right?"

Her fear was quickly replaced with anger. "I'm not sure how I should respond. I'm barely breathing. When will the witch give up on her blood sports?"

"When she accomplishes her goals."

"She must hate me. I survived the scorpion's sting in the

valley. I avoided drowning while crossing the rapids of the Lew River."

"The water rose so suddenly, the current quick, too, but we can't blame the queen for natural events."

"Can't we? Do you really believe these *natural events* are at the hands of Mother Nature? That sarding rock fell from above our heads, has it rolled because of a natural incident, too? I have half a mind to turn my horse around and confront the witch, and I would, if I knew I could win."

Garrett shook his head. "The queen had nothing to do with the landslide. Maybe the sound waves from the thunder wrenched the boulder free. I'm only stating the possibility as I don't believe her powers are equal to what we experienced."

"Maybe," Ruby said, reasoning that her accusations didn't make sense. "I understand what you're suggesting, but even so, she's responsible, no matter what you say, as I would not be traveling through this pass if not for her scheming."

"True enough," Garrett said, studying the mountain face.

Ruby inhaled frosted mountain air while wisps of white vapors escaped from her mouth, too shocked to think about the circumstances of smaller sized shale breaking free from higher peaks, then bouncing and sliding down the mountain.

"Rubessa…"

Ruby groaned, sniffed. "Look, I understood why you've chosen to call me by another name, even why the subterfuge might be necessary, but the name Rubessa fills me with anger."

He seemed confused by her disclosure. "Although I understand your dismay, given our recent incident, I didn't expect…"

"Each time you mention that horrible alias, I'm reminded of the material possessions the *witch* has stolen from me, stolen from my family, and the wrongdoing that has committed us to traveling this trail in the first place." She pointed at the ridge. "I could have died."

"I know, but you're safe. I want to know if you're okay."

"Am I okay? What kind of question is that? How do you think I should feel? My life just flashed before my eyes. Break free of this farce and call me by my real name."

"You know why I can't."

"For goodness' sake, Garrett, what demon can hear the regal sound of 'Ruby' on a mountain pass? What demon even cares? We're high in the clouds where millions of rock bits litter the landscape." She paused, thinking. "It's cold. The spruce trees are less frequent now that we've left the lower hills behind. Surely we are safe from those who would cause us harm."

He took a deep breath. "Calm yourself; you know who could hear your name. No matter where we travel, even here, that woman is a threat."

"Honestly," Ruby said, her voice quivering while staring at his austere expression. "We've crossed land, rivers, and mountain trails for too many days, and frankly, it might be better to end this frustration before the sun sets on our ill-fated ride. Save yourself. I'm a burden too heavy to safeguard. Send me over the edge to lie among the wildflowers and put an end to your chaperoning." She examined yet another rock face and pointed in its general direction. "Permit that monstrosity of a rock giant to win. Let it fall, too."

"Don't chance fate; don't seek bad omens," Garrett

offered, staring at the mountain in obvious alarm. "She shall come if you call."

Ruby scrutinized his concerned expression then glanced beyond their mountain trail, eyeing the valley floor, far below them. "So much has happened. If the queen is responsible for our trials, she won't give up until she wins. Maybe I should join that boulder, slide off my horse and jump. Don't you see, we can't win. Sooner or later, her exploits will catch us unaware."

When she panicked, her chest suffused with heat, struggling to breathe let alone talk, he urged his gelding a step forward. His leg brushed against her lower thigh. She wouldn't tell him she felt fragile, weak, that fear caused her head to ache, that tears were threatening— Nor would she confess that his pressure on her leg, that simple touch he gave, lessened her worry. His touch was human and comforting. She searched his concerned expression for signs of hope.

"Come on," he consoled, grasping her hand. "This pass is dangerous, but no more hazardous than the witch who forced us into this journey in the first place. It's not much farther. We'll reach safety; I promise you we will." He squeezed her fingers. "I've brought you safe this far. Don't you trust me, Rubessa?"

"Stop calling me that," Ruby protested. "I hate that name! If you must shield my identity by using a descriptor separate from my own, at least select a worthy name."

He smirked, releasing her fingers, obviously contemplating. "All right, I'll play your woman's game, but only to set your fears aside. Let me think," he considered, rubbing his bearded chin. "Possibly the name Willow, for you are tall and thin, and with your penchant for anger, you have the need to whip and wallop with your insolence. Willow would be an apt substitute."

She chewed on the name, nibbling at her lips and appreciating the distraction, but then glared at him, giving the impression she had actually considered it. "I don't know, Garrett. I'm made of a far more complex bark than a piece of stripling that can bend with the breeze."

"'Tis true," he whispered, seeming to contemplate further options while studying her facial features intently. "Maybe a name akin to your spirit, such as Bera."

She grimaced, shaking her head in defiance of his ill humor, while fearfully studying the mountain face.

"Maybe a fighting name," he said with a chuckle. "A name that matches your sense of adventure, such as Brunhilda."

"That's a terrible name, Garrett. If you ever have children, leave the name choosing to your wife. But your conversation assists my heart's murmur to return to a normal beat, so please continue with the possibilities."

He regarded her intently, becoming quiet in his observation. Her breath caught in her throat; his sea-blue eyes studied her so. "How about a name worthy of your esteem, your title, your beauty and earthly desires?" he whispered. "A name like—Amira."

"Amira," Ruby considered, tasting the syllables on her lips and scrutinizing an unspoken question lingering in his observation. "I like the name. Perhaps your suggestion holds merit."

He smirked at her in appreciation, sucking in a breath to probe far more than her woman's beauty, as his curious expression toyed with her eyes and warmed her heart. Sensuality rose in his quiet observation; a heated connection made more compelling when he broke their eye contact to stare at his gloved fingers.

She blushed, supposing he knew it was wrong to stare at her like that, given that she was a princess and he no more than a guard paid to protect her. Even so, she was almost saddened when he returned to his protective role and glanced away, clearly avoiding her womanly sight.

"I'll find hope when you're safe, Amira," he stated softly, too softly for a guardsman.

Always watchful, her warden shifted away from her to stare at the mountain, his forehead lined with concern while surveying the upper cliff edges. Tiny fractures of shale broke off the rim and fell. Ruby watched Garrett assessing the larger mass, its strength to stay in place, or not, as well as what could tumble next, then he urged his gelding a step backward. He reached for her reins and ushered her mare forward, leading them farther along the rocky trail. Ruby had been with him long enough to know she was confident in his guidance, his protection; she would follow him wherever he led her, although she had no choice but to accept his care. No other option existed but to be the goat and proceed through the pass, urging her mare carefully forward on a slippery slope.

Garrett offered her a quick wink and then returned her reins. She watched him maneuver his horse. Facing north again, he urged the equine onward and she followed him at a discreet distance. Although, in her current state of fear, she couldn't help herself from glancing at the mountain from time to time, or staring at the pathway they had ridden across, stubbornly searching for the next danger, which she knew could happen at any moment.

THE TRAIL POSED no great difficulty for a time, but regardless, Garrett and Ruby rode cautiously. Ruby noticed a distant flash on the horizon. The light altered, dimming at first and then shifting from a bright cerulean blue to a cool ashen gray. The wind picked up, which concerned her when she observed dark green clouds swirling in the sky. Her mare's ears alerted, standing straight and tall; she whinnied, as if the horse sensed a rising force that couldn't be seen or heard by human senses.

Soon, the airstream whooshed cold against Ruby's skin and pelted her flesh with freezing rain. She cried out in alarm, straining backward on her mare, as frozen sleet whipped at her face. Lowering her head, she shielded her eyes with her hands, but she couldn't protect her hearing as gale-force winds threatened, whistling in the midst of crevices in the mountain peaks, and the sharp, hard, darkening rock. She sucked in a slight breath as the sun retreated behind the clouds and a dark fist shot through the shadows in the sky, its force sweeping closer, swooping toward them like a bird of prey, and shrouding them inside its swirling fog.

"No escape, this time—"

The wind menaced, muttering tales of hatred. Ruby searched for reality in a menacing situation that couldn't be explained. She scanned the mountain pathway, searching for something more solid than a witch's voice, but her hair obscured her vision, the strands flying wildly around her face.

A pressure needled her waist as if prying fingers grasped at the fabric, threatening to pull her off the horse and throw her over the cliff's edge. Her woolen cloak, edged with fur, shifted away from her figure. She couldn't seem to bind the fabric layers around her neck, and she was bitterly cold. She tried breathing normally while suffering from a stifling terror that pressed against them and complicated their breathing as a blanket of snow began falling.

Ruby gasped…

Shaking, she removed a glove and placed her fingers against her freezing skin, now cold to the touch. Pulling a scarf over her head, she wrapped the woolen fabric securely around her neck, pulling the layers more firmly over her nose and mouth, and then returned the glove to her hand. Garrett gazed at her as if from the shadows of the Netherworld, trying to keep his hood on his head. If he had appeared concerned before, now his brow was lined with worry, causing Ruby's anxiety to rise, too.

"We're in for rougher weather," he yelled. "Either a storm is coming or sinister Cynara has pulled a magic trick from her book of spells. We're in for a difficult ride."

Ruby tried to smile, but fear creased her facial features. Her voice fluttered, cracked. "What should we do?" she shrieked, trying to be heard above the screaming, retching wind.

He pursed his lips, releasing a stream of curse words; she watched his breath, steaming from his mouth.

"We ride, but the journey will be difficult," he responded,

his voice strained and his expression grave. "But we don't give in; we fight the storm."

How does one fight a storm?

Garrett turned in his saddle, plucked a length of rope from the front and came close to her, soon tying it to her pommel. He didn't look at her as he wound the hemp. Ruby didn't say a word while waiting for him to speak.

"I'll try to keep you safe, but our best course of action is to keep moving. If we stop anywhere along this trail, we could be swept down the mountainside." He paused, looking at her intently, his frustration etching the seriousness of their plight. "Cynara would like that, but just in case the witch makes an appearance, I want to know you're attached to me."

Ruby scrutinized his eyes, not seeing signs of hope. "We're in trouble, aren't we, Garrett? What are you hiding from me?"

He fashioned the knot without saying a word. He glanced at her briefly then cinched the hemp, tight. A forlorn expression gave her cause for concern. "I had hoped to arrive at Prince Rudrik's castle before nightfall, but nightfall seems hell bent on finding us first."

"What's coming," she asked him, shaking, "and how can we survive it?"

"We're not giving in without a fight," he muttered, swearing under his breath. "But we had best be moving. I fear our time is running out."

Great gobs of snow found them.

Garrett appeared as if he wanted to say more, but he didn't speak. He merely pulled a hood over his head, turned his horse around and merged with the storm.

"It's going to hit hard," he yelled above the sudden howl

of wind. "Cover yourself, Amira. Bind yourself in your layers. Your mare is connected to my horse; so you won't have to face the cold. I'll face it for you and do my best to keep you safe."

"I won't be able to see…" The snow amassed, and drifted forward in thick, white waves. She blinked, trying to see through the white, trying to see Garrett, her only hope in this chaos, but his shape had merged with the shadows.

"I'll be blind—"

"You don't want to see. Protect yourself," he said, bellowing, "here she blows!"

Afraid, her mare lurched forward. Ruby grasped the pommel, not knowing what was worse: shielding her face from blindness and not being able to face the mounting evil, or keeping her eyes wide open, *uncovered*, and trying to see the storm that already stole the breath from her lungs.

Why am I so weak?

She pulled the scarf around her face but left a small opening, so she could see the pommel.

"Please, keep us safe," she implored of the gods in the Otherworld, though if truth be told, she didn't believe in gods. *Not any longer.* Who could believe in a god who had not intervened to protect their flock in times of struggle? Still, she prayed: "Please, keep us safe."

RUBY FELT TWO SENSATIONS: the muscles of her mare rippling beneath her buttocks and inner thighs, and the cold. She gripped her woolen cloak, *tightly*, but even so, the frigid air reached between her fabric layers, assaulting her chest and stealing warmth from her lungs. Time seemed to have no mercy or meaning as they slowly made their way through the pass.

The snow fell thicker, the sheer wall of it almost blinding her. She'd chance to look up, her eyesight blurred, her head dizzy from the snowflakes. Now and then she'd search for Garrett, unable to see him at all, nor the horse he rode on. She'd remember the length of rope that bound them together and was grateful for the bond that disappeared into the ether, or else they would have been lost to each other. She would have gone over the edge.

The cliff's edge—

She tried not to think about how high they had climbed above the valley floor, but from time to time she'd glance to where the ground should be and not know where the edge lay. A shaky threshold she preferred not to think about, nor wanted to glimpse at present, lingered nearby—the long slide downward. The valley below where rocks had already fallen.

Please keep me safe. I want to live!

The fleeting sense of falling caused her anxiety levels to rise. The ledge seemed too narrow, and she guessed they had come close to kissing the sky.

Ruby closed her eyes, too frightened to look. And then, her horse stopped moving. She jerked when Garrett came into view by her side. When had he left his horse?

"Come to me, Amira," he yelled, reaching for her waist. Ruby tried to talk to him, but her voice was stifled from the cold. She tried to lift her leg over the mare's back, but numb, she couldn't move her limbs.

"Are we at the castle?" she asked, trembling. He pulled her from the mare.

"No," he responded, his tone grave. Ruby slid from her horse and collapsed in his arms, her feet soon touching the ground. "We won't make it to Prince Rudrik's castle, but I've found a shelter. We will stay here until the storm passes. Come with me."

But Ruby couldn't move. Physically shaking, she collapsed to the ice and rock-laden pathway, her gloved hands molding with the snow. She barely felt the grip of strong masculine hands clutching at her waist and pulling her from the ground.

"It's all right," Garrett whispered in her ear, his lips skimming a lobe. "I have you. I will take care of you, Amira."

She liked his warm breath against her skin. She leaned into his strength, permitting Garrett to pull her closer to his side, supporting her weight and almost carrying her as he led her through a swirling tunnel of white. She couldn't see the pathway they navigated across. Her fingers were frozen, her legs were numb, but she clutched at Garrett's arm, holding tight to his strength, so deep her trust in him had grown.

"It's not far," he seemed to whisper, "a few steps more. You can do it."

He tried to hurry her along, urging her to move quickly on a pathway that must have broken away from the main trail. The snow blinded, threatening her sight with thick white waves, but then the shadow of a cave emerged in the distance and he led her inside its opening. Once standing inside, she turned in his embrace and pondered his expression.

"How did you find this place?"

"It's the best I could do on short notice," he responded, not answering her directly. He motioned her away, leaving her to support her own weight. Yet, she clutched at his arm. "It's all I could do."

"But how did you know? How could you have possibly known this cave was here?"

"Stay near the mouth of the cavern," he warned, his expression not able to hide his worry. "We're not safe yet. And I need to retrieve our supplies from the horses and settle them near the cave entrance. Try to protect them as best I can from this foul weather. I'll return as soon as I can."

"Okay," Ruby whispered, trembling with cold. She released his arm and stepped farther away from the cave entrance to escape the blinding snow. The whistling sound dimmed, but only slightly. When he turned to leave, she couldn't bear being locked inside this hole without him.

"Don't leave me, Garrett," she begged him, reaching to her protector, grasping his arm. "Please, don't leave me alone."

His stern facial expression didn't change. Ruby searched his eyes for signs of hope and contemplated the strong man she had come to admire. He paused, hesitating. "I have to get our supplies. I have to shield the horses from the storm. You'll be safe; I'll only be gone a moment."

Ruby's mouth chirruped involuntarily. She thought about pleading for Garrett to remain inside the cavern, but she saw the wisdom in retrieving their supplies, so released him and watched him leave the cave. Hope held no bearing as she waited for him to return. She paced back and forth, lowering her animal hood, rubbing her hands together and trying to restore sensation to her frozen fingers. She pulled off one of her leather gloves and slid her fingers across unfeeling cheeks. Stiffened from cold, she barely felt the life flowing within her limbs. Her legs stung from sitting too long. Bending slightly, she rubbed her inner thighs, trying to return feeling to them.

She gazed at the cave's entrance and only glimpsed a shadow of dark fate. The snow may have been white, but it might as well have been blackened coals falling beyond the entrance, sifting along the mountain, dirty shale threatening them still.

Tears pooled in her eyes, blurring her sight, and worry caused her head to ache.

Please hurry, Garrett. Hurry—

He strode inside the cavern and dropped two saddlebags on the ground. Ruby stumbled backwards, nearly tripping on the rock-strewn surface.

An ebony figure shadowed Garrett inside the cave. Ruby screamed when she recognized the female. Queen Mother Cynara, cloaked in the ghostly apparition of the witch, stood behind Garrett. It was the witch, yet, it wasn't the witch. *How could such a visitation be possible?*

Seeing Ruby's startled expression, Garrett pivoted, then stumbled backwards in response, too, noticing the apparition.

The witch raised her hands, muttered her evil incantations, her vile enchantments, and a rumble of sound exploded beyond their shelter.

"Bury them, alive!"

When thunderous fire rocketed from her fingertips, Garrett rushed toward Ruby and threw his weight against her tiny figure, driving her to the ground in his attempt to shield her from the pending collapse. Shale broke free of the ceiling.

Ruby screamed—

A horrible noise, a grinding and juddering separation, rumbled throughout the cavern. The ceiling fell.

Covering her head with her hands and closing her eyes, Ruby curled into a fetal position, aware of Garrett's weight pressing against her back and upper shoulders, his hands gripping her head, his fingers twisting into the strands of her hair and pulling her close. She welcomed the crushing pressure of his massive chest, the slimmest touch of warmth in his grasp while hoping he could still protect her.

A rock struck her leg. She winced in pain, pressed against the rock-hardened ground with the smell of frozen earth, dirt and decay, filling her nostrils.

These earthly elements and the coppery stench of blood and magic, too—

As Ruby struggled beneath Garrett's weight, the reality that the cave entrance had collapsed shook her to the core of her being. She tried to rise, twisting beneath Garrett, but she soon realized that more than human weight pinned her to the ground.

She tried to see among twisting, swirling shadows, but blindness and grit stung her perusal. Waves of matter and pigments of dust floated in the air; shale split and settled between the larger boulders. When the cavern succumbed to silence, with only the occasional tap of a rock striking a limestone surface, she permitted herself to lay her head on the littered floor.

"Garrett," she whispered, aware that his body had become a dead weight against her own. *Silence.* No response from him.

Coughing, choking on dust, she became acutely aware that her head hurt. But as she attempted to see in the darkness, she noted one important factor: her own breathing escaped raggedly from between her lips. She was alive, alive to hear a sound that bathed her soul with fear and sadness.

Alive to hear the queen's all-encompassing trill of laughter.

PRINCESS ROSE

R ose gasped, *dreaming*— Dirt and rock were falling from the sky. Lying on a bunk bed, she gasped for breath, yet she couldn't breathe, couldn't draw air inside her lungs. Raising her hands to protect her face, she tried to shield herself from injury, and though pain battled with an imaginary fear, protecting herself from the illusion was futile.

Fateful images aroused her consciousness, burying one sister, drowning the other—

"Ruby—"

Rose screamed, opened her eyes and thrashed in her bed sheets, fighting unseen demons, telling herself *'it's only a dream'* while sucking streams of wet ocean air mixed with the odor of ship-wood polish, cheap aftershave, and her own grief.

She ceased her struggles, feeling as if an anchor's weight compressed her chest and complicated her breathing. Her head arched against the pillow; her eyes glazed white. The vision persisted and a third eye refocused, gaining sight to hidden caverns inside a mountain fortress, a place where ice, snow and rock tumbled from a hole in the sky.

An opening in the sky? Rose whispered, regaining a sense of reality. *How could an opening in the sky offer hope if her sister was trapped, nay, buried, inside a mountain?*

Rose tried to withdraw from the event; she twisted to her side and knotted the sheets in her hands, hoping that Ruby was alive and safe from harm. But what if her vision was true? She hoped her vision was nothing more than a nightmare, but her visions were often correct.

Ruby might be dead—

Worrying, she scrutinized the captain's quarters, studying the space of her confinement, knowing she was housed in her own dream-world, with thoughts of her sister—hurt and suffering, struggling to breathe, coughing up dust and dirt— echoing in her mind.

Shuddering, Rose shook her head, knowing they were both held in dire circumstances, and sadly, she must focus on her own state of affairs.

She contemplated the sea captain's desk and items of the mariners' trade: a captain's journal, a compass, a candle holder and a shiny gold sextant, all lying on an old outstretched map. She reflected on one missing item. The telescope. The captain, likely on deck, probably held it in his hand to view the open sea, hoping to glimpse land.

She didn't know how long they had been at sea. She had stopped counting the days after illness had confined her to bed. Visions had come to her then, too.

"Another vision," Rose whimpered. She glanced at the front of the cabin, just beyond the captain's desk where the sun streamed inside the captain's quarters through square glass windowpanes.

Only a dream, she assured herself, reflecting on the light. *Ruby is safe—she was safe!*

It was better to focus on her current circumstances, such as the whooshing sounds of the *Sea Monster* as the ship cut through the water. The vessel must have caught moderate airs, for her bow seemed to plow quickly through the oceanic waters. Rose enjoyed the sway, preferring not to rush from the bunk, instead allowing her heartbeat to return to normal. She listened to the creaking of the outer planking, the wash of water spray against the hull, and the sound of men's voices on deck, muttering, laughing, keeping to their duties while she lay in the captain's bed.

Rose sighed, studying the room, still not accustomed to the lot that Theodore had sold her to. She'd maim the man with her bare hands, fell him with a sword if she had the strength, but he was far away from her now, and she was not as brave as her sister, Scarlett. The warden must have returned to the queen's kingdom, the bastard, to support and serve a witch's evil. She'd rather serve the needs of the pirate squanderer, though she could see he was trouble, too.

Help me, Gods of the Otherworld! She didn't know who she could trust.

She saw the manner in which the captain regarded her; she also understood how his crew examined the curves of her womanly figure. She was not yet sixteen, but her bosom was full, her shape perfect, and all the men lusted after her with a disgusting heat that marred their eyes with sinful desire; she knew the miscreants desired more than she could offer.

Rose hated the situation, but she was helpless in their proximity and forced to resist their advances. She could only thank the captain for keeping her safe from debauchery. But she saw the way he watched her, too. He wanted her; she knew he did. Still, he had promised Theodore to make her walk the plank, to throw her from the ship. And although he searched for land, somehow, she knew he would keep his promises.

When a key pressed inside the lock, she glanced at the door. The locking mechanism shifted, clicking, then the knob turned. Captain Edwin Perrow peeked inside his stateroom and then entered his quarters, carrying the telescope and expressing a zest and energy for life with his step. When he noticed she was awake, he paused in his pursuit and permitted the door to shut of its own accord while studying her in a racy and absorbed kind of way; his lips rose upward in a wry grin.

"You're awake, my briny Bella Rosa," he exclaimed, standing near the entryway. No rush to approach her, yet he scrutinized her with the same blue desire she had become accustomed to. A woman could tell.

"Why do you call me by that nickname, Captain Perrow? You do know your charitable acts of kindness will not garner my attention toward your affectionate nature."

Chuckling, he momentarily glanced at the plank flooring, but then shifted closer, nearer to her, his smile broadening. "Lassie, I know you consider my attentiveness toward you scurvy at best, but I assure you, my care, of a sometimes sweet and sometimes sour woman, is honorable."

Rose sat up in the bunk and pulled the covers against her

chest. When his eyebrows rose after the gesture, she wasn't amused. Clearly, he studied her attributes, no different than the rest of the rapscallions who travelled with them aboard the vessel.

"Honor?" she replied, venting her frustration. "I see the way you look at me."

He grinned, bowed, and made a sweeping gesture with his hand. "I don't deny it. A man would have to be a fool not to notice you. Permit me to reveal one of my more masculine qualities. When Captain Perrow finds a golden nugget lying within his bed sheets, a woman cannot blame the man if he has a wanton need to gather the treasure? Perhaps touch it, hold it—"

Rose couldn't help herself; she blushed. "You'd have a better chance of minding your telescope. I'm not a piece of gold, Captain Perrow."

"You're a stunning creature, yet you don't understand the significance of beauty, or how a man might measure it in terms of wealth. You're comparable to a yellow-boy, a guinea tucked inside a man's pocket."

Blushing, she glanced away when his expression suffused her with embarrassment. The forward man had spoken the words so casually, comfortably. Focusing on her coverlet, she tried to hide her innocence, tried to dismiss his scrutiny, but like a moth drawn to a flaming wick, she couldn't help herself. He'd said she was beautiful. She lifted her lashes to stare openly at his visage, studying the heat held within his handsome blue eyes. As much as she wanted to hate this man, day by day, she grew closer to him.

"I know what I am; a woman alone at sea. And you, the captain of this vessel, are my only hope."

"I promise to keep you safe."

She longed to believe the captain, but Rose didn't know if she could trust him. "Will you? Or do you have a different strategy in mind? A slow plundering of my soul, perhaps, a sidestep of manly scrutiny to get closer to my masthead, to penetrate my perimeter with no one the wiser to your actions."

"It's not like that."

"Isn't it?"

"You suggest I'm playing games with you. I don't play games with women or the men I command. I lead; I make acquisitions."

He seemed serious. Rose knew she should proceed carefully, not permitting intrusion of her boundaries. Trust was a factor as well and she didn't know who she could rely on in her current circumstances. But for now, what could it hurt to entertain his hospitality?

She smiled sweetly, studying his sun-dappled face, chuckling nervously. "You amuse me. Life is a game, to you."

"Bella Rosa, you don't know me well enough to make a statement like that. I'm a captain. To me, life is a voyage of discovery while sailing on open waters with no sense of direction."

She scrutinized his blue eyes; a deep mercurial blue that matched the color of the sea. At times, his pupils exposed a gradation of color, dark and mysterious; she was compelled to search within its central dark spot, and longer than was wise.

Likewise, she was intrigued by his endearments, and especially by the way 'Bella Rosa' slipped so easily from his lips, the sound so sweet she likened it to her fingers caressing the edges of fine silk. She liked—*damn her soul*—liked the endearment too much. Its necessity weakened her. An act of kindness she'd never met before. Still, one must be alert to proper courses of behavior.

"It's no more than a matter of faith," Rose said, sighing, "as well as placing my trust in you, or any other man, as well. I like to know which path I'm traveling and the port of call I'm bound for. Not knowing amounts to uncertainty. No one enjoys suspicion or doubt."

"Darling," he whispered, traipsing toward his desk. "I can plainly see you're frightened. But you might as well place your hand somewhere, so why not entrust your care with the captain of this ship."

"I want to trust you," she acknowledged, while watching him slide the chair out from beneath his desk. He sat. A long dark surcoat molded to his figure, dappling about his legs; the mahogany leather vest, age-worn from salted winds, fit him admirably, too. She blushed again, noting the shoulder-length dark hair, curling at his open nape. She returned her sight to his full lips, waiting for him to speak.

"We've known each other for longer than a fortnight. Would it hurt to say my name? Edwin?"

She chose to be honest. "I wouldn't want to grow too accustomed to your grace, for fear you would betray me."

He turned away to place the telescope on the desk, and then gazed at her again, cautiously, tapping his fingers on the desk.

"Still, you think I would betray you. I, the man who talks about your beauty."

"Endearments alert a woman to a man's true intentions," she whispered, sighing again, "but there's more to it than that. A woman can never trust a pirate."

He chuckled at her comment and placed his booted foot against his knee while embracing her attention with a serious mien. "Oh darling, you're sadly mistaken. While I'm not afraid to search for treasure, I'm merely an explorer, a merchant sailing on the sea—searching for land, gold, and other treasures I might find."

"So you say. I've heard you sharing the desire for pillaged loot while conversing with officers aboard this ship. But I know that Theodore paid a pirate, not a captain or a merchant, or whatever you choose to call yourself, to drop this golden nugget, this yellow-boy, into the sea."

"Aye," he admitted. "The man was a scoundrel, but he trusted in the wrong captain. If I were to admit to you that I was indeed a pirate, a dangerous thief, a cunning bastard of robbery, well then, Bella Rosa, you should know that a man of indiscriminate tastes would never drop a pretty piece, such as yourself, into the ocean. It would be a waste of currency."

He winked at her, making a funny clucking sound on the roof of his mouth.

"But you will achieve the task for which you were paid," she said, growing angry, "because Theodore paid you well to do so."

"He compensated me. I won't disagree on that regard," he said, grimacing. "Even so, maybe the pirate robbed him of his cash to finance a trip to undiscovered lands. Have I told you that I have an interest in botany? I search not only for minerals, but also medicinal plants."

Rose openly giggled. Surprisingly, the man's furrowed brow led her to believe he was serious, and annoyingly so. "You're toying with me. I can't imagine you searching for vegetation. You wouldn't know an eukarya from a weed."

He placed his foot on the planking, stamping it slightly in the process. "I assure you, Bella Rosa, I do understand the genus of the eukarya plant."

Rose stared at him with a serious expression, choosing to say his name. "Edwin, if you don't send me to the bottom of the sea, you can never return to the Kingdom of Velez. The queen would have your throat."

"Perhaps," he whispered, musing, clutching his chin. "I never planned on returning to that dark place anyway. And I might add, you may have mistaken my relationship with Theodore and the job he paid me to do."

Rose studied his expression for signs of insincerity, her brows rising in question. "What exactly are you talking about?"

"You shouldn't be concerned about walking the plank. Your fate doesn't wait for you in the blue abyss beneath the surface of the sea, but on new land, when we arrive at the shoreline."

"At the shore?"

"Yes. For whatever reason, the queen didn't want your fate to be death. She wants you reduced to a peasant. All your riches stripped away."

"You'll drop me on a shoreline and leave me?"

"I honestly don't know what I'm going to do. But if I

should accomplish the goal for which I've been paid, you'll be left in a new land to become a wife to a native chief. You might want to jump overboard, after all."

"You'd sell me to an aboriginal war chief?"

"Well, you're a princess, darling. I couldn't sell you to one of lesser rank."

Anger quickly changed to fear. "Captain Perrow, is this the truth of it, or are you playing games with me again?"

But Rose could see by the way his eyes darkened, by the way his brows drew together, that he was serious.

"I've decided to be honest with you. Were I in your position, I would want to know the truth of my circumstances. I will usher you to an undiscovered land, to the New World, and sell you to an aboriginal chief."

Rose's hand went to her lips. She didn't know why she was surprised to hear such a declaration from him.

"I can see you will do it, too."

"Well, there's the rub, Bella Rosa." He stood, walked to the bed he had given her, and sat beside her thighs. He drew the fingers of his right hand along the side of her face. The tenderness, the warmth, caused her flesh to tingle and butterflies to quiver in her stomach. "I've taken a fancy to you. My interest puts me in a difficult position."

"What will you do?" Rose asked.

"I dare say, I don't know. Maybe you should consider giving me a reason to change course and have a more purposeful passage. I can see that you appreciate a route of direction."

Rose didn't know what to think after his statement. Had he told her the truth, or was he dallying with her affection to gain her trust? She watched his lips lift upward in humor. Damn the man, he was as wily as a pirate after all.

"A pirate!" Rose stated, suddenly irritated. "I knew it all along. You're trying to pillage my larder."

Howling with laughter, he dared to press closer, coming nearer to her lips. "Sweet Bella Rosa, you don't know how much I wish I were a buccaneer of the sea, for if that were true, I'd plunder your lips right now, causing them to swell with desire, and I wouldn't stop pillaging your lift until my rudder—"

Rose puffed with indignation, having heard enough. She pushed him off the bed and he fell to the floor, landing on his back, but being a good sport, he didn't anger, merely stretched his arms wide and hooted with laughter.

"Oh, my darling, I thought I had you; your breath was coming in delicious stabs of affection."

Rose threw off the covers, jumped from the bunk, and then walked toward the standing trifold panels for privacy. "It's time I dressed for the day, Captain."

Edwin rose from the floor. "I agree. You've been abed for too long."

Retrieving an emerald green surcoat from a trunk, Rose held it to her chest, while scrutinizing Edwin with an avid interest. Not with the desire that she saw he misconstrued, but with the hope he wouldn't deal her an unkind fate, as he had stated. To be sold, to anyone, upset her very much. The status of the man who attained her attention didn't concern her overly. It did matter that her future husband would care for her needs in a kind manner.

Rose went behind the trifold screen where she attended to

her ablutions and then dressed. She heard Captain Perrow settling himself at his desk again. She heard his drawer opening and knew he placed the key inside. And then, pieces moved around the top. When she left the screen, she saw that he was studying the map. He raised his eyes at her in concern.

"Please, Edwin," Rose said, appealing to him. "Please don't sell me."

Edwin lowered the map. "I'm sorry, Princess Rose, but you've left me no other option."

It wasn't lost on her that he had avoided the use of his endearment. Maybe this was on purpose, but she could see by his quick return to the map that his attention no longer focused on her. Perhaps she wasn't his golden nugget after all.

Chapter Five

KING LOWELL

Lowell enjoyed the thrill of the chase and normally took pleasure in Drakones' hooves pounding against the ground as the horse charged forward, but this day tendered a different beast. Clinging to the equine's back, Lowell held the reins while bearing the stride of powerful legs, carrying man and animal across infertile land and taking them closer to the break in the trees. Lowell clutched the coarse mane and arched forward in the saddle, giving the stallion the freedom to run.

Nothing sweeter existed for him than the excitement of prevailing winds streaming through his hair, exhilarating his senses, *freeing him,* enabling him to experience the thrill of life while tearing across the moorlands, racing toward the king's forest on his steed. He reveled in the ride and took pleasure in the chase, but all too soon, the forest encroached on his joy.

He pulled on the reins and urged Drakones into a canter. Ahead of him, the king's men had entered the forest. He could not see his privy councillors any longer, but the sound of baying dogs could not be disguised, and he listened to them bawling, yowling and yapping in the distance, man's best friend searching for prey along the blood trail. He had no doubt the mongrels sniffed out their foe. They were persistent, slobbering beasts, as hungry for the chase as their instinct was to kill from hunger. The blood trail urged them onward, their small bodies knowing no rest or release from the hunt, not until their prey was captured and their appetites were satisfied. It was wicked of him to disallow their feeding prior to the hunt, but he knew, ah, he knew they would find their sustenance, and mongrels tearing a victim apart, to satisfy a queen's appetite, did not bring him joy, but joy had no bidding in judgment and a king had his responsibilities.

When man and animal came before a gap in the trees, Lowell eased Drakones into a trot. Unchaperoned, he entered the forest, following the beaten path. The temperature seemed to fall after passing beneath a canopy of outstretched branches. The dogs' baying became muted and distant. The royal councillors had gone on ahead, matching the pace of the dogs, but Lowell was in no hurry to see this business achieved; even so, achieved it would be.

He rode at his own pace, breathing deeply of damp decay while meandering along a well-trod pathway. A gateway of some sort, a place where shadows cast dark figures on jade shrubbery and the occasional bloom burgeoned for light. Lowell swallowed his fear. His anxiety sang from a place he could not define, spiriting in the air, and maybe his cautiousness or an overly ripe imagination pondered the gray bark from taller oaks—stretching closer, nearer to him—causing the hairs to rise at the nape of his neck.

The temperature seemed to slip by the slightest degree as he rode deeper into the forest, and the light, already dim, grew dimmer still, filling the forest with disturbing gray shadows. The slight croak of a toad in the distance and the occasional snort from Drakones was the only music to fill the woodland. The forbidding ambience cultivated his fears the farther along the trail he went. He sensed Drakones was experiencing a fear response, as the horse snorted, sniffing a presence that Lowell could neither see nor hear.

Shying away from the pursuit, Drakones pranced backward. Anxious, he whinnied in alarm. When Lowell tried to force the animal onward, prodding him in the flanks and slapping his neck with the reins, the horse reared on his hind legs. To remain seated, Lowell arched forward, digging his feet into the flanks.

"Easy boy," Lowell said, stretching forward, patting and stroking the horseflesh about the neck. He rested in that place for a time, permitting the animal to calm, listening to the air puffing in and out of Drakones' nose. The equine pranced on the spot, daring to rear again.

"No harm will come to you." Lowell reassured his horse. "It's okay, boy."

When Drakones seemed calmer, Lowell urged him onward, but the horse's anxiety rankled again.

Drakones fought the hand wielding the reins and paced backward, squealing in fright, dancing on the spot and rising upward on his rear legs again. Frustrated, Lowell considered whipping the animal into obedience, but couldn't bring himself to strike his beloved steed. He also reasoned that he couldn't return to the entrance of the forest, which would amount to neglecting his responsibilities.

Mother be damned, anyway—

He wished he could return to the castle, forget the hunt and consign this ugly business to his king's men. Instead, he sat on his horse's back and waited for the stallion to quiet, while surmising where Drakones' ire arose from in the first place. Lowell wasn't a fool. The stories of the forest had reached his ears; stories of his mother. Though he didn't believe half of the tales that had been woven—or was there some truth to the fiction?

Lowell knew a king could not retreat from gossip or wicked stories, but he had chosen to ignore the rumors. Now, however, a mystery existed that he couldn't entirely understand, and though he believed himself to be of sound mind, he wasn't immune to foul gossip.

Drakones surely felt this mystery.

The peasants whispered tales about the king's forest, believing the woodland haunted. They alleged that evil resided deep in the forest, in a brief expanse of valley beyond the hollow glen, and especially when the moon waxed full and the haze drifted across the ground to catch intruders unaware. The queen mother further assisted the myth, perpetuating cruel stories for her own twisted amusement and gain.

As such, many peasants avoided the king's forest, but not the victim they currently hunted. This traitor to the kingdom had been unafraid to enter the woodland, and Lowell hadn't thought to ask himself why. Why would anyone who held a fear of this place cross its path? And by what means had his *mum* found the traitor?

Lowell didn't believe the heresy for a minute, but he knew his mother had begun traveling into the forest. He often saw her from a vantage point inside the king's tower, her shadowy figure riding among the night shadows, a time when the sun sank beneath the sky, with only the white light of the moon to guide her footpath. Sometimes, a strange obscure light, often tinged with a mossy green glow, could be seen burning in the forest. Although he was curious to understand the sorcery divining in the forest vale, like the peasants, he had been too fearful to question his mother's actions. For Queen Mother Cynara had changed since red whiplash wounds had marred her flesh, and he cringed, understanding the change had not been for the better.

If the people of Velez had been frightened of the queen mother, prior to Scarlett surviving the black curse, now they were terrified of the woman they had silently named *the Ebony Queen*. Lowell understood their opinions; he felt anxious himself, and with good reason: Sometimes in the dead of night he'd awaken from a bad dream, only to find his mum standing over him, staring at him. He witnessed the madness in her soul and saw a reason to be frightened. On nights such as these, he missed the wisdom of his father.

Lowell cast his dour thoughts aside, grateful when Drakones gathered the courage to meander farther along the forest trail. He gently pressed the stallion onward, not rushing the steed, letting the horse trot at its own pace. The baying of the hounds had lessened.

Nevin, blow your horn!

Lowell arrived at a meandering stream and saw the hoof markings that indicated his king's men had passed this way, marring the clay earth with their trod. Just beyond, he glimpsed a fallen tree that had bridged the stream. He slid from his horse to the ground, tied Drakones' reins to a tall oak, and then strode toward the log.

Branches broke beneath his feet as he neared the wooden bridge; tiny pebbles ground beneath his leather boots. He maneuvered around the larger rocks, soon stepping into clear flowing water to climb on top of the tree bridge.

He stood on the wooden plank for several moments, swaying slightly, listening to the trickle of running water while studying the opposite shoreline, which continued downstream in a southernly direction. He contemplated clay banks on either side of the waterway, studying larger rock surfaces for wear, scrutinizing tiny pebbles ground into the shoreline, and undisturbed blades of grass rising from the watery bed.

Which way have you gone?

A tiny speck of red caught his attention, farther along the tree's limb. He sidestepped closer, soon bending downward to inspect the droplet. He drew his finger through the moisture and studied a smear of blood on his fingertip.

"So, you came this way," he muttered, rising, rubbing the red between his fingers.

He searched the immediate area, again, scanning the length of the log, but he didn't see tracks in the earth or on the muddy shoreline, nor any disturbed foliage or rocks, on this side of the stream. He stood up, retracing his steps to his horse. Untying the reins, he surveyed across the creek to the forest on the opposite bank.

"A smart fox," he whispered, contemplating the opposite bank and scanning the length of the stream. *Which way has the prey gone, left or right?* Lowell pulled Drakones forward and led him across the watery break.

"You think the dogs won't smell you in the water, but I will smell you."

Farther away, the horn sounded, its trumpet trill urging the dogs to return the way they had come.

"Come on, Drakones," Lowell whispered in his ear. "Gather your courage, boy. We must find the prey."

On the opposite bank, Lowell observed the end of a fallen tree. The trees were embedded together, tightly, too close for a horse to tread between. The foliage had been disturbed; a trillium flattened to the ground. It appeared the prey had moved south, trekking downstream. Lowell held Drakones' reins firmly and led the animal around the tree bridge and along the stream, hoping the prey would cross the water again.

Lowell searched the mud, rocks and sediment as he tracked a strip of land beside the water, scrutinizing the landscape, but not finding disturbances on the stream's shoreline.

"Which way have you gone?" Lowell wondered aloud, gazing downstream, but believing in his initial hunch, he maintained his footpath. He had walked a few paces when he noticed a second break in the vegetation: a swath of big blue stems, with their spiky leafage crushed. Nearing the break, he considered a rock that had been booted from its spot. He grasped the gray cobble, and soon massaged the circular smoothness in his fingers. Frowning, he placed the stone inside his pocket.

Lowell crossed the stream, believing this was the intent of the prey. Farther along still, the evidence of a second droplet of blood, dissipating to a lighter shade of pink, muddled on the shoreline's edge.

"I'm on your trail," Lowell whispered, bringing his crossbow into his hands.

Broken stems appeared, again, on the other side of the stream. The clever fox kept crossing back and forth across the water. However, the prey was not clever enough for the hunters. Once a tracker discovered the pattern, the chase became easier to piece together. The king would find his prey; it was only a matter of time.

King Lowell bellowed into the forest. "This way, our poacher is near."

Lowell reached for Drakones and swiftly climbed on his back, urging the stallion to a quicker pace beside the stream. Reaching for a whistle in his pocket, he blew several short blasts, signaling for the hunters to return. And then he waited.

The sound of the dogs, distant at first, grew louder as they came closer, yowling and yapping, soon closing the distance. Lowell watched the hounds break through the bush and careen through the water. The king's men followed, close behind, stampeding through the bush, crashing through the water in their rush.

"This way," Lowell yelled, pointing at the break in the foliage where the prey had passed through. But he didn't need to show the dogs; they charged through the water, yowling and yapping, picking up the scent. Hungry, they raced forward.

Lowell fell in behind his king's men, racing through the forest, twisting this way and that through the brush. He wouldn't be left behind again now that the hunt was in earnest.

They heard the sound all at once: the thrashing of limbs as a man jumped from his hiding spot and ran through the bush in a desperate attempt to get away. But the dogs moved faster and soon found their foe, muzzle after muzzle, gnashing into the flesh of his legs.

A man screamed in desperation.

The dogs ripped and tore at his flesh.

The poor bastard attempted to climb a tree in his fight to find freedom. He fell.

Lowell bit his lip, trying to ignore the terror-filled screams that were hideous to the human ear, but the dogs knew no such compassion. They were hungry and tore at the victim's flesh, repeatedly. One after the other they lunged at the victim, surrounding him in a swarm of sharp muzzles.

"Enough!" Lowell slipped from his saddle and approached the carnage. The victim collapsed on the ground, screaming, curling into a ball, trying to protect himself from the dogs. Lowell couldn't watch this horror any longer.

So much red...

"Call the dogs off!" Lowell screamed, running forward, but frantic, not sure what to do. He searched for Boyce, the grand master of the hunt.

Boyce Burleigh complied with the order, calling the dogs to return to his side, but the pack was hungry, and the men had to jump from their horses to assist, grabbing the animals and wrestling the beasts from their prize. By some horrifying miracle of fate, the thief still breathed.

Lowell approached where the serf lay on the ground, gasping for breath, whimpering, blood oozing from his wounds. Somehow, Lowell maintained a serious expression as he spoke.

"No man poaches in the king's forest. You took the life of my stag, a bounty that was meant to feed the king's table and the king's people. For this crime, I have ruled that you should die a traitor's death. Say your prayers, man. You go to meet your maker."

Lowell raised his crossbow, directed the arrow at the center of the man's chest and let the arrow fly. He didn't shy away from a knowing expression in the victim's eyes as knowledge suffused the poor soul that he would die.

"You know not why I entered the forest," he rasped. "I die with the secret buried in my…"

Lowell disregarded the final words, believing them to be a fool's quest.

"I want everyone to watch," Lowell growled, fixing his sightline on the victim and then the king's men. "Watch," he reiterated, "as this man takes his last breath. This is the decree a king must make when a man defies the rules of the kingdom. You are my witnesses, my Privy Council officials, who shall acknowledge to the people of Velez what has happened here, so they will never disobey the rules of the kingdom."

Henryk shook his head in disgust and stepped forward, moving to the injured, and thereby defying King Lowell. The constable of the armed forces knelt before the victim and grasped the man's hand, whispering words of compassion that only he and the wounded could hear.

"Step away from him," Lowell commanded.

"Have you no mercy, Sire?" Henryk replied. "You have wounded this man in the cruelest way. And when the victim would confess his crime, you place an arrow in his heart. Now the true motive for the theft dies with the man, and you will never know the secret he takes to his grave."

Lowell stepped closer. "I know all I need to know; he stole from me."

"Perhaps," Henryk agreed, "and perhaps not. But let him die with dignity."

Lowell stepped closer, listening more to the shallow breathing than the condemnation that shook his commander with rage. "I will forgive this slight, Henryk, as I'm not immune to compassion. However, the role of king does not permit me to bend my back, not by the slightest degree. I must be firm, as my father would expect me to be."

"Your Majesty," Henryk barked, perhaps attempting to reason. "Your father would never have hunted this man with dogs."

"The former King Rickard would have taken this man's head off with an axe."

"And in that act," Henryk beckoned, pivoting to sight the man whose breath weakened, "death would have gained mercy."

"Death is death. An ending not much different than any other entrance to the Otherworld or the nether lands," Lowell grated, carving out his idea carefully. "No matter how it comes about, the penalty inflicts the same ending."

Henryk harrumphed, placed his hands on his hips and didn't speak further, while the king's men waited for the final breath to expire.

Once Lowell was certain of the peasant's death, he climbed on Drakones' back. He searched for the grand master of the horse.

"Keldan, I considered feeding his carcass to the dogs, or placing his body on the barbican as a warning to other wrong-doers, but I've taken pity on this man's soul. For the sake of his wife, return his body to his family home. But drag his carcass behind your horse and through the crowd. I want the people of the Kingdom of Velez to understand what happens when the king's rules are disobeyed."

His command was greeted with silence. No one responded to his counsel. Not Keldan, nor Nevin, or even the war bear, Henryk Thayer. The king's men stared at him, judging him, refusing to release him from this death.

"I want you to know," Lowell explained, swallowing, attempting to hold his head high. "I take no comfort in this man's death. I will pray for his soul."

When the silence stretched, Lowell retreated from the men, fearing they would glimpse his weakness. He pressed his knees into Drakones' side, urging the horse to leave. The animal responded as it always did when given a command and it ambled through the brush. He felt no need to hurry, so permitted the stallion to trudge across the ground at a slower gait.

He tried to maintain a stern expression, but his facial muscles betrayed his inner mien and twitched and bunched beneath his left eye, suffusing him with guilt, making him feel like a criminal, given the crime he had committed. He had condemned a man to die, killing him with his own loosed arrow.

"*Sard it*— Damn it!"

The hardest kill to achieve was *the first,* but after this day, Lowell had no doubt he could execute a death sentence again. If he had to. Still, he must live with the death, despite the circumstances. Yet, once he was alone and away from the king's men, he let the stress escape his lips in a whoosh of air and considered what his sentence had wrought.

A mother and child would sleep alone in their bed tonight and for the loneliness they would suffer, he sympathized. He survived without a father; he missed his father still.

Henryk was correct in his estimation, so he would say no more on the subject. No mercy hailed from this ending.

He rode through the forest, listening to the pounding of Drakones' hooves, and was grateful when the field light grew and the spirit of green forest had been left behind. He never wanted to enter the king's forest again. It was marked with evil.

He fetched the cobble from his pocket and massaged the stone in the palm of his hand, letting it roll freely between his fingers. He would remember the discovery of this clue. Always.

Chapter Six

QUEEN MOTHER CYNARA

Queen Cynara watched the royal courtiers from her vantage point inside the king's tower. They progressed across the farthest field, parading her fallen enemy behind a horse. Her son, King Lowell, led the column of men returning to the castle with their bounty, their track forward much slower than the earlier rush across the moorlands. Assuming a scathing expression, she chuckled with ill humor while scrutinizing the bleeding carcass of a piteous pawn, his body dragging across the ground. Even from this viewpoint, high in the tower, she saw that he still bled.

She mused that Lowell had achieved his first victory by carrying out the sentence. Unbeknownst to her son, the queen mother had put this chess game into play when the spy, now being unceremoniously dragged behind a horse, threatened her secret to be revealed. Silencing the pawn's discovery had been successful for two reasons.

First, the kingdom was no wiser to her invocation scheme,

and second, Lowell, her son, had released the thief to be hunted, obviously capturing and killing the culprit, and thereby achieving his first royal decree within the Privy Council. And now that he had killed by his own hand, the next death sentence would be easier to execute.

She would never tell her son the man was innocent. He didn't need to know that a traitorous spy, pulled behind a brown steed, had never entered the forest to search for the king's stag. He had been looking for *her*, the queen, and the *pawn* had come close to discovering her secret.

Cynara left the window and walked to a side table, where she sat to break her fast. Reaching for a piece of cheese, she contemplated the night to come. While nibbling on the aged cheddar, she considered Nevin Islip, the intendant of the civil list and the kingdom's adviser on energy, science, and culture.

Nevin, a frugal spiritualist, had consulted with her ages ago to share his scientific theories and knowledge. He foretold a time when the earth would align with the sun and the moon, a day when the sun would be turned to darkness and the moon into blood. He shed dire predictions and warnings that their world would end. Foul vapors would rise from the sea, bringing serpents to their sandy shores to devour men, women, and children. The world would shake, the land would spit fire from the mountains, and dragons would awaken from cavernous dens to enflame the night with crimson fire, maybe bringing the devil, *Daemonis*, to the mortal world again.

Cynara chortled with laughter, remembering his abject fear. *Silly buffoon.* The world wouldn't end, but she had listened to him intently, growing more and more intrigued with the conversation as Nevin revealed each piece of scientific knowledge. She didn't have the heart to tell him he was right in his estimation—the dead would live again—as she didn't want to worry the intendant unnecessarily. After all, the scientist had provided a golden nugget of information that would seed her ultimate revenge.

When the hour catered to darkness and the earth begged light from the sun, the moon would be caught unaware in the resulting flare. The triad would make a different hunt possible. On this one night only, and within a breath of minutes, she could cast her spell and call the spirits of the underworld into her vale, and only then would she summon the god Odin as he thundered across the sky, searching for a wild boar to hunt or a young maiden to ravage.

Come to me. I am ready!

Cynara reached for a pewter goblet of wine and sipped the ruby red liquid, finding the taste rather pungent. The foul brew parched her mouth, reminding her of the past, and one reason for this risk.

Scarlett, Princess Scarlett— The woman who had punished her skin with a red whiplash tattoo.

Cynara recoiled in anger, reflecting on the woman. How had she broken Nicolai's curse? She had thought the black curse impenetrable. And now two enemies had banded together, likely plotting revenge against her and her son. They must be stopped and prevented from causing further harm.

Unconsciously, she reached for her neck. A wide Elizabethan ruff was bound tightly around her neck, concealing lesions and welts that marred her skin. Cynara wanted retribution for these wounds in the worst possible way. She had already waged war against Princess Ruby, and would not stop until all three sisters had experienced a worse fate than a sacrifice of scarlet welts.

Allegiances were forming…

The evening of the alignment was in sight.

Chapter Seven

PRINCESS SCARLETT

A nipping wind stole inside the bedchamber. It caressed her cheeks and fluttered wine-colored draperies speckled with gold. Nestled comfortably in the coverlet of Nicolai's four-poster bed, Scarlett wrinkled her nose, stretched her arms toward the canopy, and appreciated the arrival of a new day. Content with her life, despite an uncertain future, she concentrated on the doorway and the sunshine streaming inside the bedchamber.

The door to the balcony had been left open, which suggested to her that Nicolai was lounging outside, and she understood why. The daylight hours were diminishing, giving them little time to enjoy the outer deck. Yet, fall winds breathed a reminder of a witch's intent, too. Evil wouldn't concede in this battle, and as if Mother Nature knew of further plans, even more so than the wintry season, Scarlett waited for acts of evil, more so than leaves skittering across the decking, which only served to remind her of past wrongs.

Her cognitive mind wouldn't let her forget past wrongs.

Worry tormented her, nagged at her, sweating her cares, round and round. The actions of the past; the possibilities of the future.

No. She wouldn't think about the arrival of cooler winds or witchcraft. Somehow, a princess had to put the burden of 'yesterday' behind her. *Let it go.*

Alone in the bed, and choosing to reflect on summer days, she supposed her lover had left her for a view of the ocean, and it seemed like a good day to observe the sea when the skies were blue and the clouds puffed with white. Though she shivered, and was left wondering if Nicolai had left the door ajar on purpose, she decided to join him on the balcony.

"Nicolai," she murmured, rising to a sitting position. "It's cold outside."

Giving in to temptation, she permitted the covers to slide away from her figure, and then left the bed to stand on a braided rug. When a gust of wind swept inside the bedchamber, shivers, more so than memories, dimpled her skin. She hurried across the short distance to the armoire where a woolen wrapper had been hung on a hook. Quickly covering herself, but leaving her feet bare, she sauntered toward the doorway and soon stepped over the ledge, to stand on a stone balcony, to breathe salty, wet ocean air.

When their eyes met, Nicolai smiled. "Good morning, my Scarlett Princess. Did you sleep well?"

"I feel as if I'm still dreaming." She pouted, ambling toward the man who had become her lover, while fastening ribbed cording around her waist. "I'm still suffering from the odd nightmare, but daylight hours offer their promise again, picture-perfect with the man I love held in my sight."

Reclining on his favorite lounge chair, he opened his arms wide and unwrapped the needlepoint coverlet. "Come to me. The view is good from here, safe, and warm, too."

Scarlett yielded to a half-smile, settled on his lap and leaned against his chest. She touched his cheeks, ran her fingers across dark whiskers, and perused a handsome expression she'd become accustomed to viewing. Her fingers slid through thick black strands of hair. "Life is good. I can't believe it. How circumstances can change when you least expect them to."

Nicolai wrapped the blanket snugly around her and she cuddled close, as near as she could get. She breathed the musk of his skin, feeling safe in his proximity, warm in his embrace, and beholding more love than she had ever received from another human being. It was natural to lean close to his mouth and kiss his lips a good morning.

It was also easy to forget… How seeds of love could be lost and taken away from her.

"Have I told you how much I love you, Nicolai Graydon? How much you mean to me?"

He grasped the small of her back and pulled her closer still. "You have shared the innermost feelings of your heart, repeatedly," he chortled, grinning. "And I enjoy the offerings. I wouldn't protest if you shared your sentiments again."

She grasped his face and studied his sea-blue eyes in a way she hoped was earnest. "I'll do that and more. I do love you."

"Oh, my darling," he crooned. "When you look at me with wanton eyes of affection and whisper tender words, I want to shield you in my arms and rush you to our bed, to claim you, again and again, as mine."

Scarlett giggled despite herself. "And I'll permit your advances, my lord. Yet, it's wrong of me to behave in a scandalous manner. We are not yet married, or even engaged. Bensen might not concern himself with our sinful living, but I'm not as certain whether my maid, Juliana, or Agatha, our good and kind cook, would approve of our behavior."

"Who cares what the household servants think. I'm the lord of this manor house and I call the shots. Furthermore, it's none of their business."

It might not matter what their household servants thought, but Scarlett wanted more from the man she loved; she deserved a commitment on her finger. It was time she told him.

"It's unseemly, Nicolai. You are consigning this princess into a fallen woman with no hope of redemption. I remember what you said to me that day on the beach, that you would stand beside me, protecting and guarding me, but not at the altar?"

He nuzzled her cheek and his whiskers tickled. "You knew what you were getting into when you joined me in my bed. After all, you were well aware of my dark reputation. And now that we've lain together, we're practically husband and wife anyway."

She curled against him, laying her head on his shoulder, her palm flat against his chest. "Our lives were darker then, Nicolai," she emphasized softly. "I'd like to call you my husband. A commitment wouldn't change our newer and safer connection."

He kissed her cheek. "But we have a commitment, Scarlett. We share a natural and loving allegiance with each other.

Birds don't meet at the altar. They fly together, free of cage constrictions."

Scarlett heard the door to their bedchamber opening, heard the servant, Juliana, moving about, likely bringing in their breakfast tray. She wasn't hungry, at least not for solid food. "Do you think I'd place you in a cage again? 'Tis not my desire to house my lover in a cage of iron. Matrimonial vows, as far I can ascertain, do not constrict a bond of wedlock."

He studied her, his fingers finding her lips, the eye contact alone making her uncomfortable. "Don't be sad. Don't permit a frown to mar your pretty face or a pout to crease your lips," Nicolai whispered, nibbling at her earlobe. "I understand why this matter concerns you. Come with me. You'll feel better and more satisfied after we've broken our fast."

Nicolai opened the woolen blanket and a cool wind brushed against her skin. Scarlett shivered, disappointed that her concern was not worthy of his attention. She rose from his lap, missing his warmth, feeling cold stones beneath her feet. She scrutinized his expression, staring at his eyes, trying to smile. She hoped her frustration wasn't evident.

"It's all right. I shouldn't expect more from our relationship than you're prepared to give. After all, I have more luxuries and comforts than a woman could ever need. I shouldn't be greedy, desiring more."

He rose from his seat; a tall man, he stepped nearer to her, reached for her and pulled her into his embrace, soon kissing her forehead. Then releasing her, he gripped her hand and squeezed. "Come inside, Scarlett. Soon your life will be better. You'll see."

She noticed that his palm was warm and slightly sweaty as he escorted her inside his bedchamber. When Nicolai closed the balcony door, Scarlett marveled at the side table, set with a fine service of cobalt blue china decorated with dainty floral petals and small acanthus leaves. A wild rose had been placed in a vase in the middle of the table. Juliana had quietly brought their breakfast tray into the room and had noiselessly departed again. They were alone.

Nicolai pulled out a chair and motioned with his hand for her to sit. An amused grin illuminated his face as he took his spot on the opposite chair, and sat, too.

"What is it?" Scarlett asked, seeing his head lower in amusement. "What is entertaining your good humor?"

"It's nothing. It's just that…"

"What? What mischief are you up to this morning?"

"Scarlett," he grinned, chuckling into his hand, "I have news to share with you."

"Well, don't keep me waiting. What is it?"

Scarlett watched Nicolai, seeing he had become serious. He reached inside the pocket of his white lawn shirt and retrieved a small item: a small blue stone reflected a prism of light; rainbows radiated throughout the bedchamber.

"Oh, Nicolai," she breathed, watching her sweetheart rise from his seat. He came before her; an expression of trepidation etched the sea-blue sincerity of his eyes. He knelt on one knee.

"Scarlett, Princess Scarlett, will you marry me?"

"What?" Scarlett tittered, shocked by the question. "What have you asked of me?"

She gasped when he reached for her hand, willingly

permitting her lover to grip her fingers. She admired the beautiful sapphire stone. She watched his shaking fingers slide the gemstone onto her ring finger.

"Will you marry me, sweetheart? Will you end my fornicating ways forever and make me a better man, an honest man, by becoming my wife?"

"Your wife?" she replied, sliding from the chair and joining him on the floor. "After the conversation on the balcony, do you mean it?"

"Darling," he growled, seeming concerned, "I'm on the floor on bent knees. I wouldn't lounge in this bird cage for just any woman."

She smiled. She giggled. She couldn't help herself, noticing the fear, the worry, the concern furrowed on his brow that she might say no. "Oh, Nicolai," she shrieked, falling into his arms and sending him to the floor in her exuberance. "Yes, oh yes, a thousand times yes."

Happiness blurred her vision; tears streamed across her face. She didn't hear the door opening to the lord's bedchamber, but Nicolai's expression warned her that they were not alone. She shifted her positioning, rolling off of Nicolai to lie on the floor beside him, in time to see good old Bensen, the butler, and Juliana, her maid, entering the room, and seeming like the cats who had eaten the canary, and both of them happy with their efforts.

"It's about time," Bensen said. "I thought this cockerel would never find a good woman, let alone make a commitment to her. I'm happy he's picked you, Princess."

The maid clapped her hands. "Congratulations, Milord, Milady."

"Thank you, both of you," Scarlett gushed, clapping her hands and glancing at Nicolai. She eyed Bensen. "It appears you had knowledge of this engagement conspiracy prior to the question being asked?"

Bensen snickered. "In this household, secretive plots do not reveal themselves without my knowledge. Now, let me see the ring."

Still sitting on the floor, Scarlett rose upward and then offered her hand to the butler. Now strong and healed from his lightning injury, he helped her rise to her feet, then held her fingers in his grip and admired the ring. "Beautiful as ever, and much better worn on your ring finger than the former lady of the manor."

Scarlett withdrew her hand to examine the sapphire more closely, and then glanced at Nicolai as he regained his footing. "It was your mother's?" she asked him.

"Yes," he sighed, unsmiling. "It's a family heirloom. My mother, the Countess Leonie, wore the ring. I hope this doesn't disappoint you as my mother was not faithful to her vows. Even so, given my state of affairs, I didn't have many jewelry options."

"Yes. I recall how the subject of wealth, more so than your mother, disappoint," Scarlett said. "Nicolai, though I'm a royal by blood, I'm equally poor. I will happily wear this ring, an emblem of our commitment to each other. And although we are not wed, so our vows do not need to be spoken, I vow to honor, love and cherish, you—only you—for the rest of my life. Unlike your mother, I will be faithful, too."

"I know you will, darling. And I vow to protect, love and be faithful, too."

"If he doesn't keep his commitment," Bensen mouthed off, "I will hurt him. He doesn't have the protective sheath of a black panther for defensive purposes any longer."

"Thank goodness for that," Scarlett blurted, laughing, nudging the butler in the side. "Well then, Bensen, shall we take our breakfast to the kitchen? It seems a celebration is in order."

"Lord Nicolai had hoped to share this moment with you, Princess, in the privacy of his bedchamber."

Scarlett winked. "It's been shared. It's time to celebrate with our family. The family who stands by us."

Bensen reached for the platter. "Milady, we are at your service; a grand gathering will be prepared to your satisfaction."

Nicolai cleared his throat. "We'll only be a moment, Bensen. Prepare our breakfast in the dining room. And yes, assemble our household staff, because indeed, you are our family."

"As you wish," Bensen said, seeming honored by the statement. "Come with me, Juliana. We shall leave the master and his fiancée, our future countess, to their privacy."

And with that they were left alone.

Once the door closed, Scarlett couldn't help herself. She pounced on Nicolai a second time, tumbling her future husband to the flooring.

"You devil," she said, kissing his lips. "You had this engagement planned all along but led me on a merry chase, seeking to capture me."

"And my love," he whispered, "surely you know by now, *everything changes with the capture*. I'll hold you close, keeping you safe, never willing to let a love so precious to me, slip away again."

"Oh darling," Scarlett sighed, close to his lips and kissing him softly. "I'm grateful Cynara sent me to your once wretched home."

He touched his index finger to her lips. "Don't say her name. Don't even think it for the evil connotations that could arise. We don't want our luck to change."

THE BRIDAL COUPLE relaxed in the drawing room, sitting on the settee with their fingers entwined. Still feeling the weight of a sapphire ring on her ring finger, Scarlett engaged in conversation, but glanced at the gemstone from time to time. Watchful, she grinned when she overheard Juliana giggling about some odd witticism in the far-off corner.

She spied Agatha, the household cook, maneuvering among their guests with a plate of appetizers. Too tempting to avoid, she accepted a stuffed egg. "I wonder when Agatha assumed the task of cooking for our guests with the lady of the house none the wiser to the work?"

Nicolai squeezed her fingers. "Isn't it obvious? I notified the staff of my betrothal intentions. You may define the act as the poets might; 'the art of love'."

"The art of love might be catching," Scarlett remarked, observing Bensen pussyfooting toward the kitchen. "Do you think a relationship might be evolving between our servants?"

"Who? You don't mean Bensen and Agatha, do you?"

"I did think about the possibility."

Nicolai grinned. "My personal butler has found favor with our cook, and why not, Agatha's recipes cause the mouth to salivate with a craving for more. Have you noticed that Bensen's waistline has increased?"

Scarlett grinned, as if the news was funny. "His waistcoat seems a bit tight, but do go on. A lady enjoys hearing heartfelt love stories."

"You just want to hear the tastiest tidbits. Admit it. The way he maneuvers himself in the larder on the pretense of learning secrets, secrets of his own love story. Bensen has discovered they make the perfect couple." Nicolai leaned closer in a conspiratorial kind of way. "Furthermore, I did once sight them engaging in a private meeting in the scullery."

"You don't say."

Nicolai placed his finger against his lips. "I shall not say more given the risk of embarrassing either party."

"Your secret is safe with me," Scarlett said, winking. "I'm surprised the villagers have traveled from Culley's Cove to celebrate with us. I had no idea they would care about our betrothal."

"Yes, well, you're a beauty and they're a curious lot. They've waited a long time to behold the next countess of Drum Manor, the woman, I dare say, who would wear the lord's commitment on her finger."

Repeated knocks struck the lion clapper, and each time, Bensen retreated from the drawing room to acknowledge the arrival of a visitor. The house became crowded, but Scarlett was grateful for each new guest. After all, these people would be her people. And she was glad of it, having no family of her own.

She sipped her wine, her facial expression waning to sadness. "What's wrong?" Nicolai asked. "What are you thinking about?"

"There's an empty space at the table and in my heart, a family lost: my father, my mother, and both sisters, all of them deceased. They can't share this celebration with us, which makes me sad. I mourn the loss of my sisters, especially so on this day."

"I know it's hard, but think happy thoughts. Try to put the past where it belongs."

"It's easier said than done."

When a knock struck the door, Scarlett was so accustomed to new guests arriving, she paid little attention to the conversation taking place, thinking only that another friend had arrived to wish them well. She observed Bensen from the corner of her eye, hurrying to the entry hall; she heard him open the door, too. Yet, when masculine voices wrestled with anger, alerting her attention, she shifted on the settee and studied the entry hall to understand the commotion.

When Bensen raged: "You're not welcome here. Leave now or pay the price!" Panic quickened her breathing.

"I request admittance inside this home. I call on the lord of the manor to speak with me. I would not intrude if my message was not important."

Scarlett cringed, feeling numb. Who was this male intruder? *A memory emerged.*

She recognized the rough timbre of the masculine voice and was surprised to hear the intonation after many months. She watched Theodore Wilkins push past Bensen to stand in the archway of the drawing room.

Terrible memories rooted from the past, robbing the household of its peace and tranquility. She held her breath. The wine glass slipped from her hand. Red liquid spilled to the flooring and with her mouth drooping open in shock, her facial expression must have manifested a mien of abject fear and dismay. The guests must have noticed her displeasure as the merriment in the room ended and all conversations came to an end.

Nicolai released her hand and rose from the settee. The lord of Drum Manor had said not to think of the witch's name, but she thought of it anyway.

Cynara—

Nicolai hurried to the entry hall and confronted the intruder. "Why are you here? You should have stayed away."

"Let me speak," he pleaded, stepping toward the lord, but Bensen grabbed his arm and twisted the appendage behind his back. "It's important. Hear me out."

"I should have taken your life when I had the chance," Nicolai said, growling a warning. "You horrible excuse for a human being. The manner in which you handled a princess of the kingdom, my future bride. Do you know what bodily harm I could do to you? And now, if you think to frighten my fiancée, I will kill you."

"Don't be a fool," Theodore stated sternly. "You need to know what I have to say."

Nicolai responded by grasping his surcoat. "I don't need

to hear tidings from the likes of a bastard like you. Your return can only bring harm to my home and my family. I won't hear a word you have to say."

Trembling, Scarlett rose from the settee, anxiety rising beneath her breastbone; she felt her golden-brown eyes transforming to a burnished yellow gold. Somehow, she found her courage. "Nicolai, whatever it is, I need to know."

Nicolai's frustration was evident when he released the one who intruded on their celebration, then slid his hands through his hair. He sighed in exasperation, eyeing Scarlett with a stern manner that cautioned her discretion, a scrutiny that could still evoke fear, despite her love for this man.

"Whatever he brings," Nicolai warned, "his news can only amount to more pain."

"The pain has arrived. I can see the turmoil in his eyes," Scarlett said, her voice quivering, her hands shaking. "I can feel the undercurrent of tension in his bearing. But I sense we need to hear whatever message he means to share."

Nicolai relented. "All right, take him to the library, Bensen. We'll question him there."

Sighing, Scarlett faced her guests while Bensen and Nicolai ushered Theodore to the library. "Please, have no concern," she said, trying to smile. "You have nothing to fear. Lord Graydon and I will attend to this matter, and we'll return shortly to share this celebration with you."

Scarlett searched for her household staff. "Agatha. Juliana. Please attend to our guests' needs until we can return."

Juliana curtsied. "As you wish, Milady."

Scarlett nodded in their direction, trusting they saw her confidence, not her fear. She also hoped the household servants and her guests did not fear the changing color of her eyes, as she couldn't control the transformation. It hadn't happened in many months, but fright always caused her eye pigment to alter.

Scarlett took a deep cleansing breath, then left them for the library. She slid the double doors together, gazing one final time at her guests, then shut the doors tight for privacy.

"You have our undivided attention," Nicolai growled. "Speak. Why are you here?"

"The queen mother has become more powerful," Theo said forcefully, trying to shake off Bensen's hold. "I've come to offer a warning."

"Who sent you, cunning lion? What hand do you intend to bite this time? For whatever news you mean to share, I don't trust you."

"Trust?" he replied, scoffing. "You have no choice but to trust me. No choice but to listen to my counsel, Lord Graydon. I mean to alert you to a course of action, an action you must attend to, should you have a care for your future bride."

Scarlett approached. She knew she should permit her fiancé to ask the questions, but she couldn't help intruding. This was her fight, her life they conversed about. "Who sent you, Theodore? I don't trust that you would travel to Drum Manor of your own accord."

"I cannot say."

Scarlett shook her head. "You need to reveal your hidden truth, for we cannot act without knowing why we should."

He studied her, a compelling disregard that gripped. "You're in grave danger, but if you do as I say, hope can still be found."

"I don't believe a word of your lies," Nicolai said with a grimace. "You came to my door, thinking to snare my fiancée in your trap. I won't let you."

"I question your motives myself, Theodore," Scarlett hastened to add. "The time has arrived to tell us the truth. Quit stalling."

Theodore peered around the room. The crease of his brows and sudden popping of the scar beneath his right eye offered the only sign that he was afraid. "A rebellion has begun, a plan to remove the improper sovereign from the throne and replace him with the rightful heir. But the hand of evil must be dealt with to enable justice to occur. The queen mother must die."

"Ambitious," Bensen said, prodding him from behind, "that you think the queen could be so easily removed, but without a plan, without magic, the throne's succession is unlikely to succeed."

Nicolai faced him. "Continue. You have not told us anything of value."

"A mole, an agent of change, has learned a vital piece of evidence, but while following the queen's movements was caught spying. Sadly, by now, he has paid the highest price for his information. I'm here because it's no longer safe to reside in the castle."

"I'm sorry," Nicolai replied, considering, "if what you say is true."

"We think the queen mother means to bring further harm to Princess Scarlett and yourself, Lord Graydon. Our spy believes the witch was courting demons of the Netherworld, but we don't know for what purpose."

Scarlett's fingers flew to her mouth. "How could she attempt such an evil feat? And why would she want to?"

Theodore placed his hands on his hips. "We don't know firm details, but what we do know raises our concern. The queen has been seen trekking into the king's forest; meeting with persons on a pathway no one has been able to locate. We don't know her true purpose. We've supposed the queen means to finish the business of harming your family. She means to murder you."

"But there's only me, and I'm immune to her powers—"

"Princess Scarlett," Theodore replied, his tone firm. "Your sisters are alive."

Scarlett pushed past Nicolai to reach Theo. *Surely he lied!* She grasped Theo's lapels. "Is it true?" she begged, shaking him. "Please, Theodore, don't play with my emotions by telling me lies. Ruby. Rose. Are my sisters alive?"

"I assure you, they are, or at least they were the last time I saw them."

"If what you say is true, where are they now?" Nicolai asked.

"I dare not say," Theodore replied. "Sorry, but with the demons the witch is courting, spies could be listening to our conversation. I can only reveal that the Yeoman Warder, Garrett, is with Ruby. And I myself attended to Rose, before she departed with a friend close to the alliance. I sincerely hope they are both safe."

Scarlett sighed; she approached a scissor chair and sat. "I fear what you'll say next," she said, her voice rising to hysteria. "I fear your words more than I can say and I don't know if I can trust you. What must we do?"

Nicolai joined her. He grasped her hand. They both regarded Theodore, uneasy, willing him to speak. "It's come to our attention that one person might be able to help, as far as we can tell. A mage, a sorceress with powers similar to the queen mother, the witch."

Scarlett nibbled at her lip. "There's something you're not saying. Who would know of such a possibility? Who would know that a sorceress could come to my aid? Our aid, if what you say is true."

Theodore eyed her in a determined, pointed way. "This is a vital secret," he said, concern written on his face. "I hope I'm not struck dead for sharing this news, Princess. But only one woman could know of such a goddess—the true queen mother, Queen Regana."

Chapter Eight

SISTER MARY MARGARET

Castle Street hummed with the preparations of trade and Mary wasn't surprised to see shopkeepers milling on the laneway, spilling gossip. What else could people do in times of darkness, but go on with their lives, go on with their work, as if nothing untoward was taking place. Yet, everyone knew blood sport had occurred in the king's forest and many were suspicious of further horrors heralding from the castle, and who might be affected by each decree.

Mary ignored the conversations as best she could while passing across the cobblestones; continuing with her life as if she didn't see the crimes or sense the fear, but she saw the sorrow in men's and women's expressions and understood the hunger where the poor huddled in groups. They, the people, murmured in undistinguishable tones, their voices lower than normal.

Whatever news they spoke about could not be learned by her and perhaps it was best not knowing as she had troubles of her own. An absence of trust had led to an underground alliance. A deficiency of confidence, bridging concern, had garnered her involvement. Mary was afraid for her life but had someplace to be, and the sharp enunciation of their vocal cues only heightened her anxiety.

Had Gill shared news of the alliance? And what innocent might be caught next?

Sighing, Mary walked faster as she moved among the villagers, nudging shoulders with commoners, hurrying across the cobblestones, scanning left and right, fretting that unknown threats hid everywhere. She tried to avoid suspicion while passing Whyte's bakery. The door was closed and barred to customers, but the aroma of fresh bread suffused the air. Her stomach clenched in response to the aroma, but she wasn't hungry; days of anxiety had spoiled her appetite. She'd lose the meager contents in her gut if she even attempted to break her fast.

When a pop of noise sounded, she jerked, then glanced at the apothecary, her hands clasped modestly at her waist, soon nodding to William the chemist when he passed through his doorway, wiping his hands on a cloth. When he raised his hand in greeting, she marveled at his dark surcoat and considered his dour appearance. Although a shiver crawled up her spine at his scrutiny, Mary responded in equal measure, lifting her hand tentatively, waving it regally, then clasped her rosary beads as if to say: 'yes, I am a nun, a priestess of a religious order, who fingers tiny rose beads to convey a purposeful and spiritual demeanor.'

When she walked past John and Will Baxter, two brothers, both local shoemakers, she told herself not to run.

Running might caution the shopkeepers to notice her, and the queen's spies could be anyone, even these two.

Someone watched.

Someone had learned the truth.

Someone knew.

Mary gripped her lip with her teeth, aware that the religious were not immune from persecution.

Fire. Flames— *An axe!*

Though she'd taken precautions the past few weeks, she lived in fear that a witch might learn her real identity. A soul had already paid a price. *Poor Gill!*

Her fault. *Her fault—*

But risks must be taken if the kingdom were to realize its true royal patronage, a boy whose name could not be revealed, and daughters who must avoid the kingdom to be safe.

Mary considered the secrets Queen Cynara held and the plot she must be planning. Surely she was scheming revenge, and new opportunities to murder the rightful heirs of the throne. *What business did the queen contrive in the forest, late at night?* Gill must have learned a vital clue.

Mary startled when a villager bumped into her. "Sorry," she muttered, knowing the contact had not been her fault. She only glanced at the peasant youth, his face gaunt, his expression hungry, his clothing ragged and unclean. Normally she'd stop and wish blessings on the orphan children, but not today. Today, she must reach her destination. Passing beneath the Water Gate, she progressed to the only safe place she and the lord chancellor could meet; the village church.

But now she wondered what further use their secret meetings could be. The witch had become a dangerous force. The consequence of breaking the curse had slowed Cynara's pursuit only momentarily. Mary knew scarlet marks hid beneath Cynara's outlandish collar. Lady Eliza, the queen's lady in waiting, had told her they were horrible.

Whiplash lacerations had only served to ignite Cynara's anger, compelling a madness that fueled unpredictability, retribution and vengeance, with no compassion for the human soul. Likely, only death could overthrow the witch's rule and Mary wondered what counsel might aid the ending.

Aniron would never leave her crystal palace.

When a hammer struck iron, she gasped, sucking in a breath in alarm. When she realized that Thom Spens had struck the anvil, already hard at work in the smithy, she calmed, glanced in his direction, and considered the manner in which he nodded in her direction. Unsmiling, serious; a stern facial expression caused her stomach to clench. *Should she fear Thom?* The blacksmith watched her pass by this way frequently; could he suspect her goings-on? Maybe on her next visit, she'd take Wexam Street past the market, and traverse the long way around to avoid his suspicion.

Sighing, she scrutinized the perimeter of the church lawn and passed through the gates of St. Sophia's Chapel. She hoped she hadn't placed the lives of other nuns at risk by entering the sanctuary, but what other choice did she have but to seek her accomplice.

Sister Mary reached for the church door's handle. Grasping it, she pulled the door open and proceeded through the doorway into the narthex, then walked up the center aisle of the nave, soon turning the handle of the confessional box.

She scrutinized the inner sanctum to ensure she was safely alone, then opened the door of the confessional and proceeded inside, closing the door behind herself. Taking hold of an ornamental cross on the wall, she pulled it from its hidden cavity and forced a secret lever downward. A locking mechanism clicked inside the wooden panel and the wall retreated slightly. Gazing one final time through the wooden slats of the enclosure, she pushed the hidden door aside and passed through a concealed entryway into a secret chamber.

"I didn't think you'd come," Mikkel Daniel, the lord chancellor said, rising from a pew. Candlelight flickered inside the narrow corridor, brightening his eyes and casting a glow against the stone wall and on the opposite wooden panels.

"I took the risk. Though one might try, it's not possible for me to hide when times are difficult. Your face bears the strain of recent crimes. Worry lines crease your face." Mary closed the hidden door. "Come to me."

The bishop offered his comfort and held her close to his chest. His mouth fell victim to her lips, and she kissed him, drowning in their sinful embrace. "I know it's wrong to want you at times like this," she said, bending her neck to permit his kisses, "but I'm weak, and I need a distraction."

"I've learned from hearing confessions that stating one's worries, one's sins, leads to deliverance. We'll mind our behavior and beg penance for it after," Mikkel replied, tugging at her veil and pulling it from her head. The coif slipped away, too, and slid to the stone flooring to pool at her feet.

"I've found comfort in your embrace; even so, I don't think the time is right for matters of the heart." She released him. "We must talk about the queen and recent wrongs against the people. Gill likely revealed information about the alliance, or those who have taken part in it."

"I have not heard anything from the Privy Council that would lead me to believe he talked, but it's a grave situation. I don't deny it."

She rested her head against Mikkel's shoulder. He was a dependable staff, a solid length of iron she could brace herself against during wicked weather.

"Mikkel—" She stared at his eyes and grasped his shoulders. "Gill will have been punished in an attempt to learn his secrets. He may have shared news of the alliance during his imprisonment. News of you; news of me."

Long slender fingers stroked her cheeks and twined in brunette strands threaded with gray. "He didn't share anything of importance, or my lady would not be here. Forget your cares, take off your robe," he said, eagerly, "I've missed your caresses."

"Mikkel," she whispered. "We must not. The timing isn't right."

He pivoted her away from the secret doorway, closer to the pew. "Forget about that evil woman. I have command of the council, command of the king. Place your trust in me. Let me stroke your petals."

Despite herself, she gave in to her lover and removed the outermost layer of her habit. That he was a religious man hardly bothered her. It was true he belonged to the gods and the gods work, but without his wardrobe he was no more than a man. And though she wore the garb of a nun, she was no more than a woman with desires of her own. She'd cope with the gods when she met them in the Otherworld, but she supposed motherly beings of a supreme nature had encouraged these gifts as well, and it was a shame to let them spoil.

"Are you asking me to love you, Mikkel?" Mary rasped, placing her surcoat on the pew and standing before him in her linen kirtle. "If the queen mother learns of our relationship, or learns my identity, I'll never couple with you again."

"In these difficult times," he said, hesitating, "I'm asking you to focus on our relationship, not of that, that evil."

Mikkel breathed huskily and his hand meandered to her waist. "A time will come when we can satisfy our desires, but you're right, we must talk about the situation to consider that poor Gill was caught and determine what further steps should be taken." He ushered her to the pew and encouraged her to sit. "I wanted to tell you a secret of great import, but the timing never seemed right."

"You seem concerned. What is it? I give you leave to tell me."

His forehead lined with trepidation. "A warrior waits to enter the battle. A young man who has captured the queen mother's interest, one who has found favor with the king."

"Who would be so brave?"

"The Master of the Horse, Keldan Ashburn."

"I know of him; the son of Lord Ashburn." At the mention of the surname, Mikkel frowned, and a regard in his expression gave her cause to worry. "Do we take the risk by sending another lamb to do battle?"

He glanced away, shaking his head. "We don't have a choice."

"There's something more. What are you keeping from me?"

"You should know the facts if we're to place another young man at risk. *Regana*, Your Majesty, I have kept a secret from you."

"Don't call me by my real name. It hurts too much to hear it," she said, becoming emotional. "Share instead your secret. Whatever it is, you can trust me."

"You won't like it."

Mary became alarmed. "Stop stalling. Tell me."

He peered keenly into her eyes. He grasped her shoulders and tenderly rubbed them.

"The boy, Mary, the master of the horse, he is your son."

Mary gasped. "What are you saying? What have you done?"

"Now Mary, calm down. Don't raise your voice or look at me as if I've deceived you."

"Haven't you? After the boy was born, you promised to keep him safe, by placing him in a home where he would never learn of his royal lineage. I hid his birth from everyone —his sisters, his father—an evil queen. I denied my son his mother's love, *his mother's love*, a huge sacrifice for me, all so a hideous witch would never find him and do him harm. And now, after time has passed, you disclose he has found favor with the witch who has come close to destroying my family?"

"I see that you're angry. Calm yourself and let me explain."

Mary stepped away, breaking their contact, wishing she could increase the space between them, but the corridor was narrow. "I am so angry with you." She reached for her surcoat lying on the pew. Mikkel stepped to her and pulled the garment from her hands, but Mary's palm pressed flat against his chest, not permitting him to come closer.

"Mary—"

"Mikkel, do you know what you have done? You have put my son—Rickard's son—in the gravest danger."

Mikkel appeared annoyed. "I placed him in a good home with a good family who had found favor with both the former King Rickard and his new queen. I understood your motherly affection and your wishes for your son to be safe in a household where no one would know his royal parentage—but a prince could never be raised as a simple country lad, especially if this reign of blood and magic was ever to end."

"I would not consider Lord Ashburn good counsel for my son."

Mikkel sighed. "King Rickard would have wanted his true born son to learn a proper education, even if it is cutting, to know how to rule in his stead, to understand how to care for his people, should he ever have the opportunity to do so. I acted as King Rickard would have commanded. Mary, surely you understand."

"I understand the anger flowing through my veins. I'm searching for a measure of restraint, so I don't say something I'll regret," Mary said, considering Mikkel's comments. She turned to the secret door, giving the man she loved her back. "All you need to understand is that I am a mother. I had enough worry, concerning myself with three daughters. Now, I need to protect my son, too. I won't see him forfeit to that, that ebony witch."

Mikkel reached for her. She felt his fingers stroke her arm

and clutch her waist. Grudgingly, she let him pull her against his chest. "Your children have the blessings of the gods," he whispered in her ear, his teeth nipping at her lobe. "As long as Odin watches over them, they will be safe."

"I don't take comfort from the gods. Odin hasn't visited the kingdom during this blight." Mary sighed, shifting in his embrace, laying her head against his chest. "What do you have in mind, then, for my son?"

"He has only been asked to keep watch over the night and to learn specific facts of value. He is not to accept risk of any kind."

Mary attempted to calm herself as she could not change the circumstances. "I suppose it's better for a true born son of King Rickard to be part of the resolution. Does he know who he is? Does he know of his royal birthing?"

"No, Mary. Keldan is unaware of his royal parents. He believes he is the natural born child of Lord and Lady Ashburn."

"The lord who gave Prince Lowell the gift of a horse on his name day? That's an interesting bit of information."

Mikkel fingered the fabric at her side, slowly pulling her kirtle upward. "Lady Ashburn's child was stillborn after a difficult birth. She still believes the son placed in her hands was her own. Only Lord Ashburn knows the truth. Your son is safe."

"I hope you're right," Mary whispered, her breath quickening as Mikkel's hand fondled her lower thigh, his fingers sliding upward, crossing her hip and fondling her belly before capturing her breast.

FOR A TIME, Mary lounged on the uncomfortable pew with Mikkel, succumbing to the weakness of desire, then lounging in the afterglow of their lovemaking, contemplating the confidence that had been divulged, but she couldn't stay away from the castle for too long of a period, and it was soon time to return to the tiny chapel in the northeastern tower. She gave her lover one final kiss, enjoying the warmth of their embrace before reaching for the secret latch.

She retraced her steps, leaving Mikkel inside the secret chamber. He'd exit through the other doorway, which led to a private corridor and his bedchamber.

She left St. Sophia's Chapel with a warm glow on her face, contemplating her return to the castle.

Prayer was foremost on her mind. A whispered conversation she'd offer to the ether, hoping the God Odin would hear her prayers and keep her family safe from harm. She contemplated her son's name and was glad he'd been given a strong title. Rickard would be proud. She promised herself she wouldn't spy on him often. He had to remain a stranger to her, but she couldn't wait to look at this man, knowing she had found her son.

SISTER GERTRUDE

SISTER GERTRUDE WATCHED Sister Mary leaving the church. When the nun had first entered the chapel, Gertrude had been cleaning the floor in the choir loft. When the door swung open, she ducked behind a pew, and unobserved, had watched Sister Mary parade up the aisle and then disappear inside the confessional box. Suspicion had restrained her from offering a proper hello.

She had waited a prolonged period of time for the sister to share her sinful confessions to the bishop, thinking the interlude inside the confessional box inappropriate. So lengthy, she'd given up on waiting for the sister to leave and had returned to scrubbing the floor.

Foul air and wicked sin, she knew something was amiss between the bishop and the sister. Sister Gertrude's estimations were proven correct when wicked sounds, guttural groans of physical temptation, wafted from somewhere beyond the confessional box. She shook her head, understanding they hid their unnatural affair in the confines of a secret chamber.

Anger contorted her face while picturing the sinners cavorting in mortal sin, and by servants who had made their promises to the gods. Such wickedness must be reported, and she knew who would be interested in learning what she had heard.

But who could she tell? The queen mother was wicked, dangerous, and more unpredictable than the human sinners. She couldn't be trusted to act in a responsible way. So, what should a nun do?

Gertrude returned to her work, cleaning the choir loft until her fingers were raw and the floor gleamed. If only a savior could see that lambs had fallen like the fallen angels.

Would the gods be willing to forgive them? Perhaps, but

surely a form of penance would be required to mitigate the sinners' actions.

Sister Gertrude considered that saving the Lord Chancellor and Sister Mary from sin depended on her. She would trust that the solution to the problem would reveal itself after a heartfelt spell of prayer.

Since she was alone in the north transept of the chapel, she prostrated herself in the shape of the cross, lying flat on the flooring, her head resting on the stones, her hands palms up, reaching toward the Otherworld, praying.

"Our Father, who art in the Otherworld, hallowed be Thy name; Thy kingdom come. Thy will be done…"

Chapter Nine

PRINCESS RUBY

R uby struggled to rouse her conscious mind, unable to recognize that she was trapped inside a mountain cavern. The chamber seemed cold and the hard rock she'd collapsed against had garnered an unfavorable position for her head. The ground oppressed her cheeks; the cold numbed her skin. She moaned, sliding her fingers through clay silt debris and tiny bits of frost-laden shale. She wept a breath, too tired to open her eyes, too weak to lift her eyelids, *listening…*

Silence.

No music tweeted from Mother Nature's hole in the mountain. Neither were earth's elements audible, such as wind or rain, or human life with its distinctive vocal cues. For all she knew, she had been lulled inside her own unconscious mind, and was *dreaming*, her body cramped beneath the columns of a massive mausoleum, squeezed between the sand pillars of a great pyramid, buried beneath triangular mounds of clay-packed soil, or worse, she lay in a graveyard, or god forbid, a tomb. A place where the wind forgot to breathe and the rain didn't have the strength to weep. She might as well be deaf, or dead. *Was she dead?* Perhaps her soul was soaring, surviving in an alternate universe. A place where noise was forbidden. A place where silence reigned and not an evil queen.

But then, she did perceive a symptom of life: the soft whooshing of her own pulsing heartbeat, the noise throbbing within her eardrums, and a quiet stream of inhalations, almost tentative, as she breathed.

Ruby wasn't dead; she was alive.

Weary, she forced her eyes open only to find blackness; an impenetrable night, an insipid curtain that extinguished the sun and banished the light. Ebony darkness wrapped her inside its cocoon. A confining place that restricted her movement. She couldn't picture so much as a gray shadow, but she could think. A memory emerged.

She recalled rocks tumbling, a curtain of debris raining on her. Maybe a rock had struck her head, rendering her unconscious, robbing her of her sight. She considered the unthinkable; maybe she was blind. *Cynara—*

A second sensory perception, *pain.* She stifled a cry. She was lying on her belly. Her head hurt. A stabbing ache tortured the corners of her mind. She tried to reach for her head, but it occurred to her that a heavy weight held her immobile and pressed against her back, her buttocks and legs; preventing her from movement. She realized; she wasn't alone.

"Garrett?" she croaked, sputtering. "Can you hear me?"

She heard a groan.

"Garrett, tell me you can hear me."

She couldn't bear his weight and attempted to free herself

from his bulk. Twisting beneath him, Ruby anguished while trying to break free of the weight pinning her to the ground. Wriggling, she edged her way out from underneath him. Once she was free, she succumbed to tears. Her head hurt. Her backside hurt, and she could barely feel her feet. Stretching onto her back, she rubbed her legs, feeling a sharp stinging sensation threading its way to her toes, and although the pain brought her to tears, she had to think of her protector. She rose to a sitting position, wiped her eyes, and leaned toward him.

"Garrett?" she asked him with concern, her voice cracking while reaching for him in the darkness, her hands examining his back, a shield of armor littered with clay and fallen rock. She brushed off the debris as best she could. "Garrett, can you hear me?"

She ran her hands over him, examining his neck and shoulders. She leaned in closer, her fingers sliding over his mouth, his nose, and a tangled nest of furry beard she could not see. She searched for signs of life; she heard a whisper.

"So, you're breathing." She sighed, relieved. "Alive but hurt. You unselfish man, injured because you tried to protect me and keep me safe."

Searching for a reason for his silence, Ruby examined the contours of his forehead, her fingers roaming into the rugged silk of his curly hair, searching. *Wet and sticky fluid.* She leaned in closer, smelling, ascertaining the metallic scent of blood. Garrett was bleeding. A lump had formed where he'd been struck.

"Oh, Garrett," she said, frightened he could not hear her, scared he might never wake up. "Please don't do this," she cried, wiping at her eyes. "I'm too frightened to be held in this cavern alone. Please, wake up. You have protected me from injury, and suffered a wound at my expense."

She needed to bind his injury to stop the bleeding. She reached for her clothing and pulled up a woolen layer edged with ermine fur, followed by her surcoat and linen kirtle. Concerned only for her protector, she ripped a strip of linen off.

"It hardly matters that you saved me," she whispered, reaching for him again, not knowing whether he heard her or not. She sought him in the night, pressing the fabric to his injured head and binding it tight. "I don't think we'll make it out of this situation. She means to see us dead. This time, I think the witch has succeeded."

Garrett groaned. "Ruby—"

"—Garrett," Ruby exclaimed, pressing close to the sound of his voice, her hand holding his head. "Can you hear me?"

"Aye, I hear you, Princess. I wish I could see you."

"You're wounded. You have an injury on your head. The witch meant to bury us alive. But we've escaped burial, and I'm tending to your wound as best I can to stop the bleeding. It's black as pitch inside this cavern. I can't see your wound to clean it."

"Pity," he said, whispering. "The wound and our plight."

"She has us. She's won. We'll die in this, this burial chamber."

"Perhaps," he agreed.

Frightened and not knowing what else to do, Ruby nestled close to her protector and stretched out beside him on a bed of rock and clay. She knew it wasn't proper to lie close to a man. It was unseemly for a young woman, but she needed his comfort. She wanted to be held, and what other choice did she have? In this world where the end seemed near, he was her only rock. And so, still holding his head, she shifted closer, pulled his head nearer to her cheeks, and came in contact with his matted beard.

"Ruby…"

And though she shifted to the somber note of his voice, she was blind to his physical form. She couldn't see his eyes to judge his worry, or his lips to consider his passion, no matter that mere inches separated them, so she pressed closer still to touch his life. So close, his breath stirred against her mouth.

"Sweet princess, you must not…"

"Garrett," she replied, her lips brushing ever so softly against his, "we're going to die, you and I, and I'm frightened. I can't bear the thought of it. You're all I have."

"Aw, darling," he replied, reaching for her, pulling her into his embrace and offering his arm as a pillow. "I made a promise to protect you. I mean to try."

"We're buried." She moaned, her voice breaking, tears welling in her eyes. "You can't protect me. I knew it days ago. That witch buried us inside this cave. We'll die in here."

"Don't despair, Amira, my ruby gemstone," he replied, pulling her closer, kissing her forehead. "I know the situation seems bleak, but if a pathway to freedom exists, have faith, have hope, for if the gods are on our side, I'll find a way out. When I've recovered my strength, I'll search for our bags and build a fire. Thankfully, I brought them inside the cavern before the opening collapsed."

"I'm not sure I'm grateful," Ruby whimpered, wiping at

her eyes. "It's as black as the Netherworld inside this hole. If only I could see you."

"There's not much to see. No more than a simple man and a princess, rooting in the dirt."

"Digging our own graves, we might as well be."

"I'll not hear talk of an unpleasant sort. You're my reason to live; my reason to try." He sighed. "The battle cry doesn't spy her last breath until the soldier accepts his final mark. We're not dead, and hardly done for yet."

"Oh, Garrett," Ruby said, despairing. "While I appreciate your attempt at hope, our mark binds us to the Otherworld. We won't make it out of here, at least not with our breath intact."

He kissed her forehead again. "It's best I find our packs and start a fire. Options won't present unless we search for them. I know it's dark. I understand you can't see, but crawl on your knees and feel with your hands until we locate our packs."

"We should wait until the bleeding stops."

"Let me bleed. We'll find our packs, then we'll worry about blood. If I'm to lessen your concerns, I need to know what's inside this cavern. I'm already weary of the night."

"I'm sick of everything black myself."

Sighing, she moved away from his warmth, settled onto her hands and knees, and began searching, her fingertips sifting through clay silt debris.

Chapter Ten

PRINCESS ROSE

A cloud-filled sky and an ocean of deep, cerulean blue extended across the seascape for as far as Rose could see. Somber, she contemplated the ocean from the vantage point of the *Sea Monster's* main deck, swaying with the ocean's swell each time the boat rose and died away. The spray misted her cheeks, and the sea air should have earned a breath of tranquility, but a mounting fear, a premonition roiling in waves tipped white, caused her stomach to clench.

She eyed the horizon, her hand holding the railing, her skirts flapping from a sudden gust of wind. A woolen shawl hugged her shoulders and she held it firmly with her free hand while braving the oceanic breeze nipping at her face, which watered her eyes and ruffled her hair, forcing vibrant red curls into her eyes. She released the railing temporarily to grasp the length, then tucked the strands behind her ear. Wobbling with the rhythm of the ship, grateful that the captain had permitted her to leave the cabin. Given the storm that was coming, she did not relish being isolated inside a captain's hold.

Grasping the railing again, she glanced at Captain Perrow, who stood on the windward side of the quarterdeck, a spyglass held in his hand and pointed out to sea, searching, always watching for land. And although Rose sighted a gull on the starboard side, which should have suggested to her the promise of ground beneath her feet, she knew they would never reach safety. She'd seen as much with her second sight.

Edwin gave up his search, hurried down the short flight of stairs, and came to stand beside her. "What's the matter, Bella Rosa? Why are you so glum?"

She shook her head, not caring what he thought. "I'm going to drown."

His eyebrows lifted in surprise; his face wrinkling, expressing his surprise. "Drown, did you say?" he asked, refusing to take her seriously. "I don't think so. Not on my watch, Princess."

Rose leaned against the railing. The breeze whispered against her skin, breathing possibility, and bringing with it the nervous scent of the sea. The whitecaps were noticeable, and she reflected on how quickly they could rise. No matter what the captain said, her foreboding could not be deterred; the ship and its passengers were bound for a watery grave.

"I thought you'd play the pirate, the one to throw me into the sea. I was wrong. You'll play no part in the wickedness that delivers me into the ocean to drown. The wind is picking up. Can you feel it? A storm is coming."

"Rose. Darling— Don't be so dramatic. Look at the sky." He indicated, waving his hand. "Blue stretches as far as the eye can see, and while there's a breeze, the wind is calm. Did you see the gull? That's a sure sign we'll reach land."

"The wind will threaten us, Captain Perrow, and before she blows, you'd best batten down the hatches." She gestured toward the crew. "In fact, you should make haste and shout your orders, advising the crew. The waves will rise from the sea, crowning the ship, and…"

"A sea monster will swallow us whole, or some other odd nonsense? I don't think so, Rose. You must stop whispering your dour theories; the crew is starting to voice their concerns about you. You're making my job more difficult."

Rose grasped his arm, her face expressing the concern she felt inside her heart. "Edwin," she scolded him, shaking him. "You fool, I have seen it," she said, hissing. "The water will rise, higher than the ship. The bow will touch the sky before she sinks into the deep, into the valley of a black and wicked sea. The keel will yaw about from side to side and the hull will be damaged. The main mast will break free from her hold and fall into the ocean. Your men will be swept away and spilled into the sea, and you and I, we will…"

"Stop it, Rose!" he said with a grimace. "You're beginning to disturb me. You sound like a witch. The men have been telling me stories of the passenger with red hair, a woman who brought bad spirits and evil omens aboard this ship. I tried to keep you from them by confining you inside my cabin, but now that I permit you to frequent the deck, you spill crazy stories, filling my crew with worry. This nonsense doesn't assist me in keeping you safe."

"I'm sorry," Rose replied, lowering her head. "I don't mean to cause concern, least of all to myself, but I have had visions." She raised her head again, meeting his eyes earnestly. "Misfortune will find us."

He glanced at a quartermaster standing nearby, then grasped her hand. "Rose," Edwin said, begging, "please don't let my men hear you speaking like this." The captain pulled her into his embrace. "What am I to do with you and your visions? Please, don't worry. I promise to take care of my ship, my crew, and you."

He kissed her forehead and then released her. She didn't know how to feel about the contact, the hug or the kiss. No man had ever kissed her before. She contemplated the affection while scrutinizing his serious mien, but an evil witch was more concerning than a man's touch, and she realized he didn't believe in her visions anyway. To him, her warnings were no more than images presented from an overworked imagination, so she said no more on the subject.

"The weather is known to be uncertain this time of the year; the sea can be choppy, but if what you say is true, you had best return to my quarters. It's the safest place to be."

"What about you?" she asked, not wanting to leave him, feeling safer in his company.

"My men need me. Now off you go."

Rose begrudgingly left his presence, walking up the stairs to the quarterdeck and soon reaching his quarters. Grasping the handle to his cabin, she glanced behind, hearing him shouting orders to his men.

"Reduce sail, batten down the hatches, and lash everything down that can move. A storm might be coming, and I don't plan on going down with the ship."

When he shouted further instructions, Rose knew he had

believed the tale. "And men, remove the main sails, lash them hard to the side. Tight, you understand, so they won't pry free."

She heard the grumbling from the crew and caught sight of their angry expressions, as they openly stared at her, but the men were soon rushing to complete their work.

"It's all right, Rose," he called to her. "Return to my quarters. Go inside. I'll join you as soon as I'm able."

Rose did as Edwin commanded, grateful that he believed her. Stepping inside his cabin, she closed the door and leaned against the frame. The tears came, but she wiped them away. Her hand went to her lips. Would his belief in her vision be enough to quell the coming storm? For she was certain Queen Cynara had somehow found a way to ride the wind, finding a direct pathway to a princess. While the boat had been aptly named the *Sea Monster*, the only *monster* on the sea was the witch, and she was soon to find her victim.

Chapter Eleven

PRINCESS SCARLETT

Scarlett waited in the entry hall of Drum Manor with her arms folded against her chest. It was almost time to travel to an unknown destination, and the thought of leaving the only place that had ever felt like home caused her distress. She tried to distill the fear, not wanting the awareness of potential danger to overrule her will to act. Leaving left much of her life uncertain, such as a vow of marriage that had been placed on hold, and the comforts of hearth and home as well. Once she passed over the threshold, her life would forever change, and not necessarily for the better.

Evil threatened and an enemy lay in wait.

A pair of marble statues, a girl on the left and a boy on the right, stared at her, making her uncomfortable. She recalled the first occasion of examining these childhood statues. They were semiprecious. How could she leave them? What if they weren't here when she returned, if she could return? She wasn't certain of anything.

Bensen was loading their luggage inside the horse-drawn

carriage while she waited for Nicolai to join her. Scarlett glanced at the drawing room and peeked inside the library, too, recalling how the chambers had been coated with dust at her arrival. Now, they were clean and inviting, but sometimes when she regarded their restoration, her mind played tricks, and she wondered if she was observing a mirage that might soon dissolve, evaporating before her eyes, leaving her bereft and unsafe. *Once they had departed, would dust mar the surfaces again?* The circumstances in the manor house appeared easily understood, but ever suspicious, Scarlett sensed the lingering dust, a cryptic reminder that forced her to address darker thoughts and a disturbing reality that past events couldn't be left where they belonged, in the past.

Dust and ash settled on her shoulders, again.

When Bensen opened the door, she startled. "Oh, there you are, Princess. The carriage has been prepared. If you're ready, I'm able to assist you."

"That's all right, Bensen. I'm waiting for Nicolai. He went to his bedchamber to retrieve an item of importance."

"His dueling pistol?" Bensen drawled, his eyebrows raised in question. "Some good that will do when the witch engages us with her company."

The frankness caused her alarm, and though she swallowed her fear, she wouldn't admit to the butler that she was afraid. "Hopefully, the mage will address our concerns before he has the need to use it, but I feel the weight of this uncertainty. If my mother is alive; I still can't believe it."

"Your mother is alive," Bensen stated, his reluctance to believe apparent, "if what Theodore says is true."

Scarlett glanced at the staircase when she heard Nicolai

hurrying down the stairs. When he reached the landing, he crossed the entry hall at a brisk pace. She reached for his hand and he grasped her elbow, urging her toward his lips. She welcomed his strength and the affection in his love, especially the kiss against her forehead.

"Don't fret over disclosures we can't prove," Nicolai said, massaging her chin with his fingertips. "I see the worry lines creasing your forehead. Think of this journey as an adventure. A destination that might bring you closer to your family."

"It could make you a richer man. Is that why you're supporting me?"

Nicolai frowned. Scarlett didn't know why she had worried him with her skepticism. They had formed a loving relationship, one in which she had made a long-term commitment. His expression soured and she wished she had kept her uneasiness to herself.

"I thought you trusted me."

"I do."

"Then don't doubt my capacity to stand beside you, no matter what happens. I support you because I care for you. If you don't know by now how much you mean to me, you never will. You crawled beneath my skin and built a relationship with my heart. Unless I've interpreted your emotions incorrectly, our love is not built on human riches."

"I understand. I'm sorry. I do trust you."

"Do you?" he asked, bringing her nearer to his chest. "You must not let fear control your emotions. We've built a strong foundation. Doubting this will only serve to ruin our happiness. Now, our carriage is waiting and we have a mage to find. If you're ready, we should begin our journey."

Scarlett placed her hand on Nicolai's arm, witnessing his sincere expression. "I'm sorry, I'm not myself. I should have more faith in what we've found together. I shouldn't let the past ruin the future."

Bensen didn't speak while opening the manor house door, wisely keeping silent while motioning for them to precede him outside.

Nicolai grasped her waist, his hand squeezing. "It's all right, my love. I understand more than you think I do. Let's focus on the issue at hand and try to forget the past."

They passed through the doorway, but once Scarlett stood on the front landing, she frowned, seeing Theodore waiting at the front of the carriage. The man averted his attention from her regard; maybe he was only pretending to safeguard the two geldings, and she was still suspicious of him.

"Must he come with us?" Scarlett whispered, facing Nicolai's thoughtful expression. "Can we believe him?"

"I trust him as much as I would a skunk, and I do worry what nastiness the weasel might spray; even so, he must accompany us if we're to learn the truth. He won't be driving. I don't trust him to take the reins, so Bensen will manage the horses."

"Don't worry, Princess," Bensen said, his eyebrows rising. "If Theo tries anything, I'll stick him with my cane."

"Always the jokester," Nicolai snickered, ushering Scarlett toward the carriage. He opened the door, and she put her foot on the rise, but then she shifted her stance to study Drum Manor one final time. The towering gables, the manor where she had experienced not only the greatest frights but also the happiest moments of her life. Could she ever return?

"Don't worry," Nicolai said, offering his support. "I see your concern. We will come home to Drum Manor. I promise you this on my life."

Uncertain, she scrutinized his eyes. "I'd never want to see you hurt, or something worse, dead. Wherever this journey takes us, we will always have a home as long as we stay together, wherever that home may be."

Nicolai gestured toward the wagon's door. "It's time to leave, Scarlett."

Accepting his direction, she shied away from Theodore's observation and climbed inside the carriage. Nicolai followed behind her and once they were both inside, he closed the door.

"Will Bensen be joining us inside the cabin?" Scarlett asked, settling on the bench.

"When he feels it's appropriate to do so, but for now, he wants to share the driver's seat with Theodore to get to know the man. See what's up, as he confided with me. As he terms it, 'get under the man's skin' in an attempt to learn his secrets."

"Our butler is wise, brave, too, but I see you don't trust the warden either."

"I don't trust certain men at the best of times, but in this instance, I don't know what to believe. Yet, I hope his statement is true. We must consider why a man would take a risk to seek you out. Maybe your family is alive like he says. It's possible."

"Do you think my mother is alive? My sisters?"

He appeared sincere while squeezing her hand. "For your

sake, I hope so. We cannot know for sure, but the truth will be revealed in time."

"Maybe," Scarlett said, frowning. She shifted on the bench to peer outside, soon hearing Bensen cluck at the horses. The carriage jostled and the horses whinnied, beginning to trot. They were on their way.

They traveled in companionable silence for a time. Scarlett stared out the window, considering the passing landscape, and daydreaming of the moment when she might see her mum again. Would she know her mother if she saw her, or would their reunion feel as if she shared a conversation with a long-lost stranger?

As the horses trudged onward, Scarlett grew accustomed to listening to the clip clop sound of hooves plodding against the hard-packed trail, causing the carriage to rock at times. She perused the view of seaside bluffs in the distance, pastures dotted with milking cows, and villagers walking along the laneway to Culley's Cove. When she tired of minding the scenery, she closed her eyes, and while holding Nicolai's hand, their fingers entwined, she drifted off to sleep.

She succumbed to dreams, her mind discovering a childhood puppet drama with snapshots of her younger life. Within a bedchamber of Camden Castle and inside a royal tower, a memory emerged of a woman brushing her hair. Thereafter, she hugged her close to her bosom and assisted her atop a soft mattress, tucking her inside the blankets of a curtained framework, protecting her from the approaching night. The memory brought comfort and a feeling of safety.

Sweet dreams, child, Scarlett heard a feminine illusion whisper.

Unable to connect with the maternal tone, Scarlett fretted in her sleep, her facial expression wrinkling, her figure twisting on the bench. The woman could have been anyone, a maid even. Servants had shouldered a motherly role her entire life.

The dreamscape shifted, and she found herself standing in a more peaceful place, a serene paradise, a biosphere of pearly white salt and azure blue skies. She swore she stood on a mercuric sea, reflecting on puffy white clouds and a perfect blue sky. An ancient mountain emerged in the distance, and she felt compelled to walk toward its crystal temple. Her scarlet dress dragged through the water, pooling at her feet, but still she trudged, scrutinizing the divide in wonder. Azure skies hovered above her head and reflected on the ground at her feet.

Hah, she considered, that which is above is below, and that which is below is above? *Where was she?* Had she died and gone to the Otherworld? The wind stirred and a familiar voice echoed in the wind-stream. Scarlett awoke with a start, a message slipping from her lips:

> *Aniron waits for you amidst the land*
> *and sky,*
> *A white world where the salt flats rise,*
> *A place where white clouds kiss the*
> *earth,*
> *And mirrored water echoes a blue sky's*
> *worth,*
> *Infinity—where beginnings have*
> *no end.*

*The temple is hidden within a
goddess's pen.*

Nicolai stared at her in a concerning way. A quizzical expression creased his brow. "Scarlett, this outburst has caught me by surprise. What have you confessed?"

She took a deep breath. "I don't know, but I think," she replied, considering, "either my mother or the high priestess, Aniron, known on earth as a mage, contacted me while I was sleeping. Aniron waits for me by the sea of land and sky."

"You were asleep. Maybe you were only dreaming?"

"I don't think so. The words were strong, vibrant, as if someone else whispered them."

"But who would whisper such nonsense?" Nicolai asked, pulling her into his embrace.

"Of this I'm certain," Scarlett acknowledged, her fingers rushing to her face. "I don't know how it's possible, I don't know if I can trust what I've been a witness to, but by some means, some method, I have heard the voice of my mother."

Chapter Twelve

SISTER MARY MARGARET

A lengthy psalm of prayer and meditation had invoked Mary's fatigue. Her back ached, more so than her knees, from kneeling against a flagstone floor overly long. Situated near the altar, a spectrum of color captured her attention. Rainbow hues streamed through stained glass windowpanes, and though an array of multicolored light wasn't unusual for the chapel, she likened it to a lamp unto her feet, a light of hope that divine intervention had not only been communicated, but had also prepared a path for her daughter to seek.

The land of sea and sky emboldened risk; even so, one powerful woman could still the coming storm, and one mark, her daughter, Scarlett, could find the divine place where a high priestess lived, the Salar de Uyuni.

Rising from the chancel flooring, Mary tried to alleviate her cramping leg muscles. Managing the pain, she clutched her prayer beads in her hand and rolled the smoothly carved roses between her fingers, while considering the obstacles in their path. Yet, when a sound disturbed the serenity in the sanctuary, she wondered if her petition had summoned a more dire presence. She shifted her stance and glanced toward the entrance of the chapel, in time to witness a noble woman and two guards parading into the narthex.

She gasped. *Queen Mother Cynara—*

Sister Mary bowed her head, abandoned all thought, and slid to her knees in a show of respect she didn't feel. *Keep your thoughts sacred,* she begged of herself, while waiting for the queen's approach.

"You may rise," the queen mother said, her tone curt.

"Your Majesty," Sister Mary offered, casting her sightline to the flooring. "How might I assist you?"

The witch snaked forward, narrowing the distance between them, honing a thoughtful expression. An emerald green surcoat sheathed her figure and trailed behind her person. Mary dared not test the queen's unpredictable nature by looking at her eyes.

"Have I seen you before, Sister? An air of familiarity exudes from you."

"We have walked past one another while exercising at court. Though you may not recall the conversation, we have exchanged greetings," Mary replied, swallowing. She met the queen's regard briefly, then glanced at the paving stones again, attempting to display a sense of modesty.

"You must remind me. I don't recall the exercise and I'm not one to forget. Where have we made each other's acquaintance?"

Mary squirmed under the pressure, her head smarting, her cheeks flaming pink. "I must have been walking to the village where I do the good work of my religious order, offering my assistance to the orphaned children, but more often than not, aiding the sick in their recovery from illness."

"I don't frequent the chapel or the village," the witch retorted, a cruel edge to her voice. "It's not my work, you see, to perform lesser duties, and your work has not gained my sympathy. I asked where we met. Is there a reason you won't tell me?"

"Ma'am, I reside in the castle, in the chapel tower. I frequent the castle corridors to go about my obligations. It's here that we met, but only in passing."

"I don't recall it, but your choice of language, more so than your speech, leads me to believe you're an educated woman. Are skilled women common among your vocation? I'd think not, which leads me to question your sincerity."

The comment angered Mary. "I don't deny I'm more cultured than some, but you don't care about my learning or anyone else's. You want your answers." Mary breathed, rolling her prayer beads between her fingers. "I'm not sure why it's important where we've met, but I also work in the royal gardens. I know you don't frequent the barbican often, so maybe you've seen me from your window in the royal apartments."

"Perhaps," Cynara said, stepping closer, "and now that you mention the garden, I have seen a nun cultivating the earth, though I'm certain I recognize you from some other place."

When the queen mother bridged the gap between them, though Mary shivered, her body flamed from her head to her toes. Uncomfortable, she stepped backward, attempting to retreat from the queen and her scrutiny. Instead of focusing on piercing, minty green eyes, Mary studied saintly paintings fastened to the wall. "I cannot know what you mean."

She adjusted her mien to a purposeful expression, but Cynara caught her off guard when she stepped closer than was comfortable. "I think you do know what I mean." The witch reached forward and grasped her cheek with a cold right hand. "You're as nervous as a peasant girl about to be raped by a gentry lord, and your anxiety causes me concern."

"Who wouldn't be nervous—" Mary stated, deathly afraid, chiding herself to hold still. "You're hurting me."

Mary searched within herself for courage. *Don't give your secrets away.*

She stood steadfast against the queen's scrutiny while the evil woman studied every contour of her face. She greeted the harassment head on, knowing she must assert her strength while forcing herself to stare at the queen's minty-green eyes. The witch's brows furrowed; suspicious still, her eyes drew closer together.

The evil woman released Mary's cheek and seized her veil instead, pulling her closer, scanning her brown eyes intently. "When doubt arouses my attention, 'tis my right as your sovereign to address the concern. Something stinks here."

Sister Mary was deathly afraid. Her breath quivered from her lips. "I have done you no wrong, Your Majesty. I'm a loyal servant, to the people, to the crown. I am clean of all sin."

"Hmm," the queen mother intoned, "I'm not inclined to believe it. No one is without sin. I have seen such eyes before; I will discover the truth you try to hide."

A click against the chapel flooring caused each of them to

angle toward the sound. "Your Majesty, I see you have witnessed the eyes of Mary," Father Clement said, calling from the turret stairs. He bowed in a show of respect, smiled slimly, then rose upward again and moved toward them. "Many villagers have told me that Sister Mary's hands empower the healing grace of the divine. Her actions are that of mercy, of kindness. A servant of the gods is not worthy of mistrust."

The queen released Mary's veil, sneering. "I don't share your convictions, Father. One never knows where schemes against the crown might be hiding."

Cynara glanced at Mary again, scrutinizing her. Though there was some truth to two women passing by each other in the castle corridors, years had passed since the witch had seen *Queen Regana.* The passing of time had advanced her appearance; wrinkled her cheeks, hardened her knees, but her mind was still sharp like aged wine or cheese. Mary bit her lip, knowing that once the queen's suspicions were aroused, the witch would be on her guard. She should have retreated from the castle years ago. It was too late to leave now.

"I have need of your patronage, Father Clement." She leveled her sights on Mary. "We must speak in private."

"As you wish. It is my pleasure to serve you." Father Clement nodded. "Sister Mary, please take yourself to the garden. Your work is needed there."

Mary responded with a curtsey to the queen and a grateful nod to the father. She pocketed her prayer beads, fetched her trowels, and then approached the arched doorway that led to the upper landing of the barbican. She attempted to cross the space in a calm fashion with a walk that would appear composed. It wasn't wise to entertain risk, but once she had passed through the archway and was out of sight, she leaned against a wall of stone and took a risk, *listening*, hoping to hear what the queen required of Father Clement.

FATHER CLEMENT

FATHER CLEMENT COULD NOT CONCERN himself with the conversation that had taken place between the two queens. Evil had made his acquaintance and he must prepare himself for battle.

"How might I assist you, Your Majesty?"

"I am in need of a spherical object, a body of celestial wonder, and it is my understanding that the chapel stores the article."

"Could you be more specific, Ma'am. A religious order has dedicated itself to preserving several items of sacred importance."

She licked her lips greedily, her desire evident. "A glass orb."

The disclosure of the orb disturbed him; his brow furrowed and his teeth clenched. He had been warned of a time when the Otherworld orb could be threatened. Had the moment arrived?

"The sacristy retains many items, but they're kept here for a reason. I cannot release them to anyone, not even a woman as great as you."

"While you attempt your niceties, your negligence and refusal to comply wound me."

"It is not negligent to protect sacred vessels, and a woman as powerful as you should understand why I must."

Cynara's face contorted with anger. The queen grasped his shoulder and he felt her nails digging into his flesh. "Have you forgotten who I am? I hold jurisdiction over you; your objections plague my patience and thwart my need."

"My apologies, Ma'am, I did not mean to offend you. I understand your disappointment."

"Do you?" An electric current vibrated his flesh and mixed with the blood oozing from his wound and seeping through his garment, but he suffered the pain, refusing to submit. "Do you understand the blood that will spill if I don't receive the orb?"

Father Clement breathed through the pain. "There are... Policies, procedures— Human judgments and strictures that limit a priest's will to obey your request. I must guard the chapel's objects. Rules have been in place for generations to protect extraordinary wonders."

"I admire your bravery, but I have needs, rules, and methods of my own, too," Cynara said, increasing the pressure. "Patience when it is required, and punishment when it is needed. My patience is at its limit. It's time to collect what I came here for."

Her nails dug deeper and he winced, weeping from the shooting pains. "It is said an orb exists that came from the Otherworld; it's precious. I will not give it to you."

"I didn't know it came from the Otherworld," she said, cackling. "It's interesting what painful pressure can release."

Father Clement collapsed to his knees, knowing he'd made a terrible mistake. "Why do you need such an item?"

"Mind your own business. I will not submit to your questioning. Yet, I am inclined to silence your tongue." She grasped his throat. "It's here inside your throat and I'm losing my patience. Do you or do you not have a glass orb in your possession—for I have been led to believe you do."

Father Clement saw he had no choice but to submit to the witch's needs and give her what she wanted, or lose his life. He bowed his head in submission. "The chapel protects a stone, a quartz orb, a perfectly circular sphere with flecks of gold, and within its perfection it is said a single droplet of blood, all contained within the glass."

"Fetch it for me."

"I vowed to protect it," he said, weeping, "vowed to keep it safe."

"You fool," she said, her voice laced with poison. "You have done your job in protecting *the Otherworld orb*, and your queen is grateful. Must I remind you that you don't own it? All objects stored in the sacristy belong to your sovereign queen."

"Ma'am, I understand."

"Do you? I could release you to run through the king's forest. The dogs like to chase the foxes through the forest. Have you heard them? Their yowling and yapping? Given you're a man of the gods, it would serve you better to collect the orb. It'll go easier on you that way."

The queen was a cruel woman, even knowing this, Father Clement relented. "My apologies, Your Majesty. I have no desire to test your anger further. I am but your humble servant, here to assist your petition."

She released her grasp on his shoulder. The priest's scarlet blood coated her fingertips. "If you're as loyal as you say, move quickly, humble servant, and give way to my needs as I tire of this inconvenience."

"If you'll wait by the altar, I will collect the orb from the sacristy."

SISTER MARY MARGARET

SISTER MARY SLID BACKWARD, retreating from the conversation as silently as was possible. She opened the small wooden door at the corridor's end and passed through the archway, then quietly closed the door behind herself. Once outside, she fled down the stone stairs to the landing, and was soon walking on a grit pathway. Deep in thought, she ambled along the barbican, scarcely noticing the perfumed smell of the garden. The fresh air had been tainted by the queen mother's visit.

Sister Mary meandered to the handrail while considering the queen's demand. *An orb?* She glanced at the flowers, at the marble statue of King Rickard, and then at the sea beyond. Gripping the railing, she couldn't bring herself to tend the flowers. Her thoughts were a jumble of suspicion, and underneath the questions her own fears hid.

What game does the witch play? And why does she need a glass orb?

When Father Clement placed the orb in the queen's hands, as he was bound to do, what would the witch do with the sacred object? Mary pondered this mystery, her mind full of questions, realizing that an association might be made between the forest and the orb. Mikkel and the spies must learn the information promptly.

She bit her lip, recognizing that the queen mother had come close to recognizing her. Gratefully, the witch had not recalled their prior association. Mary reached for her rose prayer beads, but with her need so great, she held them too tightly. The strand broke. The beads spilled to the ground and scattered along the gravel pathway. Some beads fell far beneath the barbican's terrace, never to be recovered.

Sighing, Mary slumped to her knees. Upset at the breakage, she picked up the tiny rosebuds as best she could, and one at a time, placed them inside her palm.

Hearing a crunch on the gravel, Mary glanced toward the sound. The queen stood on the landing, her hand atop the railing, scrutinizing her; a knowing expression, wrinkling her face.

Why hadn't Mary heard her approaching?

How had the witch moved so silently?

Mary winced, sucking in a breath, breathing air that seemed to spoil as the queen mother breached the gravel walkway, moving closer, offering nary a word. She paused in her step, bent downward, then picked up a single bead. Rising, she studied it closely, intimately rolling the rose between her fingers.

"A pity." She was irritated and stepped closer. "What will you count with now to ease your worries?"

Sighing, Mary rose from the ground. She retreated to sadness, opening her palm, praying for aid, gazing at the beads that lay wasted on the ground.

Odin, please give me the strength to survive this ordeal.

Mary took a deep quivering breath for courage. "My father gave me these prayer beads when he brought me to the nunnery. He carved them with his own hands, giving me a gift I could hold when the nights were long."

"Your father gave them to you?"

"Please don't think of his gift as a blessing, Your Majesty. I was simply a mouth to feed and an expense he could no longer afford. He called me an old maid, a woman unable to find a proper suitor. He related; I'd never amount to anything."

"But you did rise to higher callings," the witch whispered, stepping so near she could cause her harm if she chose to.

"What do you mean?" Mary responded, looking sadly into the queen mother's piercing eyes, hoping the witch wouldn't respond with her real name.

"Sister Mary, I would think the answer is obvious. You're a nun." The queen snarled. The witch reached forward, placed the rose bead in Mary's palm, and then grasping her hand, squeezed it inside her fist and held the appendage cruelly tight.

Mary lowered her head in shame. "I would not have chosen this life, Ma'am."

"Sometimes, our life does not choose us, so we must choose our life. I give you permission to leave the habit, the nunnery, too, if it is your intention to do so."

"It's been too long," Mary countered. "I would not know an alternative to this life."

She released her hand. "Lies. You don't have the courage to face my scrutiny, nor the poise to straighten your back. I don't believe one word of the sentiment singing from your tongue. I know you from somewhere, and though I can't recall the exact place, I promise you this: I will remember you and your relationship to me, and when I do—your best hope for salvation is that your story is true."

"Your Majesty—"

"I'm giving you until midday tomorrow to come to me with the truth. You'd best not visit the village during this time. I recommend you restrict your activities to the bedchamber, where you best abide in solitude and prayer."

Mary bowed her head. "As you wish, Your Majesty. Do I have your permission to take my leave?"

The queen mother stepped backward, gesturing at the staircase. "You do."

Mary kept her head downcast as she walked past the queen. Tears filled her eyes while taking her leave.

"Sister Mary?" the queen called.

Mary wiped at her eyes, facing her. "Yes, Ma'am?"

"What about these counting beads you leave scattered on the ground? Your father made them. Will you not pick them up?"

Mary sucked in a breath. "Perhaps they're more of a sorrow than I thought. It's time to leave them behind."

The queen's eyes drew together. "If that is your decision, then be on your way."

Leaving the garden, Mary fled up the stairs, retreating

through the arched doorway that led inside the chapel. Father Clement waited. He was sitting on a pew with his head hung in despair, holding a small square box. He glanced at her, and she reflected on the priest's dour expression and the orb concealed in his hand.

She thought of Mikkel.

Instead of rushing to the lord chancellor with her news, she climbed the turret stairs to her bedchamber and locked herself inside. She knew risks must be taken; the queen's visit to the chapel must be shared with the alliance, but going against the queen's directive, and venturing to the village to disclose this orb association, could put another life at risk. And presently, she must think of her own.

Chapter Thirteen

KING RICKARD

A spectator in a royal confrontation, the bait and trap conflict played out between Cynara and Regana had been an interesting diversion. The two women had entertained him, offering something more than a mental image of his own mortality, solidity and pain.

Two royal paths were bound to intersect. Why had Regana chosen to reside in the chapel? The risky move lacked intelligence.

Fortunately for Regana, it appeared as if Cynara had not recognized the woman who had veiled herself inside the costuming of a nun. Even so, a witch had her vices and his wife wasn't blind to human disguise. He saw her suspicious nature had been aroused, and like a dog hungry for a bone, the witch liked to chew. The wheel in her wicked mind would keep on spinning until a nugget of truth was revealed.

A once dearly beloved woman had fled the barbican, and with the nun's departure, he focused on Cynara instead. Fashioned regally, a wide collar circled her neck, only serving to highlight her stern facial features. Though the binding seemed excessive, even for a queen, the pleats didn't diminish her dark beauty. She hadn't aged and was as beautiful as the first day he'd taken her to his bed.

An insufferable mistake. Her bitter expression reeked of ugliness, and now, as if hearing his thoughts, the vile woman approached him.

"How goes your watch, Rickard?" she said, snickering, sauntering toward him. "Your people have not responded to your son's rule or my influence in a respectful manner. It's your fault. I should have placed you on the platform sooner. Yet, the coming week will serve our deficiency adequately, or so Nevin has led me to believe. A queen's ambition might be possible."

Sard off. He'd tell her if he could.

She paced closer and sat at his feet. Repulsed, he watched her take hold of his leg, her fingertips stroking the immobile appendage. He barely felt the sensation and feared his awareness of human touch, heat or pain, was diminishing.

"You're weathering, Rickard," she said, her fingers wandering the length of his hardened legs, picking at solidified flesh and flicking its pieces to the base. He hated her for what she had done to him.

"You would be proud of your son. He's achieving the kingdom's work in an admirable way. In his free time, he has taken up the pursuit of hunting," she said with a satisfied grin. "Our boy is an excellent marksman, if I should say so myself."

When she rose to scrutinize his face, anxiety stirred inside his dead heart and barren gut, making him feel uncomfortable.

"That nun," she said, her hand gesturing in the direction Regana had fled, "do you know her? Have you engaged her in conversation or had an association with her? You're not the type of man to feel desire for a plain, ugly woman." She smirked, her lips rising oddly. "I bagged your vanities once, so I understand your taste in women, and I must say, you would *never* have coupled with a boorish woman."

Though desires of a sexual nature don't concern me at present, I don't deny that your statement is somewhat correct. Regana isn't a beauty. Yet, her temperament holds other characteristics that I should have contemplated. Human qualities could have satisfied my appetite.

"I'm questioning your silence, Rickard. Who are you shielding with your stony posturing? I wonder if you might be hiding valuable information. Protecting someone, maybe?"

She laughed at him, a horrifying expression of disregard that grated his ears. Cynara was despicable. He hated her more than the soldiers he had faced in battle.

Someday, your cruelty will earn a fitting retribution. Not from me, of course, women like you eventually meet a worthier opponent.

"Forgive me, Rickard. I had forgotten that your speech had solidified. Your plight is understandable. You cannot possibly know who Sister Mary might be."

I'd never confide the truth, you sarding bitch!

"I could revive breath to your lungs." She seemed to

ponder, gazing at him intently. "But that would be impossible. I shouldn't tease you with possibility."

She traipsed to the stairway. He didn't sense her emotion while watching her leave him, though he did contemplate the growing divide, and the increasing gap that came between them with each step. She grasped the handrail above the stairs and took her first step upward, her mind in concentration. She pivoted, facing him.

"Didn't Regana admire the garden, Rickard?"

A knowing look brightened her wicked face as a thought took shape. "Is it possible?"

She sneered, climbing the stairs, shaking her head. Still pondering, she glanced at him again, her facial expression revealing an evil mien he'd become accustomed to. "Would your former queen be so stupid as to live inside the castle, all this time, posing as Sister Mary? She should have left the castle, her presence threatens me, and my son."

He agreed. Regana should have left.

"Lies find their way to the truth. Maybe for your birthday, I'll give you some company to assist in the cultivation of the garden. It brought your former queen joy to admire the flowers, too." The witch left his company then, her amusement angering him. "After all this time, I'd like to be the one to entertain a nun's company."

Rickard considered: *Run, Regana. Your time for hiding is at an end.*

———— ⚜ ————

QUEEN MOTHER CYNARA

WHEN CYNARA REENTERED THE CHAPEL, Father Clement was waiting for her. The poor man, his sadness could have reflected the loss of an only friend. Alone and sitting on a pew, his sullen expression irritated her. She didn't care about his need to protect the past. It only mattered to her that the priest gave up the orb without further interference.

A wooden box rested in his hand. "Is that the orb?"

He lowered his head, clutching the box. "Yes."

"Father Clement, your glum disposition won't change my mind."

"It's a sacred object, Your Majesty. Surely you, more so than anyone else, would appreciate the importance of a revered possession."

Cynara stepped closer to him. Reaching the priest, she took the box from his hands. It was surprisingly heavy. "I understand this orb is of great import to both of us. I promise you this, I will take good care of it."

Cynara couldn't help herself; stepping a distance away from the father, she opened the lid and peered inside. "Strange, but this glass ball doesn't look like much lying inside this fur-lined cask." She glanced at the father. "Where is the glow? Are you certain this is the orb we spoke of earlier? The Otherworld orb?"

"It is, Your Majesty."

Cynara snapped the lid shut. The click echoed in the chapel. "Then my business is concluded here, Father."

Eager to leave, she pivoted to walk the center aisle, with her surcoat trailing behind her, but when the religious man cleared his throat, she paused, and glanced at him.

"What is it?"

He rose from the pew and faced her. "Ma'am, I must warn you; advisors, priests before me, priests who pledged their lives to keep the orb safe, that enchantment, perhaps evil, hides inside the orb. If it were to be opened…"

"Father," she ground out cruelly. "I have no care for a religious man's sermon. Worry about your flock. I'll concern myself with the Otherworld orb. Do you understand?"

"There's a single drop of blood inside the glass. If it were to be unleashed…"

Cynara had heard enough scaremongering from Nevin, so refused to pay heed to nonsense contrary to common sense, rather than intelligence from a priest. This man was quickly becoming an irritant. "I command you to silence."

He nodded, saying no more, his expression grave.

"One more request, Father."

"Yes, Ma'am?"

"Sister Mary is to be confined to her bedchamber. She is not to leave the chapel tower for any reason."

"Has she given you cause to confine her to her room?"

"Let me be clear on this issue, Father. The people do not ask questions of their queen; the queen asks questions of the people. Is that understood?"

He stumbled backward. "Understood."

"Now, I have business to attend. Good day to you, Father."

After leaving the chapel, Cynara conversed with her guards and instructed them to arrest Sister Mary and confine the nun inside the prison tower.

She didn't stay to watch the commotion. She had to hide

the orb in her chambers, and after that she must talk to her son. A former queen required a fitting retribution.

Chapter Fourteen

KING LOWELL

The queen mother entered her son's drawing room so quietly, Lowell barely heard her footsteps, but a sixth sense, which he'd probably inherited from her, warned him of her arrival.

Sitting at his desk, he shifted documents to hide the telltale information, then greeted his mother with a grimace. Her cheeks were uncommonly pink; her mint-green eyes bright with mischief. It was abnormal for her to be so uncommonly happy. *What had she done?*

"I need to speak with you. Are you busy?"

He glanced at her, curious about his mother's purpose, as her association with him was usually secondary to a formulated plan. If he were to be honest with her, he'd reveal he wasn't interested in a courtesy call, learning her mischief or speaking of it either. "I have matters to attend to, and they're important."

"Your paperwork cannot be more important than your mother."

"Don't be so dramatic," he said, shielding the papers. "You've left me and the privy council to cope with the kingdom's work, *alone*, for the last fortnight. I'm not ending my work the moment you entertain me with your company."

"You're an ill-mannered brat."

His cheeks heated with anger, bearing a lengthy and uncomfortable period of silence while studying, yet not really studying, the names scribed on the parchment. He wasn't sure if he should disclose the search for a partner, but maybe he'd tell his mother about this matter after all, if only to enforce his independence.

"What do you require of me? You're not here to speak to your son."

Stony silence greeted him. The information must be gratifying as she seemed in no hurry to disclose it. Nearing him, she rubbed her hands gleefully. "I have news of note to share with you."

"Tell me," he said with interest, leaning backward in his chair, and placing his feet on a rounded spot on the desk. "It must be a disclosure of great worth for you to stare at me like a cat who's eaten a delicious bird."

She grinned, meandered closer, and reclined on a scissor chair beside his desk. "I have located your father's former queen, Regana."

"Is that so?" he stated, unimpressed. "You disappoint me. I thought you might have entered my apartment to visit your son. You've been absent from the kingdom's affairs, which isn't like you; maybe you've been taking up sporting activities in the king's forest, engaging in wicked plots instead."

"I do what I must, and I don't council opinion from you."

"But now you've uncovered another conspiracy, would you have my dogs chase the former queen through the woodland, too?"

His mother had the audacity to laugh. "The idea does amuse me somewhat."

"Really? Do you not have enough blood on your hands?"

"You are not my son." Cynara's face crinkled with disgust. "Sitting on the throne comes with responsibility, burdens that can be fatal. Must I remind you, the woman is our enemy."

"I need no reminder that she is the former queen, and as such is more your enemy than mine. It seems to me you robbed the poor woman of her crown. A husband, a royal title, and her children, too. I don't care that you did it; the affair has served us well, but would you steal her life, too?"

The statement caused his mum to anger, but he was frustrated, too. She measured him with disappointment, her forehead lined with wickedness, her cheeks reddened with hatred; bringing to his attention the physical attributes that once caused his father angst—and maybe harm, too.

"These games have become tiresome," Lowell said, shaking his head. "I sit on this throne to rule the kingdom, and I mean to act on my own terms, without your meddling."

"I bring you important news and you disregard it. Instead of showing your care, you give me indifference. You're not a child. Don't speak to me like one. I'm your mother; respect your elder."

"I respect you, admire you; fear you—but I don't have to agree with your opinions or your decisions. Where did you find her?"

Her expression softened. She leaned backward in her

chair. "The most unlikely place of all. The chapel tower, living a new life with a new name. A queen has shed her crown to become a nun, and taken the name Sister Mary."

"Huh!" Lowell chuckled. "A brilliant scheme. You never frequent the chapel. It is said not even to marry my father, which leads me to ask, how did you find her? Why did you go there?"

She glanced away, rolling her eyes. "The reason for visiting the chapel does not concern you."

"Did you think to confess your sins?" Lowell asked, finding humor in the situation. "Did you partake in prayer?"

"Don't irritate me," she said, glancing at her fingernails. "Not that it's any of your concern, or your business, but I needed to discuss a matter of importance with Father Clement."

"A conversation that you're not willing to share with your son or the privy council. Am I right?"

"It's private, Lowell. The subject does not concern you."

"Will you at least tell me what you have done with the former queen, your nemesis, Regana?"

"A guard has taken her to the tower to be imprisoned."

"Probably the best course of action, given who she is. But your work ends here, Mum. I will make further judgments regarding this woman's situation."

"Don't test me. You may weigh the scales of justice, but my counsel forms a part of the resolution."

"You, Mother, need to mind your own ambitions. Meddle less in my affairs and choose more womanly pursuits. The court might talk about you less if you did some stitchery."

She glared at him. "Feminine crafting? Don't mock me. I will not be told by my child what to do."

"Look at me, I've grown up while you've been hunting for power. Surely you see a man before you, a man capable of making his own decisions."

"Let's get back to the sisterly imposter and her punishment."

"Take your worries to your bedchamber and sleep on them. In this regard, and all matters of the throne, I alone, with the guidance of my Privy Council, will weigh decisions and their subsequent judgment calls."

"Do you think to ignore my counsel?" she ranted, her tone sharp.

"I think to rule. And if need to, I will rule my own mother, too. You have no power over me."

"I would not test that theory."

His mother's comment silenced him. It seemed wise to divert the conversation to a safer subject as her ugly demeanor frightened him. "There's another matter you should know."

"What would that be?" Cynara said, glaring at him. Lowell realized he hadn't deterred her one bit. Inside that scheming mind, she plotted.

"I have begun the search for a wife."

"I can assist in that regard. I have some considerations on potential fiancées, which I would like to share with you."

He showed her the papers. "The lord chancellor has given me names of several eligible women of royal birth. I've been considering their qualities, and whether or not I'd like them, as the lord chancellor has been trying to arrange for one or two of the prettier girls to visit the castle."

"Why didn't you tell me sooner?"

"I don't know why, or maybe I'd rather not say."

"You wound me. I see you don't trust your own mother."

"It's not a matter of trust. You above all women understand the importance of a king finding a wife. A queen to give me a son to pass on my father's good name and his crown, such as was passed down to me."

"I understand the importance, but I had names in mind, too."

"Present them to me. I will consider your selections."

"Lowell," she said, rising, attempting to intimidate him, "I will have the final say."

"Why?" Angering, he stood. "That comment upsets me. You don't hold the power over me that you lorded over my father. I will select my wife, and should I choose to, similar to my father, I will have mistresses in my bedchamber, too." He sneered at her, afraid, almost daring her to object. "A noble woman to carry my children and lesser women to bear my play. I've placed a guard at my door to ensure you cannot control who I entertain inside my bedchamber."

"Guards ignore my passage. I have created an ungrateful monster," she hissed. "Have you not learned anything I've taught you?"

She prepared to leave him. "I'm warning you, Lowell. As easily as you've been made a king, your powers can be stripped away, removed. Don't mistreat your mother, or you'll rue the day."

"You're the least of my worries. I don't fear you."

She traipsed to the door and glanced at him with a consternation that should have warned him. "A mother knows when *her* kid is lying, so I'm giving you fair warning; you should fear me, Lowell."

"Oh, Mum, enough of these games," he called after her. "Where did you imprison the former queen, Regana be her name?"

"Where regal prisoners are placed; the prison tower." She stared at him, making him uncomfortable. After a time, she pivoted, offering her concern to her son. "Why?"

"I'm curious to see this woman. The woman that gave birth to my half-siblings."

"There's no need for you to bother yourself with her."

Lowell rose from his desk and threw the papers on the surface. Rolling the top down, he locked his private papers and other important materials inside. It seemed the names must remain private from his mother's prying eyes.

"A good evening to you, Mum," he said, escorting her out of the drawing room. "This matter is a concern of mine; I will tend to it."

He motioned to his guard. "Please escort the queen mother to her chambers."

She glared at him with such hurt, he almost wished he hadn't been so hard on her. Even so, his mother had to know her place in his life and it was long past time someone taught her a lesson. Who better than her son.

Lowell turned away from the queen mother, showing her his back, then proceeded to the prison tower, but he knew his mother's regard followed him, until she could see him no more.

Chapter Fifteen

LADY REGANA

Forlorn and held inside the prison tower against her will, the former queen peered through square windowpanes, mindlessly regarding the courtyard below. She had once cried beneath this sullen place while grieving the loss of her husband, the dead King Rickard. Now, she mourned the loss of her former self. A nun no more, a lover no more; she had no one to blame but herself. It seemed the evil queen had won.

The guard opened the door and she glanced his way. She'd been expecting to see the witch. The boy-king was an entirely different surprise.

The guard announced his arrival. "His Majesty, the King."

Regana lounged to her knees and bowed her head in a show of respect she didn't feel, astonished to greet King Rickard's son. "Your Majesty," was all Regana thought to say.

"You may rise," he commanded, and so she rose to her feet, slowly meeting his dismay. A look no different than his father's, no matter that Lowell's eyes were steely blue, and Rickard's had been a hue of emerald.

"What name do I call you by, Sister Mary or Lady Regana?"

"I suppose, Sire, it serves no purpose to lie about my identity," Regana said, sighing, choosing to reveal her true appearance. Her hands quivered while removing a white veil and a cap of similar color from her head. She stood there, suffering his silent stare, her head barren of a nun's habit, knowing her brunette hair was threaded with gray. "You may call me Lady Regana."

He stepped closer. "Lady Regana, why have you hidden yourself away as a nun all these years? I'm certain your children believed you were dead. It's unkind of you to put them through such misery. Rumors persist that my mother dealt you an unkind fate. Why would you have the people believe such lies?"

"I have no care for what other people believe. I feared your mother, so I hid to protect my children."

"You abandoned your daughters, but you didn't wander very far. You assumed a new identity. A new name?"

"There is far more to this story than a name." Regana sank into a nearby chair. "I don't mean to disrespect you, but the queen mother robbed me of my royal household, and all I held dear. My husband. My children. The prospect of a comfortable future, too. I couldn't take another husband, so my shameful regard led me to the only recourse I could think of to save myself—the nunnery."

"The queen may have stolen your husband, but not your children. You left your daughters behind, to be raised by servants. It was cruel. Your lack of motherly instruction led one of them to act like a monster. Why would a loving mother do such a thing?"

The question made her uncomfortable. He stared at her with eyes of steel, seeking a truth she wasn't free to divulge. "How could you understand? A boy yet to seed passion, yet to father a child? Oftentimes, a mother must hide her heart to be kind, but I didn't abandon them, not entirely. I kept watch over my children in my own way."

"How did you mind them? Through prayer?" he chided, sneering at her. "Did you think the gods would watch over them, too?"

"Do you care what becomes of my children?"

"Not particularly," he said. "I would see your daughter dead for the harm against my father, the treason she committed against the throne."

"Your Majesty—" Regana thought she should tell him the truth, that his mother had rooted the evil in his father's death. What did she have to lose, since she was locked inside the tower? She decided to take a chance. "You couldn't be more wrong. You should be aware of the true situation, which made you a king."

"Don't be vague." He scoffed, minding her unkindly. "Do you care for your daughter still, after her treasonous act? She robbed you, too."

Regana knelt before him, then lowered her head submissively. "A real mother minds her children." She glanced upward, scrutinizing his face, making her point. "Not all mothers have the same tenacity where their children are concerned. Please, Sire, my daughter is innocent of the crime of which she was accused."

He stepped away, his hand rising to his forehead. "Don't be absurd. I saw the scene with my own eyes."

Regana squinted, beseeching. "You saw what your mother wanted you to see. Her spirit has turned to blackness, and she uses dark arts to give rise to supernatural powers. Surely, you're aware of her evil deeds, aware of the reason the people call her *the Ebony Queen*. Have you been listening to your people? On that terrible day, Scarlett may have thrown the serpent, but the queen's dark magic pierced King Rickard's wrist. The queen mother committed treason!"

"I won't hear your lies. She did nothing of the sort!"

"She did. I cannot prove it, but I would bet my life that it's true."

He stepped backward in horror; his hand slid through his hair. Regana could see the boy-king had never considered the possibility of such an evil act. His anger rose quickly. He pointed at her, his fingers quivering. "You crazy woman, don't wound me with misguided intent!"

"Mercy is mine," she said, whispering her prayers, opening her palms and raising them skyward. "Please, permit the truth to be known to King Lowell."

"Don't play the nun's role now," he criticized, sneering. "You're no more than a common woman, performing a dramatic role on a stage."

She should have remained silent. The boy was an impertinent fool with no ear for the truth.

"I spoke the vows that a sister must speak to become a nun. For all intents and purposes, I am Sister Mary Margaret.

For more years than I'm willing to count, I have lived my life serving the gods and their people. I have no regrets. I have lived my life humbly, as you humbly serve the kingdom. I pray you serve it *far* better than your father ever did."

He glared at her with his mother's anger, but she knew her story had been heard. A seed of mistrust and doubt had been planted. She knew this by the way he looked at her.

"Guard!" he ordered, his tone stern. "Open the door."

After the king left her company, Regana returned to the window. What would her revelation gain or lose? The truth bartered an unmeasurable price, one expense dismissed her freedom while the other ordered her death. A former queen had committed treason against the queen mother and with one disclosure, one thought was certain: a heady price would be paid.

Chapter Sixteen

PRINCESS RUBY

Kindling burned within a hollow of limestone, giving off heat and light. Ruby watched the flames flickering, casting waves of uncertainty against the cavern walls, which only served to alert her to a dire situation. The chamber was depressive, disheartening, the atmosphere more appropriate for a vault or a tomb. A place where humans didn't have the capacity to leave.

What would she do when the fire died down? What then?

Garrett had faced the inky blackness in a braver manner, scrambling on the rock-strewn ground on his hands and knees, patiently searching until their supplies had been found, timber, too. He had built the fire in a charcoal pit, a depression in the limestone surface where travelers before them had fashioned flame. She'd stood near him, silent, feeling as useless as a worn-out shoe, but once a spark had ignited to shoulder a feeble flame, Garrett, being an unselfish man, had retreated into the bleakest fathoms of the cavern to investigate avenues of escape.

Not only for him, but for a princess, too.

What will I do when he learns freedom from this place is not possible? The theory rankled her, numbed her, robbing her of the ability to act. *What was the point?*

She waited for Garrett to return, burdened with a bleak reality. Alternatives to lessen her sorrow didn't seem likely, so watching a dancing illumination softened the blow and assisted the passage of time. The light should have radiated a beacon's comfort—warmth, too—but instead of focusing on the positive, that they were still alive, she reflected on misfortune. Once the flames had licked the logs clean and tinder was reduced to ash, she would find herself here; buried alive inside a cavern, shivering with cold and with no good prospects for the future.

When she heard Garrett's footfall, she was eager to hear the sound of his voice. "We can't stay here," he offered, his tone dire and echoing off the walls. "We will die if we don't find a way to leave this mountain."

Fearful of what he'd found, Ruby reclined to a large boulder. "Have you found clues that might help us?"

Garrett paced to where she sat and held his hands above the fire. "Yes, I have discovered a tunnel that extends farther inside the mountain."

"Is it worse than you're telling me? You look as if you've sunk your teeth into a bitter lemon, or broken a tooth while chewing on stale bread."

He glanced at her and then returned his attention to the flames. "I didn't expect to fight my way through the darkness. No man or woman wants to crawl inside a mountain, not knowing the danger that lies ahead; where we might stumble, where we might fall, or if one faces the worst knowledge possible, that hope arrives without mercy, cleaving to the deader end of a tunnel."

Ruby shivered after his comment. "I knew our circumstances were bleak. What can we do?"

Garrett sat beside her on the boulder. He grasped her hand. "I'll not lie to you. The witch buried us well. The entryway is blocked with rocks too large to shift aside. Sure, there's good news, too. We're shielded from colder elements like ice and snow, but there's no chance of leaving the cavern the way we entered. We have no choice but to inter ourselves inside this bitch, hoping we'll find an alternate exit."

Her world collapsed. "I didn't think you'd be so brutally honest," Ruby said with a grimace, her tone laced with sorrow. "Yet, you carved out our situation in the gravest way. It's almost unkind. Escape doesn't seem possible. Do you think Cynara knew of this cave and took advantage of it?"

He embraced her, hugging her to his chest. Ruby welcomed his strength, comfortable in his arms, while being grateful she wasn't alone and that a champion accompanied her still. "Wicked schemes stir inside the witch's brain," he said, appearing thoughtful. "I hope she has no knowledge of the passageway, or the fact we survived the collapse."

Ruby shook; a shiver of sound escaped her lips. "You're taking me deeper inside the cavern, aren't you?"

He patted her hand and then clutched it tightly. "What other choice do we have but to trek inside the witch's throat."

"An ugly proposition, but what if we can't find a second opening? After an indeterminate effort, what if we learn the tunnel doesn't lead anywhere?"

"What are you suggesting, that we watch the flames until lack of fuel, lack of oxygen, starves the light?" He shook his head. "When I promised to protect you, I knew this wasn't going to be an easy quest, but I don't resign from duty, give in or give up, when times are tough."

"I appreciate everything you've done for me. I need you to know that."

He squeezed her hand. "I need you to understand that I'll do everything possible to protect you, but I won't delude you with false promises, or lies, either. We find a way out—or we don't."

"We could die."

"Everyone dies, sooner or later. It's fear we must master, not the ending of our lives."

Ruby fretted as the reality of the situation took hold. Death was a real possibility. It marked the end. *What did dying feel like?* Life might be a constant struggle, but she was too young to die.

"I won't give up, not yet," Garrett said calmly, his tone offering little comfort, "there's always a chance we'll survive."

Suddenly, Ruby was eager to try. "When do we begin?"

"In the morning, after we've had a night's rest. It's been a trying day. There are supplies left. Dried meat, bread, water and cheese. We'll feast tonight and ration our supplies tomorrow."

"Garrett?"

"Yes?"

"I've never been so scared."

He hugged her, massaged her arm, and she welcomed his embrace. "I'm out of my element as well," he said, sighing. "I have endured horrible circumstances before, but if there's hope to be found, I promise you, I will find it."

WHEN RUBY AWOKE the next morning, ebony darkness permeated a cavernous Netherworld. One wouldn't know whether it was night or day. Sunlight might bridge the distance between land and sky, but inside this place, inside this tomb, the absence of light—or even the warm glow of a fire—frightened her. Blind, she couldn't see her hand in front of her face and the fear of the unknown caused further tension, tying knots inside her gut.

The fire was extinguished; not one ember was glowing in the pit to offer heat or light. She shivered, lying on the cavern floor, pressed close to Garrett for comfort. She lay against him, listening to his breathing, borrowing his warmth and desiring his strength.

When they were both awake, they silently broke their fast, each consuming one strip of jerky and two swigs of water from a leather flask. Soon after, Garrett combined their supplies inside one pack, and then they prepared to investigate the passageway.

"Are you ready?" he asked, feeling for her hand.

"As ready as I'll ever be."

"Here's what we're going to do," Garrett said, squeezing her fingers. "I will lead us through the passageway. I'll warn you of obstacles as best as I can. We'll take small steps, baby steps while walking."

"I understand."

"Do you? We'll be blind. Unable to see what's in front of our faces."

"It's obvious the night is dark. I can't see you."

"Amira, caves are a dangerous place and we're without light. We don't know where we're going or what we'll find, so we must trust each other, care for each other, and move together as one, feeling with more than our hands."

"Have I ever said that I didn't trust you?" she replied, sighing. "You have guided me well and kept me safe. I'm grateful."

"I have done a terrible job, but I'll keep trying." He sounded grave. "The cavern pathway is uneven. Use your hands to find stability, your sight if at all possible. Grip the tails of my surcoat and hold on tight. We'll proceed at an easy pace. Do you understand?"

Ruby stood there in the darkness, scared about what might be coming next, but she wouldn't confess this. "I understand. I wish there was light to mark our passage."

"So do I," he murmured. "If you're ready, it's time to leave."

When Garrett rose, Ruby rose, too. She listened to him collecting their belongings, slinging the pack on his shoulder. She clutched the fabric of his surcoat as he had instructed.

"Let's go," he said, calling out, "we're walking now."

She matched his step, clutching his leather coat. The ground was uneven, slippery from the sleet that had breached the cave and frozen. Blind to all but the proximity of her protector and the placement of her feet, she worried where they were wandering. A chill coursed along her spine, penetrating her flesh. Wrapping her woolen cloak tightly around her shoulders, Ruby swayed on her feet, slipping, but having a grasp of Garrett's surcoat saved herself from a fall.

"Are you all right?" Garrett asked, pausing.

"Yes, please continue."

"Once we near the tunnel, you'll be able to touch the cavern wall. The rock wall will assist your balance."

She stumbled forward, searching for the limestone. She touched an abrasive edge and a chill penetrated her fingertips. She didn't want to touch it, not knowing what she'd find, but having no other choice, she grasped the limestone. Convulsive shivers threaded up her spine.

Garrett led her forward like a beacon in the night, shepherding her deeper inside the cavern. She gripped his coat with one hand while her fingertips courted the cavern's edge. Apprehension seeded fear. Darkness distorted reality. Nary a sound exuded from the cavity; even so, she became accustomed to the rasp of her breathing, inhalations and exhalations, whispering between her ears.

I hate this night. I'll die in this nether worry of a place.

Her fingers slid along the cavern wall, feeling the coarse, rugged surface. A furry creature wriggled beneath her fingertips and she screamed as it ferreted away.

"What is it?" Garrett asked. "What happened?"

"I don't know," Ruby replied, her voice strained, fright singing from her lungs. "A small creature, maybe a mouse."

"You scared me. I almost jumped out of my skin. Please, don't fret about it. Take it as a good sign, a sign that occupants, other than two blind humans, are stumbling in the dark. Plus, a mouse won't hurt you."

"It will if it bites me," Ruby shrieked, shuddering from

the stress, but she trudged onward, tentative and afraid to submit her fingers to the rock wall again. "For all you know, that creature could have been a bat."

"Must have been a mouse, or at the least a rat. I don't hear the flutter of wings, a good sign, by the way. A bat might suggest a way out."

"One we cannot reach," Ruby replied with a grimace, traipsing on a rock-strewn trail. "The entrance is buried, even for furry creatures. I don't like bats, rats, or animals I cannot see."

"Don't think about it. Save your breath. The surface is uneven; focus on maintaining your balance."

THE CIRCUMFERENCE of the tunnel was shrinking. Ruby had to stoop or hit her head against protruding rock.

The air quality lessened, too, older and staler, reeking of dank earth. Her breathing became more labored as the walls narrowed. Panic warred with common sense and Ruby fretted inside the putrid place, filling her mind with visions of death and dying. She panicked, struggling to breathe, suffocating inside a constrictive black tube. Though her imagination shouldn't have given rise to hysteria, she feared what she couldn't see, no different than when she was a girl, a time when imaginary monsters hid under her bed.

What monsters hid in wait now?

She paused in the middle of the passageway, afraid to touch the bedrock, in time to hear Garrett muttering a stream of curse words. Ruby placed her hand on his back.

"Damn it!" he growled, bending downward. "The passageway degenerates, and extends toward a lower cavity. It's just beneath my waist."

Ruby's head hurt. She worried what this meant. "Can we get to it, can we pass through?" she asked, wishing they had light to guide their way. It would be so much easier if they could see. She nestled closer to Garrett, clinging to his coat, perceiving him bowing to his knees and stretching forward, stretching inside the tunnel.

"I think so. The passage seems to continue. We'll duck and crawl through the gap, but be careful."

When Garrett stooped downward, her fingers lingered on his back. She replicated his behavior and bent downward, too, soon kneeling on the cavern surface. Inching forward, she reached above her head, her fingers trailing the rocky lip of limestone protruding from the ceiling, somewhat blocking their path forward.

When had the upper surface descended so low?

She ducked her head and attempted to crawl underneath the ledge, but wearing a thick cloak and a woolen surcoat, proved to be a problem. The crawl forward became difficult.

Sighing, weary from her struggles, Ruby returned to where she had been before and sat there feeling like a ninny. Leaning against the limestone, now accustomed to its cold temperature, her emotion engaged with fear and tears threatened. Her head hurt. Her chest expanded, laden with anxiety, but lacking of breath. The only release from this prison seemed to be the normal human reaction to sit on this gravel surface and cry.

"What's wrong?" Garrett called to her, waiting on the other side.

"I need a break from this. I can't crawl anywhere in these layers. I wish I was wearing a man's breeches, at least then I could move freely without the encumbrance of skirts barring my way."

"Remove your cloak and gown." His voice was kind, but firm.

"That would be improper, Garrett."

"It's as black as a witch's heart inside this hole. Your modesty will be protected; I won't see you."

"But you'll know."

Garrett didn't say anything for the space of several seconds, and during this uncomfortable pause, Ruby wondered if her struggle to crawl while wearing feminine garments annoyed him.

"Garrett?"

"Devil strike me for admitting this, though you're uncomfortable stripping down, it would be a pleasure to envision your beauty, more so than this bloody prison," he said, coughing up cavern dust. "Take off your cloak, lay it on the ground, and I'll pull you through the gap."

Ruby closed her eyes and pressed her fingers against her temples.

"Did you hear me? I'm here. I'll help you."

"All right," Ruby said, relenting. She removed her cloak as her protector had requested, shivering when only her woolen surcoat shrouded her figure. She reached inside the cavern tunnel and laid the garment on the limestone floor, stretching it along the passageway as best she could.

"Are you ready?" Garrett asked.

"Yes—" She positioned herself on her belly and gripped the cloak with her fingers.

Garrett pulled her forward, and her upper body bore the brunt of discomfort while grinding over the oppressive surface, yet, she soon passed under the outcropping to the other side, coming face to face with her protector.

She couldn't see his eyes, but his warm breath fanned her lips. Though she was buried inside a mountain, confined between a rock and a hard place, she knew his closeness should make her uncomfortable, yet his nearness garnered her gratitude and she was fascinated by his proximity.

"We can do this, Amira. I promised to protect you. I'll help you as best I can."

"I know you will." She whimpered, his caring fueled her emotion and caused tears to well in her eyes. He touched her face, discovering the liquid collecting on her cheek.

"Don't cry. It pains me to know you're sad. Hurts me to know I can't keep you safe."

Ruby took a deep, shattering breath. She leaned against his forehead and closed her eyes. "I needed a moment to collect myself. I needed a moment like this. You're a patient man, Garrett."

His warm hand embraced her jawline, and she leaned into his strength. "When I need to be. Are you ready for more adventure? Excited to see what waits for us deeper inside this mountain?"

"Hah," she scoffed. "There's naught to see and I fear where you'll take me. Though, I suppose there's no other choice but to wander about while being grateful for your guidance."

Into a deeper, Netherworld of darkness.

"Here's what we're going to do. The cavern is wider now, but houses rocks of all shapes and sizes. You'll have to crawl without the encumbrance of your skirt. I'll descend backward, pulling you on my coat."

"I hope it doesn't rend."

"You're not that heavy and the leather is strong. You'll raise your skirts and crawl forward on your knees, using my coat as a barrier. It will shield your skin, somewhat. I won't lie to you; passing over this rugged surface will hurt, but at least your skin will be protected."

"Thank you for thinking of me. Let's press onward."

"All right," he whispered, giving her cheek a pinch.

Still facing her, Garrett slid backward and pulled the coat with him. Ruby missed his nearness, though the distance separating them was slim. Sighing, she pulled her skirt to her waist and then crawled over the first stretch of leather-draped rocks, her flattened palms and knees bearing the weight of her body.

She closed her eyes while bearing the touch of sharper rocks against her hands. When sensitive skin came into contact with stones, the pressure was unbearable. She held her breath, fighting the painful sensations, regardless that a fur hide covered a portion of the trail.

Sharp and jagged, the aggregate tore through the leather coat and scraped her palms and raked at her knees. Ruby sucked for breath. Fluid slid along her leg.

Bloody nether lands!

Ruby cried out, wincing. Struggling— She reached blindly, her hands aimlessly searching, unsure of where to place her knees. Inching forward, slowly, they maintained a painful hodgepodge, wrestling with the ground, fighting exertion and nausea, while Garrett constantly repositioned the coat.

The ceiling intruded against her back. She was sick with worry. *Was she crawling through a coffin to her grave?* Constant pressure; constant strain. *What lay in wait around the next bend?* The mortar restricted her movement and scored her palms. *She was bleeding.* The temperature increased and she labored for each breath. The unwelcome taste of blood coated the passage to her throat.

"Amira, you can do this. You're stronger than you think," Garrett urged, his voice belying his fatigue. "Come to me. One hand reaches forward, a knee after that—Baby steps. *Remember?* Don't give in. Don't give up!"

"It hurts."

She huffed with frustration, wincing when she missed the leather hide and a sharp boulder scraped her knuckles. Her surcoat had come loose from her waist. She crawled on it, her feet catching in the hem. She swore, and though her hair was bound, strands escaped the bun to wisp against her forehead, straying into her eyes. Not that it mattered, as she couldn't see.

Garrett stopped. A stream of curse words exploded from his mouth.

"What now?" Ruby fretted, fearing what predicament they faced next.

"The pathway is littered with boulders. All shapes and sizes. Prepare yourself for a sharp descent."

"Okay."

"We can't know what's at the bottom. Be careful. I don't want you to fall. Shift backward onto your buttocks; with your feet placed in front of you, then slide forward. You shouldn't need your cloak, take it off and give it to me. I'll manage it for you."

Once Ruby found enough space to shift her position, she did as Garrett requested, but she hated the passage across larger boulders, and descending across the stones proved difficult. Shooting pains in her arms and legs, and injured palms, caused her eyes to tear from each rock she touched, and each boulder she maneuvered across. Tentatively, she stretched her leg forward, reaching with a leather-covered foot, her toes searching for a stable surface. Maintaining an upright position proved difficult. Twice, her equilibrium failed and she lost her balance, collapsing against the rocks.

Marring a leg; striking her head.

"I don't want to do this anymore," she whimpered, her right shoulder stinging from two solid blows, her head smarting, having careened against a limestone wall more than once.

"Do you want to take a break?"

She shook physically, fighting tears and fright. "I don't know. I'm scuttling across the rocks like a stinking crab, but not going anywhere."

"Crabs have it better than this. Light, and an ocean at their scuttling feet."

Ruby slipped and fell against her back. "Sarding nether lands!" she cried out, screaming her frustration. She lay against a clay bed, her back screaming, her eyes straining to see something more than illusions of the night. Tears leaked from her eyes and she let them collect on her cheeks. The situation as helpless, hopeless.

"Bugger it all!" Garrett ranted. "Bloody Netherworld, piss and vinegar. A black hole. Its width, not much wider than my chest."

"Must we pass through it?" Ruby cringed, squeezing her palm into a bloody fist. "That *sarding* witch. I might as well remain here, lying on my back."

"No." He grumbled, his anger echoing among the rotten space. "You know what we have to do. Despite the fact we're facing a tight squeeze, a damn wormhole."

"I'm exhausted," Ruby said, panting, "I don't have the strength to crawl, nor lift my body. I have fallen against the cavern wall too many times." She closed her eyes against the panic, her breath rasping from her mouth, her heartbeat striking a dangerous rhythm. "The atmosphere inside this casket waxes heavy. The night weighs on my courage. The situation boils my fright. I want to hurt the witch for burying us—and I will, if I ever have the power to do so."

"Aye," Garrett said, growling, "I'll assist you to do it, too. I'll add the muscle to light the fire. But we need to escape this place. Best to keep our minds healthy and not on revenge. The timing isn't right. Have you had enough of a break?"

"I need a moment more," Ruby whispered, trembling, "to overcome my fear, and maybe to take a sip of water."

"I wish we had stronger spirits," he whispered, his tone full of longing. "I could use a strong ale right now."

He slid backward and sat beside her on a boulder, then

removed his pack from his shoulders. Searching for the flask, he soon passed it into her hands. "Take a drink."

Ruby's hands shook while holding the flask, but she removed the cork and took a swig. It felt refreshing to hold the water in her mouth and feel the moisture against her throat, despite how stale the water tasted.

"Thank you," she whispered, "take a drink yourself."

"There's not much left. I'll leave it for you."

"Satisfy your thirst, or you won't be able to care for me."

"I don't want to see you thirsty."

Ruby snickered, though the sound wasn't funny. "You won't see my thirsty expression, Garrett. You won't see me at all."

He groaned, reluctantly taking a sip. Ruby heard him replace the cork, heard him place the flask inside his leather pack.

"The tunnel is too tight for extra clothing. Wad your cloak into a ball. You'll push it ahead of you as you crawl through the tunnel."

"And our strategy in this situation?"

"To wiggle forward like a worm, like a snake," Garrett grumbled. "Your sister would be able to interpret the movements of a serpent."

"Don't mention her." Ruby growled, anger causing tears to form in her eyes again. "Don't foul the air with her name. She betrayed me."

"Amira, the air already stinks of a garderobe's dung, and your sister does not contribute to the stench."

"Scarlett's a factor in our situation. If she had only heeded my warning, and left a wicked, royal family alone, I wouldn't be worming my way inside this trench."

"You were in grave danger before King Rickard's death, but whatever the reason we find ourselves inside this shit hole, let's not waste our energy on anger. Myself, I want to see what demon lies in wait at the end of the tunnel."

Ruby bundled her woolen cloak into a ball. "Let's hope it's not our own mortality."

Chapter Seventeen

PRINCESS SCARLETT

The group traveled for several days, continually driving the horses in a southerly direction, venturing toward an unknown destination. No one knew whether the salt flats were real, so Scarlett was grateful that her companions upheld her vision. Yet, despite their support, she wasn't certain of the revelation, and found herself continually pondering if her circumstances related more to an overworked imagination. Whatever the regard, some force led them, and presently beside the ocean.

Traveling near the water gave Scarlett time to reflect on past and future days. She hardly minded the carriage wheels bumping and grinding against the lane while admiring the sea. The nonsensical journey aided her mind to wander while studying a raised strip of land that rose above rippling, cerulean-blue waves. The ocean had always been a calming influence, so when she wearied of travel, stopping at the beach provided ample space to breathe and stretch her legs.

The horses partook of briny, verdant grasses salted with sea air, while she escaped to the beach. Standing on the shoreline with the wind nuzzling her face, she contemplated more than a distant sea, and recalled a time when Father Clement had offered her a promise: *a blue current of love where worries have no hold.* She didn't know if it was possible to find the affection he had spoken of, but she welcomed the nearness of the water. The waves gently rolling in, gently rolling out; breathing against the shoreline. Mother Nature's gesture calmed her mind; delivering peace, mental health, and bliss, too.

Despite the autumn chill, Scarlett wedged her toes in the cold, wet sand. Fine particles flirted with the ocean's current, splattering against her face. She squinted, shivering involuntarily. The strong breeze caressed her face, mussed her hair, and caused fresh tears to escape from her eyes. Already, she sensed, more than felt, frost in the air. The change in temperature promised the return of snow with the fall season shifting to winter. The daylight hours were lessening, increasing the promise of gloom and darkness.

Frowning, Scarlett gripped her cloak and held it tightly around her front, and strolled along the beach, following the break in the shoreline, listening to the gulls, letting her skirts drag across the sand. She considered the plight of her sisters, and a mother who had inspired this journey. Visions were leading her to an impasse.

Aniron waits for you.

Theodore had finally admitted he did not know which route they should travel as the true Queen Regana had confided to his contact that the direction to progress would present itself in its own good time.

Scarlett believed his assertion might be true, given the dream or vision she had experienced. Her mother had told Theo that the pathway would come from Scarlett's thoughts, and she hoped she had the faith to discover the place.

A place where white clouds kissed the earth.

She couldn't envision this place offering the serenity that Father Clement had described, but her intuition foretold she would appreciate the place all the same, if she ever arrived there.

"Scarlett!" Nicolai shouted from a distance. She pivoted toward the sound of his voice, grinning. *She'd walked farther than she'd realized.*

Waving one hand in the air, she sauntered toward Nicolai, but she saw his face was lined with concern. He pointed. Before she could consider why, he broke into a sprint.

"Don't turn around—" he yelled. "Run, Scarlett. Run!"

She knew she should listen, but curious, she faced the rising storm.

Confused, Scarlett watched the sky darken, felt the wind spit sand against her face. A destructive force soon lifted a large mass of sand and water from the ocean floor into the air. Grains of sand merged together and formed a whirling, funnel-shaped mass. Astonished, she watched the twisting, gyrating tornado rushing toward her. Helpless, she glanced at Nicolai, the man she loved, and then she faced the oncoming evil.

Her eye color changed. She swayed on her feet like the

cobra would do if threatened, and then she swallowed her fear.

The sky succumbed to darkness. Squinting, Scarlett struggled to see the threat against a noisy, pounding beat that overruled the ocean sounds. She feared the weight of it would burst her eardrums as slashing winds wrapped around her figure, threatening to pull her apart, limb from limb, and lift her off the ground.

She despaired. There was nothing to hold onto—

Bending forward, Scarlett wriggled her feet in the sand. Somehow, she rooted to the ground as grains of sand molded together, forming the face of an evil queen.

"I have come for you," the witch screamed, her voice screeching. "Let go!"

Strong and unafraid, Scarlett glared at the queen's evil eyes, swaying on her feet. "You have no power over me, devil's spawn. Leave me. Leave this place!"

Scarlett reached for the witch, but the whirling sand sculpture of a queen fashioned into the shape of a hand and reached toward her neck.

Scarlett tried to retreat, but she wasn't fast enough to forestall tempestuous winds. The witch's hand grasped her neck and choked off her breath.

Cynara's cackling laughter resounded in the air. "How does it feel, grains of sand cutting at your flesh, marring your skin?"

Scarlett wanted to respond, but she was drowning, and soon lifted off the ground. *Odin...*

"This is the pain you marked me with; these are the scars

you've placed on my neck. I've had enough from you. Welcome to the end of your miserable life."

I'm innocent…

Scarlett reflected on the witch's anger while experiencing a strangling grip that crushed her windpipe. She struggled inside the funnel, trying to break free of the punishing hold. Her hands penetrated sand, filtering the particles, but soon the storm's strength expired her worries and her spirit rose above the storm. She knew something was wrong when she glimpsed Nicolai, fighting his way inside the spinning mass.

She stared at the scene in confusion. Having been freed from her physical self, Scarlett's spirit tried to return to Nicolai, but she paused, surprised to see that her human form was turning blue.

One breath entered her lungs, and she jolted back into her body, recognizing a harsh cacophony, and contact, too: Nicolai hugged her on the ground. *Why had the queen released her?*

Lightning streaked through the ether, followed by the crackling sound of thunder. The electric current illuminated the funnel-shaped cloud with light. Scarlett heard Cynara scream and watched as the whirlwind shifted away, leaving Scarlett gasping on the sand, nestled in the safety of Nicolai's arms.

She realized a power stronger than the evil queen had saved her from certain death. The god of war, Odin, raced through the clouds astride Sleipnir, his large warhorse with eight legs. A long red cape trailed behind his massive shoulders. Two black ravens flew by his side and two hungry wolves raced forward, teeth gnashing. Scarlett was grateful, watching

Odin fly through the firmament, speeding through the sky, carrying his magical spear, Gungnir, with a practiced hand.

Scarlett scrutinized his brawny arm, large muscles rippling, as he pulled his spear backward and prepared to throw the weapon. Gungnir sailed through the air, delivering an electric current inside the funnel, and blanketing its churning mass with thunder and lightning.

"Be gone, evil witch!" he yelled, his rich, melodic voice rumbling in the ether. "Do as I say, or I will bury you in your evil work."

"Odin!" she screeched, her power weakening. "How dare you interfere with my business."

"I have watched you at your worst. You've toiled too long with your witchcraft. A lesson needs to be learned."

"A lesson will be learned," she said, ranting. "Soon!"

The grains of sand stopped spinning in the air, and in one great whoosh, fell from the sky, their grains forming a hill of sand on the shoreline. Scarlett breathed a sigh of relief, supposing the evil queen had departed.

Nicolai assisted her to rise, soon pulling her into his embrace. "Are you hurt?"

She trembled within his arms, her hand flying to her neck. "Minor injuries," she replied, unable to stop the tremors.

Scarlett watched in amazement as Sleipnir galloped closer, soon landing on the ground near her, and carrying Odin on his back. The wolves raced along the beach and farther along the shoreline, perhaps chasing the evil. One raven settled on the god's left shoulder, the other landed on the beach.

Scarlett studied the god of war, captivated by his age-worn

face. A full graying beard and longish strands of silver hair enveloped his shoulders. She would have been frightened by his appearance if not for the compassion radiating from a single blue eye. She twisted within Nicolai's embrace, her focus on Odin.

"How do I thank you?"

"I have permitted the witch to go about her nasty business for too long," he said, calling to her, "I'm sorry for your troubles, Princess."

"No one is sorrier than I," Scarlett replied. "On this occasion, I thought I was dead and bound for the lands of summer, or the Otherworld."

His brows drew together, wrinkling at the bridge of his nose. "You're too young to feast at the table of the gods. I won't let the witch hurt you, and I know the path you must take."

"You do?"

"Your mother has prayed long and hard for you to find your way. A more determined woman I have yet to meet."

"She can't keep me safe, but since you have rescued me, may I ask a favor of you?"

"One may always ask. What do you need?"

Scarlett left Nicolai's embrace and approached the god, hoping he wouldn't say no. "I require a safe manner of travel to arrive at the home of the white goddess. She exists in a world where salt flats rise, where white clouds kiss the earth."

He grinned, nodding. His rosy cheeks wrinkled at the corners where a single blue eye and an empty socket lay. "I know of such a place."

Scarlett nibbled at her lip, hoping he'd help. "Can you

take me there? Can you provide safe passage? I know that once I arrive at the Salar de Uyuni, the queen can no longer hurt me."

Odin nodded. "I can. I will."

The raven, a large bird with beady black eyes, sat on his left shoulder. "Caw!" the bird said. And Scarlett was certain that the creature nodded, too.

Chapter Eighteen

QUEEN MOTHER CYNARA

Cynara withdrew from her incantation in a fit of anger. She stared at five flaming wicks that illuminated the glen, furious that her conjuring spell had failed. She sat in the center of a three-ringed circle hidden deep in the king's forest in a brief expanse of valley beyond the hollow glen. She swept her hand over the flames, casting the wind element, which caused the fire to expire and black wax to splatter on the forest floor.

"Why?" she screamed at the half-light of day, wringing her hands. Why had the god of war interfered on Scarlett's behalf?

Why had he done it?

It didn't matter. This was not a time to worry about subjects that were at an end. She couldn't concern herself with uncontrollable circumstances. It was better to divert her attention to her future ambitions instead.

Rising, she paced outside her circle, studying the circular shape, scrutinizing the triangle at the head, the pentagrams on each quadrant of the outer curve, and hexagons carved inside the three-ringed circle. She knew the entire design had to be perfect in scope and measure to achieve her purpose.

Still, she wondered: *What was the god's motive? What was Scarlett to him that he would save the princess?*

She supposed his reasoning didn't matter. She glanced at her hand with satisfaction, considering that whatever his motive, she had obtained the item sought: a single strand of auburn hair. She only wished she could have completed her mission, but once again, Scarlett had thwarted death.

Even so, the failure could not rob her of greater rewards. When the alignment happened, Odin would be sorry for getting in her way. He had an ability, a power she desired, and she meant to obtain it, no matter what she had to do.

"Ragnarök!" Cynara yelled, cackling, gesturing with her fist. Her expression was crazed, her mind unbalanced and enmeshed with the psychotic belief that she would not fail again. "I will bring your destruction, and soon."

Chapter Nineteen

PRINCESS RUBY

Ruby was concerned she would never reach the end of the tunnel. *How far had they progressed? How much farther did they have to go?* Hot and sweaty, she likened the physical exertion to that of captured prey; two human animals seized by evil who suffered the physical sensations of claustrophobia, but still managed to crawl through the belly of a snake. If not for Garrett's constant persuasion, forced encouragement at times, she'd have given up and allowed herself to be consumed by an appetite much greater than her weakening willpower.

No one would ever know what she had suffered, or how difficult it was worming her way forward, her abdominal muscles protesting the exertion while pushing a balled-up cloak, and though she was grateful for a smoother, less obtrusive passage, by the time Garrett slipped from the cavity at the bitter end, exertion had bathed her face with sweat.

She lay near the finish, exhausted, with moisture dripping

from her forehead and falling into her eyes. She didn't have the strength to crawl farther.

"It's okay, Amira," Garrett said, coaxing her to come to him, his voice a soothing balm in the night. "A few more feet and you can rest. You can do this. You're not alone. I'm here; I'm waiting for you. I'll help you."

He crawled back inside the tunnel, reached for her cloak and removed it from her hands, then pleaded with her to come to him. *So close, but so far.*

"I can't do it." Ruby gasped, her heart beating too fast. "I'm exhausted. I don't have the strength."

"Yes, you do. Yes, you can."

When she was close enough that Garrett could touch her fingers, he stretched farther inside the tunnel and grasped her hand, then pulled her to the edge.

He grasped her underneath her armpits and pulled her forward, then assisted her to escape the tunnel. Free of the constriction, she wobbled on legs too weak to support her weight. As if Garrett sensed her instability, he held her close to him. She laid her head against his chest, her equilibrium unsteady, her balance threatening to give way. A buzzing sound echoed in her head. She felt dizzy...

She fell.

When Ruby later opened her eyes, it was still night. She lay on the hard ground of a cavern bed not knowing where she was, but soon realized that Garrett knelt above her, holding her in his arms and frantically calling out her name.

"Amira!" he said, shouting, his voice laced with concern, his hand lightly patting her cheek. "Can you hear me? Amira, please, wake up—"

"I can hear you."

"You've taken a fall, but you're safe. Are you hurt? Anywhere?"

She was not only aware of his human contact, but also how good it felt to be held in his arms. "Everything hurts; my hands, my knees, my head—no part of me has escaped from injury."

"I'm sorry for what you've suffered. I wish our circumstances were different, but let's not dwell on bitter passage. You're too warm. I want you to drink some water. I'm putting the flask in your hands."

Ruby accepted the flask and did as he urged, but she only took one sip. "There's only enough water for one of us. You take it. I'm going to die anyway."

"Don't speak like that! We're not going to die, no one's going to die. I won't let it happen," Garrett said, his tone forceful. "You've exerted yourself too much, and it's my fault. We should have stopped. We should have rested more."

"We should never have left the castle. We've been on a fool's journey. I should have given up days ago."

"Stop. It's dark enough inside this cavern. Don't permit darker thoughts to control your mind. The night already weeps of despair. Focus on this moment. Amira, you're thirstier for life, drink it."

He passed the flask into her hands, and Ruby did take a sip, but felt guilty for consuming what should have been shared. "There's no water left now," she said, weeping, "none for you."

"It's okay, don't cry. I may have heard water dripping deeper inside the mountain. It's a good sign."

"I don't have the strength to find it."

"Not tonight," he said, stroking her hair. "I'll search for it in the morning."

"We'll never see another morning."

"No more talk of ugliness. A few hours' rest will make a difference in how you feel."

Ruby nestled her head against Garrett's chest, and cradled into the comfort of his arms. He was the only strength she was certain of and she trusted in him. "I'm tired, Garrett."

"I give you permission to sleep."

"I'm scared, afraid to close my eyes. Please, don't release me."

"I will hold you all night long. We'll take a break, have a rest, and we won't go thirsty. I'll find water in the morning."

He massaged her cheek, his fingers stroking her hair, and she wondered if he knew how much his kindness meant to her. She listened to his breathing, her eyelids heavy, her heartbeat returning to a normal pace.

"If we see another morning, Garrett."

He stretched out beside her and pulled her closer to him, tucking her head beneath his chin. "Look, I know you're tired; I know how hopeless our situation seems, but we cannot give up. If by chance we can leave this nastiness behind…" He paused, and when he did, Ruby wondered if he trusted in his own lecture. "Listen, I promise you, I'll find a way out."

She didn't believe him, but it didn't matter. His attempt at gravity earned her gratitude all the same.

"Garrett, I hope you're right."

WHEN RUBY AWOKE the next morning, she was wrapped inside her cloak, and lying on a stony bed with her head resting on Garrett's pack. The environment had not changed while she'd been sleeping. No light, but she didn't sorrow over it. Alone, yet she didn't panic. Garrett must have journeyed farther inside this cavernous maze to study their mountain prison, while she lay on the stone floor, quietly considering, until she heard him returning.

"Are you awake?"

"Yes," she whispered.

"Are you ready to see where the pathway leads us?"

"I'm ready if the trek takes us somewhere better than this black monster. Have you discovered anything positive in your recent quest?"

"I found water. It's a promising sign." He passed the flask into her hands. "Drink as much as you like."

"I can't believe it." Ruby brightened, reflecting on the weight of the flask resting in her hands. "I recall you saying you heard water dripping. I thought you were imagining it."

"Drink," he urged. "You didn't consume much water yesterday and I don't want you to faint again."

Ruby rose upward to a sitting position, then removed the cap and drank deeply, surprised the water tasted so fresh. "What else have you found along the path and where will you lead me today? Surely no more wormholes, as I don't think I could take the confinement or the physical exertion."

He retrieved the flask, then passed her a slice of jerky and a wedge of bread and cheese. The bread was crusty and the cheese had hardened, but she ate the foodstuffs anyway.

"The pathway continues, but it divides into two separate corridors."

"Two possible routes out of here. Which one do we take?"

"I chose the one with the water, though it's a crapshoot either way," he suggested, sighing. "Even so, two options are better than one, for if one fork doesn't work, we can return to the trail-head and take the other."

"I don't know if I'm ready. My muscles are hurting in places I didn't know I could feel pain, but I know you'll want to continue with our explorations."

"We don't have a choice. We can't stay here. I'd like to leave soon, if you're able. Are you strong enough to stand on your own?"

"I'll accept your assistance if you're of a mind to help me rise to my feet."

"When you're finished breaking your fast, it would be my pleasure to help you, Princess."

GARRETT MORRIS

GARRETT GRASPED Ruby's hand and assisted her to rise to a standing position. When she swayed, he urged her closer to him, worrying she might faint like before, but her strength of mind belied signs of languor. When she didn't succumb to weakness, he hoped it was a good sign.

"Should I wear my cloak?"

"A damp cold exists where I'm taking you. You'll want the protection of a wrap."

"I'll take that as a yes," Ruby said, grasping her cloak and placing it on her shoulders.

"Permit me to take your hand. I'll guide you through the night. I don't want you to fall again. Do you remember the rules?"

"What rules? The only guidance I require comes from my guardian warrior. I placed my trust in you when I grasped your hand. Lead the way, Garrett. I'll go wherever you take me."

Ruby's trust consumed him with guilt, as even though they had travelled long and far, he had failed in keeping her safe. Sure, he'd discovered options that could lead a princess to safety, but two trails inside this maze could also lead to a path unsought, and that crux squeezed at his conscience. He remained hopeful, though the situation might not resolve with a good outcome.

"I'm grateful you trust me to chaperone our foray into the unknown. Especially since the previous hours have challenged each of us."

"There's no need to hide the truth from me. The dour sound of your voice tells me everything I need to know."

"A man has his weaknesses. This fight has diminished my spirits, and challenged me more than any other problem I've faced before," he said, sighing. "I feel as weak as a leg of mutton. I worry that at some point there will be no more corridors to find. More often than not, there is only one entrance in a mountain and the previous one may have sealed our fate."

The princess laid her hand on his shoulder. "I know you won't give up on me, or on our survival."

"'Tis true. As long as I have a princess to guard, I'll never give up on your care."

They traipsed toward a narrow corridor, and then meandered through a widening canal of limestone, the entire time descending farther inside the mountain and not once in the moments that followed did the princess complain.

He jumped when Ruby clutched at his arm. "Did I frighten you?"

"You, frighten me?" He chuckled, squeezing her fingers. "Never."

"I scared you. Admit it. I'm sorry if I did, but it's comforting to hear your laughter."

It gave him comfort to feel her fingers, if only to know she was nearer to his protection. Together, they progressed through the dark, their senses alert, until he heard the telltale sound that *might* give them hope.

Drip. *Drip.* Drip.

"Is that what I think it is?" Ruby said, surprise in her voice.

"You're listening to the sweet sound of water. Finally, this cavern gives us a surprise, and we'll be near it soon."

They took tiny steps forward, baby steps, slowly trekking toward the trickle. The cavern narrowed, but he didn't notice it as he was more mindful of the feminine fingers grasping his biceps, slick with moisture.

"The water's a relief, but I don't much like the sour smell of egg."

"It's better you care about your next step. Bend down, Amira. We're descending a waterfall of rocks on our bottoms."

"This sarding nether land. I have had enough of rocks and hard surfaces."

"Then you'll be grateful that the boulder stones are slick with moisture, coated with lichen and running water."

"Ew," Ruby said, touching a jelly-like topcoat. "I go from the tight squeeze of a tunnel to the cold, grimy surface of a trickling waterfall. What's next?"

"Getting wet by sliding downward on your rear quarters," Garrett chuckled, not minding the wetness soaking through his breeches. "Pretend your fingers are meandering across a treasure of seed pearls."

"Strangely, the surface does feel rich and nubby."

Once they reached the bottom, they found the water, too. Garrett was grateful to hear Ruby giggling, cupping cold water in her hands and thirstily drinking. While kneeling at the edge of an underground sea, he did the same.

"You don't disappoint," Ruby said. "Maybe after further exploration we'll find our freedom, too, just like you promised."

"Maybe after we've passed through an underground sea. I'm sorry to tell you, but to progress farther, we must wade through it, which means we'll get wet."

"Why am I not surprised?" she said with a grimace. "Though the water quenches my thirst, I don't want to pass through it. What if it's deep? What if it's impassable? I can't swim and the water is cold to the touch. I don't want to be cold."

"It doesn't matter what you want."

"I thought our luck was changing."

"Luck has little to do with our circumstances," Garrett offered, "but maybe hope does lie ahead. I'm surprised you have not noticed. There's a light in the distance."

"A light?" A faint flicker of bioluminescence emanated from a distant cavern ceiling. "How can that be?" she asked him, seemingly astonished. "A starry night sky hidden deep inside a cavern? I've never witnessed a sight as wondrous as that."

"I don't know if I'd describe it as wondrous," Garrett said, his hand on her waist. "It's unusual, and strange to find in the darkness. I hope it's safe and doesn't poison our breathing."

She smacked his shoulder. "Yes, there was that egg smell, but don't frighten me unnecessarily. Surely it's natural?"

"Whatever mystery compels the light, it's time to move toward it. I don't know how deep the water is, but sorry, princess, we'll have to remove our clothing before wading across the sea to reach it."

"You want me to do what?"

"We need to wade through the water."

"I understood your directive. Why must I remove my clothing?"

"They can stay on if you don't mind your garments getting wet, but I personally don't think that's a good idea."

"My bottom is already wet."

"Mine is too, but soaking our garments completely is inconceivable."

"Very well," she grumbled, sighing, but then reluctantly obeyed.

Garrett removed his clothing as well, aware that the

princess was undressing, too. She removed her woolen cloak, her surcoat and then her kirtle. A feminine shadow stood near him, and he knew she was only clothed in a bandeau and panty braes. To stop himself from contemplating her nakedness, he bound her clothing into a ball and then passed it into her outstretched hands.

Standing in the dark, he couldn't see Ruby clearly, but he knew she was as naked as himself. His groin throbbed to life at the thought.

"Are you ready?" he asked, shifting the pack to his back.

"I am."

He took hold of her hand. "Sorry, Amira, I know this swim won't be pleasant."

He didn't give her time to fear the cold water before pulling her into the underground sea. When they splashed through the surface, she uttered an instinctive cry, and the fright caused him momentary guilt, knowing he must lead her through the standing water. Cold liquid prickled his skin, prickled the princess's skin, but they scrambled through the water, searching for stable footing.

"It's cold. *So cold.* I knew it would be…"

"You can do it," he said, feeling chilled himself. "I can hear your teeth chattering. Breathe through it."

He ushered her forward, noticing her skin when she briefly came into contact with his arm, firing his emotion. He stamped the awareness down, knowing he couldn't concern himself with the proximity of her nakedness, but the water's chill did little to stem his longing. He had to distract himself from temptation, and the woman he cared about from a cold reality.

"Look at the ceiling," Garrett said, gesturing. "Focus on the light, not the chill in the air."

"Sa-sard the ceiling," Ruby replied, her voice stuttering. "I'm uncomfortable. Every part of my being wants to leave this rock-strewn place. Are you not cold, too?"

"Sarding freezing, but we're approaching the other side; we'll be there soon."

When Ruby slipped underneath the water, Garrett didn't panic. He not only pulled her from the recesses, but also swung her upward and held her in his arms. He should have been a gentleman and carried her sooner. *What was wrong with him?*

"My clothes—" She sputtered, spitting out water. "I've dropped them."

It was his fault, but he didn't admit it. "It's okay. I'll find them. Here, hold the pack."

Garrett ushered her to a place in the water where she could stand safely. She held the pack and shook like a leaf in the wind while he returned to the water, not feeling the cold any longer, and diving repeatedly until he rose to the surface with her clothing.

"I found them. Damn it. My clothes are probably wet, too."

He swam the final length to where she waited, and then together, they waded the final few feet to the waterline, where the water receded to a limestone ledge. Garrett offered her his hand and helped her to leave the underground sea.

Cold and dripping, the princess stood on the water's edge, shivering so badly he could hear her teeth clattering. Hugging herself, she appeared like she might cry. He didn't want her to cry, didn't want her to be chilled to the bone. Garrett dropped his pack on the ground, followed by her garments. All landed with a squish.

"Not a promising sound," he grunted, coughing. "But with luck, my clothes are dry."

"We're soon to find out."

Garrett tried to distract himself from the situation, from her nakedness, by studying the luminescent miracle of light on the ceiling. He grasped his leather, long coat, which had been attached to the pack.

"Luck is on our side, for at least the inner lining is dry."

He came near the princess then, and beheld the beauty standing before him, then drew her close and wrapped his coat around her shoulders. Taking her in his embrace, he massaged her back, his fingers stroking the outer layers of the coat while wishing he stroked her skin instead. His awareness ignited, understanding that Ruby was naked.

"You're an unselfish man, Garrett. To stand before me unclothed, protecting me, trying to gain my warmth, while you leave your own skin bare. While your caring compassion warms my heart, you must protect yourself, too."

She shared the manly long coat with him then leaned her head against his naked chest, perhaps listening to his racing heart, placing her hands around his waist. He sucked in a breath when her fingers entertained little circles, exploring his skin still wet from the underground sea they had passed through.

"Surely you realize it is wrong for a young maiden to be held so intimately, but the embrace warms my heart."

His fingers wandered to her lower spine—

"What do we do now?" Ruby said, shivering, though she was held in his embrace.

He pulled her closer, molding her to him. "We warm up, we let our bodies dry, I seek a place to hang our clothes. Hopefully, they will dry."

Garrett squinted, peering at Ruby. Although the cavern was shadowed with gray, he was able to see her earnest expression. Underneath the mysterious ceiling, he contemplated this woman and her passionate nature. He had saved her from drowning—that and many other obstacles.

"What is it? Why do you look at me with wonder in your eyes?"

"I don't know what I would have done without you as my protector," she said, touching his cheek, her fingers tracing the curve of his jawline to his mouth. "I look at you with the eyes of a woman, a woman who is grateful for your courtesy, and kind, caring ways. You have saved me, more than once. For this reason and many others, I think I love you, Garrett Morris."

He shook off a breath, permitting her to explore him still. "You don't mean it, Amira. You only think such thoughts because I've taken care of you, as I should. It's my responsibility as your protector."

"I know what I said, and I meant every word."

The princess rose up on her tiptoes and bravely kissed his lips. He closed his eyes, savoring the sensation as she rested against his chest. "While the kiss is pleasurable, it's wrong."

"Did you hear what I said? I love you. Do you not have kind words to share with me, too?"

Garrett closed his eyes, sighing, leaning against her forehead. He wanted to respond in equal measure, but he couldn't. The beauty he held wasn't just any woman. "Any man would bow before you, even I would beg for your hand, but I can't return your affection. 'Tis my duty to guard and protect a princess. I have sworn an oath. I won't take advantage of you."

"I'm naked. I'm a woman in your arms, and if truth be told, I have not been a princess for many moons now. We are all that there is and all there will ever be, a man and a woman, two fragile human beings yielding to each other beneath a mysterious ceiling."

"I understand what you plead for better than you know, but human desires do not change a man's responsibility. Whatever happens, I will always be your guard, but you—must remain a princess to the kingdom and a ward to me."

Garrett damned his manly nature that intruded on his willpower and twitched to life, throbbing with his need. She smiled, and he supposed she marveled at the firm shaft rearing against her belly. Ruby wasn't an immature girl; she knew what he disguised, the desire to protect her virginity.

"This is not a kingdom we find ourselves inside. Here, I'm a woman bereft of a castle or a throne. Even so, I feel your guardianship, pulsating against my skin."

"You must not tempt me. I'm a man with a man's nature, trying to shield you from the cold. I can't hide the need my body betrays, and I know I hold a precious gift."

Unrelenting, she kissed him again. "A gift melds to my arms, too."

"Sard it all." Garrett muttered, succumbing to a nether land atmosphere prior to kissing her lips and tasting her sweetness. She hesitated when his hand cupped her breast, giving rise to sensations that desired to find release between her legs, but he sensed her inexperience and her excitement, too. He couldn't do it. Couldn't betray the princess or her mother's guidance, so he retreated from her lips to kiss her forehead. "I care for you. I would protect you even if the work resulted in my death. Yet, I won't take advantage of this situation. If you were to give yourself to me now, I could never let you go."

She stared at him with a longing that caused his heart to beat faster. Unwilling to give in to what he supposed was a mutual desire, she reached for his face and pulled him back to her lips.

"Never let me go, then," Ruby said, pleading with him, her breath quickening, her body warming. "Keep me close to your heart, permitting me to know, I'm still alive."

Garrett weakened to Ruby's demands and kissed her, offering the princess the sensual pleasure she sought and an eventual release, but he denied his own gratification. He would not mark his precious Amira with his seed.

Chapter Twenty

PRINCESS ROSE

Rose stood on the *Sea Monster*'s main deck, bearing the back and forth sway of the vessel as it traveled through rough seas. The skies were contaminated with cumulus clouds; cotton-like puffs, furling and rolling flat, sanctioned by the wind to deliver a chilling breeze. She knew the boat was in trouble and the frightful expressions of the crew only accentuated her belief that these men acknowledged a dire fate, too. They had worked diligently to prepare the ship, but Rose worried their efforts were in vain.

A storm brewed on the horizon.

A noticeable change in the weather had compelled her to silence. Tears leaked from her pale blue eyes while staring at a gray sea. The waves rolled across the ocean, building one to four-foot whitecaps, stretching as far as the eye could see. Their curls misted her face and threatened to rise higher. For the first time in her life, she was deathly afraid of the coming hours.

"Gods of the Otherworld, please save us."

Kenneth Hayes approached her. "Princess Rose, the captain has ordered all but the ablest hands below deck. Return to the captain's quarters at once."

"I want to see it come." She shouted at the wind. "I don't want to drown inside a stateroom."

"Quit the hysterics. 'Tis the captain's orders, and if you don't obey him, I'm to drag you there myself."

Rose glared at the short, portly man while perusing his angry expression, a dour look rounded out with a full graying beard. "Why do you care for my well-being? You've called me a witch yourself."

"Oh, aye," he replied, sizing up her feminine shape. "I've called you that and worse. It wouldn't bother me none if you were swept overboard. You, Princess, have earned us a rough sea. The captain should never have brought you aboard this vessel."

"I don't bring the storm," she said, huffing.

He grasped her arm, cruelly pinching. "Don't you? If you didn't invite this foul weather, why then, does she come?"

Rose gave into his demands, reluctantly being led away. "Why? I'd tell you, but a simpleton cannot be depended on to understand."

She appealed to Edwin who stood on the quarterdeck, waving to get his attention in the hope the captain might assist her, but Hayes ushered her toward the stateroom and her need went unanswered. The ocean's spray misted her face prior to passing through the quarterdeck doors and entering the captain's quarters.

"You'll stay inside if you know what's good for you."

She knew she shouldn't test the quartermaster, but she did so anyway. "And if I don't do as you say?"

"You're a bad luck coin. As I said before, it wouldn't upset me if you were swept overboard and buried at sea. It's only the captain's rule that keeps you safe. Should you disobey his command, I might see it done. After all, sacrifices are necessary to save the ship."

Rose knew she was beaten. She scrutinized the swaying floor, listened to the rising wind. "Bastard!" she uttered angrily. "You win. You horrible churlish man. I'll do as you say, I'll stay inside."

He muttered unintelligible language under his breath and then left her standing near the entryway. She watched him leave the way he'd come, tottering through the doors. Sighing, she retreated further inside the quarters, but unwilling to dismiss the trouble, she sought the aft lookout and climbed the stairs of the captain's quarters, progressing to the upper windowpanes.

The boat rocked.

Lurching forward, Rose unbarred the middle panes and peered outside. The sea was ugly. The clouds formed into a towering squall-line, and in the short period of time she'd been inside the cabin, the whitecaps had grown higher and were giving off spray. Unstable, she rocked with the vessel's irregular motion, seeing the wind had increased as well.

"Close the shutters, foolish lass," Edwin yelled, hurrying inside his quarters. "Should the glass break—"

When the ocean heaved upward, Rose lost her equilibrium and fell backward, soon finding herself lying on the cabin's flooring. Dazed, she watched the wooden slats swinging above her head, soon contemplating the boat as it bucked a monstrous wave.

Edwin somehow closed the window and latched the wooden panel. When he finished the chore, he glared at her in a meaningful way, and then knelt against the floorboard and grasped her hand, while expressing his concern.

"Bella Rosa, what were you thinking?"

"It's dark inside the cabin with the windows barred. I knew a storm was coming," she said, fearing the worst. "The sky darkens. I did not want to be caught unaware."

Edwin assisted her to rise. "Princess, no man or woman wants to see the devil's sea rise up. Come with me. Come sit on the bunk. It's the safest place to be during a storm."

She nodded in agreement, accepted his outstretched hand and squeezed it tightly. He escorted her to the top landing. She reached for the railing, wobbling on her feet, but once she was able to grasp it, they hurried down the staircase to the lower portion of the stateroom.

A howling and threatening wind made her presence known.

"She's come," Rose said, her voice quaking, "the storm is here."

"Just as you foretold. I wish we were safe at port."

A consternation written in his eyes compelled her to believe a man was as frightened as a princess, but whatever emotional distress an officer might be feeling, she saw he fought to mitigate his fear.

"Every captain worries about bad weather, and though we cannot control heavy seas, we can trust in our training. We'll ride out the storm as best we can, but you, Bella Rosa, must trust in my guidance, leadership I have gained from other able-bodied seamen. Please remain inside the cabin."

"Where can I be safe if I do as you say?"

He took her hand, his expression grave. "I told you, my bunk is the safest place. You best climb under the sheets and hold on for dear life, for if what you foretold is true, we're in for a rough ride."

She nodded, taking his arm. He guided her toward the bunk. "I need to return to the quarterdeck to watch over my men. Please, stay here. Despite what you believe, I will protect you. If you leave the stateroom, I can't promise your safety."

"And if the boat should break apart, what then?"

"Rose, we're at the mercy of the sea, but focusing on the worst outcome doesn't protect your mind. It only serves to confuse a difficult situation."

Compelled to silence, she nodded at Edwin, then watched the man who had promised to keep her safe, abandon her, to return to his post. She curled into a fetal position in the blankets and fisted the woolen fabric in the palms of her hands, waiting for the storm to worsen. She didn't have long to wait.

The wind increased, howling with her fury, tossing the *Sea Monster* in the ocean currents as if the boat were a child's toy. Frightened, Rose gripped the edges of the bunk, listening to wooden timbers creaking while fearing the boat would break apart.

The vessel heaved up and then plummeted again. The constant rocking and instability earned her a queasy stomach. Understanding sickness was fast approaching, she climbed from the bed to fetch a bucket. When the sea rose up again, compromising her balance, she collapsed to the floor.

Crawling across wooden slats, she seized a bucket and lost her morning meal.

Raising her head, she wiped her mouth and crawled to the bunk with the bucket held in her hands. The sea heaved, and she followed suit, retching.

Sweating, fretting she'd be sick again, she imagined Captain Perrow at the wheel, setting the bow into the wind, climbing white-capped waves. She pitied the captain and his crew, brave men fighting inclement weather, but without their struggle and hard work, the ship would surely be lost.

The *Sea Monster* rose upward again, then fell hard, striking the trough at the bottom of a crest, the hull taking a loud and decisive pounding.

What further violence could the Sea Monster endure?

Time slipped by but the storm didn't lessen. The winds grew louder, *shriller*; the storm attained gale force strength.

Rocking. Rolling— The vessel pitched to its side.

Disaster slammed against the boat, striking from a different angle. The thrust forced the *Sea Monster* onto her side and threw Rose from the bunk. She slid across the cabin and came to a rest, to lie haphazardly against the opposite wall. Stunned, *hurt*, she rubbed her head, then attempted to crawl toward the outer door.

Even so, the boat swung wildly to the other side, and she fell again, striking the lip of the bunk on the opposite wall.

"Rose!" Edwin screamed, rushing to her.

Crumpled on the planking, she rose to her knees to face the captain, glimpsing a wild and raging sea behind his back.

The *Sea Monster* rocked up and down; water splashed over her railings.

"The boat might be lost," Edwin shouted, rushing to her, taking her hand and lifting her as if she were a rag doll. "She's taking on water. We might not be able to save the boat."

Rose cried, tears blurring her vision.

Water surged inside the captain's quarters, streaming across the wooden slats. Rose tried to scramble away, tried to retreat from the terror, but slimy tentacles streamed against her legs, so cold against her flesh, the water almost burned.

"We don't have a chance inside the boat. Maybe no chance outside of it, either."

Rose nodded, accepted Edwin's support and held his hand tightly. While attempting to leave the cabin, following the captain toward the unknown, she stumbled, swayed, and strained to maintain her balance. The wind howled on the open deck, whipping her hair, thrashing her skirts around her legs. An angry ocean compelled her attention. Its ugly swell rose up—and she slipped—

She fell to the decking and screamed from a rising fear, soon slumped against the railing. Separated from Edwin, she rolled across the quarterdeck and struck the outer lip of the railing. He tried to reach her, but a second swell threw him in the opposite direction, leaving Rose clinging to the railing's edge and pressed too close to an angry sea.

"Goodbye..." She mouthed the sentiment to Edwin Perrow, the captain of the *Sea Monster*, as she was swept into the frigid waters of the open sea.

"Fight! Swim!"

Shock took hold of her. Ice-cold water chilled her to the bone.

Fool. Edwin dove into the churning abyss and fought to

reach her, following her down. Attempting to swim, Rose extended her fingers toward him, wanting to reach him. *She wasn't ready to die.* She desired a better life, but the chill paralyzed her movement, and the weight of her dress only served to heft her deeper. She swallowed saltwater and fought the current, kicking until she rose above the surface. She spit ugly brine from her lungs, choking, but then fell deeper still, breathing saltwater inside her lungs.

Sinking, *burning*, yet consciously gazing at the surface above for her only hope. For *Edwin*—

Floating—Weightlessness. No further struggles, only silence.

Chapter Twenty-One

LADY REGANA

Regana stood near the tower window, studying the courtyard below. A sudden pressure wrenched her arm and constricted her heart. Grimacing, she fell to her knees and collapsed against the cold, flagstone floor, while understanding that a horrible fate had come to pass.

"No…" She wailed, tears forming in her eyes and blurring her vision. Unconsciously, she reached for her rosary to count her worries, but the prayer beads were gone, just like…

"Rose."

The grief took hold of her emotions and she screamed, *wailing*, her sorrow flooding the chamber.

It cannot be…

Regana hoped it wasn't too late to pray for her daughter's deliverance.

Gods of the Otherworld, please save my child. I beg of you, don't let her die!

Chapter Twenty-Two

KING LOWELL

King Lowell stood on the threshold of his mother's bedchamber, contemplating how she might react to his query. He considered the reason he broached the subject of his father's death in the first place, the comment made by the woman held in the prison tower:

The queen's dark magic pierced King Rickard's wrist.

He didn't know why he concerned himself with the remark, didn't understand why the statement goaded his conscience. *Surely, the former queen lied.* But something about the way she had held his regard and the certainty of her opinion, had concerned him for days.

Normally he would bring the king's men to the privy council chambers to discuss and resolve courtly issues, but subjects involving his mother came with complications. The only option left to him was to speak to his mum.

When the foot guard allowed him entrance into her chambers, she was sitting at a small side table. When she noticed him, a cynical smile lifted her lips. "This is a surprise. To what do I owe the pleasure of a visit from my son?"

He approached, stopping in front of her, staring intently at her eyes. "I must speak with you regarding a matter of concern."

Her eyes narrowed. "What matter concerns you?"

He grabbed a scissor chair and placed it nearby, sitting opposite his mother. He searched for the right approach. "Someone has accused you of duplicity in my father's—your husband's—rather, King Rickard's death."

"A traitor to the court, no doubt," Cynara replied, seemingly unconcerned. "And would this traitor currently reside in the prison tower?"

"Is Sister Mary a traitor, Mum? Or is there some truth in the matter of my father's death?"

Lowell measured his mother's expression, watching for signs of guilt, but her brows merely rose in interest, her serious regard not giving her veracity away. "The former queen is guiltier of duplicity than me. I don't know the woman, so I can't presume to understand what her motive might be or why she accuses me. Mind you, she hid herself away for nearly fourteen years, changing her identity—for what reason?"

"Yes, but does she lie, Mum?"

Lowell hated asking the question. Hated he had begun to mistrust, but the queen mother had changed, and not for the better. Anger illuminated her eyes as he waited for her to reply. She rose from her side table but said nothing. Uncomfortable with the silence, he reflected on a basket full of greens beside the table.

"What do you have there, Mum?" He gestured, pointing at the basket.

She reached for a stripling branch of berry vegetation, and carefully held the scaly bark.

"*Prunus spinosa*, blackthorn," she replied, studying the wooden length full of small blue berries, as well as wicked sharp thorns. "It reduces the redness and swelling on my neck and shoulders."

"And that?" he asked, pointing at an ugly brown root.

"Angelica," she replied. "Are you interested in knowing why I have this medicinal herb in my bedchamber, too? You enter my room full of distrust, searching for my guilt, asking disrespectful questions. Should I reveal my scars, too? If only to prove they exist?"

"A dramatic display of outrage won't be necessary, Mum. After all, I've seen your scars, but some might question if you use these ingredients to concoct a witch's spell. Did you know you have become known as the Ebony Queen? In earlier days, I would have told naysayers that they fashioned lies for their own purposes, but now, seeing your basket of ingredients, it gives me cause to wonder."

"*The Ebony Queen?*" She rolled the words as if testing them and seemed to derive satisfaction from the moniker. "If what you say is true," she mused, "what do you have to be concerned about? You know who I am. You know what I'm capable of."

"So it is true. You use these ingredients to spin another web."

She frowned. "Lowell, you need not concern yourself with what I do. I am the master of my own purpose."

"I am the king; it is my responsibility to know what people and servants alike are entertaining in my court. This duty applies to my mother, too. I need to know. Did you murder my father?"

She turned her attention to the blackthorn, addressing the barbs, then contemplated him purposefully, her lips pursed together. "You were there, Lowell. With your own eyes, you witnessed the crime. One person is responsible for your father's death, and it is not I."

"Are you certain?"

"After what I've done for you?" she said angrily. "You may leave my chambers, Lowell. Take your accusations with you, and don't return until you can offer an apology to your mother."

He stood, preparing to leave. "I'm sorry. You know I had to ask."

"You had to do no such thing. To take a traitor's word against your own mother is an injustice. You should be ashamed of yourself."

Lowell's face flamed with anger. She treated him like a child, but he was the king. He had a right to ask questions.

"I have not taken a side; I came to seek your counsel, not your disrespect."

"Now that you've heard my response, you may leave. I'm busy. Good night, Lowell."

He left her apartment no closer to the truth, but although his mother had been adamant about her innocence, something didn't seem right. She hid a secret from him. He knew it, but did he have the courage to ferret out the truth?

Chapter Twenty-Three

PRINCESS SCARLETT

"Haw!" Odin shouted from the driver's seat.

Scarlett heard the baritone singing from the god's voice while reclining inside the conveyance. She was peering through the windowpane, concerning herself with travel, when—*Thwack!* The rein's *snap* prompted Sleipnir to squeal.

The shrill cry of the horse, more so than a god's directive, colored Scarlett's fears, but there was little time to contemplate. The carriage lurched, rolled forward, and then shot off, traveling at an abnormal rate of speed.

She gasped, worrying the wheels would break. "What's happening?"

Nicolai grasped her hand. "Don't be frightened. I know we're accelerating swiftly, but gods travel faster than mortal beings."

"This isn't only about the pace. Something more is happening."

"Yes, it seems you're right," Nicolai breathed, excitement

accenting his voice. "The impossible has become reality. Sleipnir is taking us into the sky."

Scarlett was flung to the backrest. "No—Someone save me."

Anxious, she glanced at the windowpane, but was afraid to peer through the glass. What if they fell from the sky? But then she saw what her mind refused to acknowledge. They had left the earth and the ground was sinking, *shrinking* farther away.

"We're not birds, how is this possible?" She searched her fiancé's expression as if he held the answers. "Nicolai, has the carriage transformed itself into a bird?"

He shook his head. "A carriage cannot sprout wings, my love, though we have left the ground and are flying like birds do. Calm yourself, our transport shouldn't surprise you, given that the god of war's horse has the ability to fly."

"We're high off the ground."

"I'm aware of the distance, but the view is compelling. See for yourself."

Scarlett found the courage to peer beyond the window. Though puffy white clouds should have inspired her imagination, a fear response inhibited the experience. Her heart pounded a beat too loud, her breath caught in her throat. Mounting worries could not be suppressed even though an immortal god drove the carriage through the air.

"Will we fall?" she asked, her eyes filling with emotion. "Could the witch force us from the sky?"

"I don't think so," Nicolai said, prying her hand off the armrest and easing her against his side. "With the god of war driving, I think we're safe from evil. Odin struck the witch with a thunderbolt, maybe she's dead." Nicolai snickered. "You'd be calmer minding the view. Be brave. See what's beyond the window."

"When Odin offered to help us," Scarlett said, nibbling her lip, "I didn't expect to be flying like a bird."

"I know, my love. You said that before. I see you're scared, but take a chance, look over there—"

She squeezed her eyes shut tight. "I can't."

Nicolai leaned toward his window and urged her nearer to him. "You can. You're made of stronger traits than girlish fears."

When the carriage banked to the right, she gasped, then gripped Nicolai's hand, almost too tightly. "How many girls can say they've experienced a true to life nightmare? My fears are not childish."

"Maybe I used the wrong descriptor, *yet*, you've faced tougher situations than this flight."

"I don't require a reminder."

"Maybe you do. You've suffered a snake bite, a prowling panther and an unpleasant incident at sea. You survived them all."

"Not without scars."

He touched the corner of her lip. "Humans carry scars, those we can see and those we can't. Come on, my love, be courageous, open your eyes," he said, begging. "Look over there, for your viewing pleasure, a coastline of natural sand beaches and a stretch of oceanic water. From this vantage point, one can see the waves rolling toward the land. And there," he said, pointing, "large plots of fertile land, farming houses, and a multitude of tiny trees dotting the ground, too"

Scarlett peeked at the passing landscape. The view was fascinating, but when she glanced downward a second time, her stomach fell at the sight of the ocean, recalling a clash with the queen. She contemplated Nicolai's knee-length breeches, but it was clear her fiancé didn't see this journey the same way.

"You seem excited about the ride."

"I am excited. When will I fly like a bird again? Manage your fears and delight in the experience."

When Scarlett saw his joyful expression, his smile should have calmed her fears, but no matter how meaningful this journey was to Nicolai, her only desire was to stand on solid ground again.

He grasped her chin. "You have to get past it. You know, my love, you're safe. Odin won't let us fall."

"I wish I could see the adventure through your eyes, but having never experienced flight before, I can't be certain of anything."

Bensen chuckled, shaking his head. "Focus on the experience, Princess, not the height above the ground. If birds can do it, we can do it."

Theo leaned toward the window and peered at distant spaces as if searching for troubles that couldn't be seen by the naked eye. "The queen has new abilities. You're safe, unless the witch can challenge a god."

"Although the god of war drives us to the land of sea and sky, are we safer in his company?" Bensen said. "The queen has become powerful. You saw the twister she fashioned from grains of sand. How was the unnatural, whirling wind, made possible?"

"If I hadn't spied the act with my own eyes," Theo said, glancing at them momentarily. "I wouldn't have believed the witch had a supernatural ability. What more could she do?"

Scarlett forgot her fear of flying momentarily. "I hope the high priestess can aid our safety, but given past experience, I'm not sure how she could assist us."

"WELCOME to the Salar de Uyuni, the home of the mage, Aniron," Odin said, speaking to them from the driver's box. "Take in the landscape. You'll never see a place as serene and beautiful as the one that greets you now."

Scarlett peeked outside the window to reflect on a wondrous tract of land. A sea mirrored puffy white clouds and cerulean blue skies, and if she were to compare its wonder to a godly place, to her, the Otherworld embodied its essence. When Sleipnir dashed forward, she grasped the armrest tightly, and breathed a sigh of relief when the carriage landed safely on the ground.

"We've landed," Odin called out. "You may exit."

Nicolai grasped her arm. "I know you're eager to leave the carriage," he said, winking, "but are you keen to experience your first glimpse of paradise?"

"I have my concerns, but I'm more intrigued by what the Salar offers, then the sky."

"Come on then, let's go see it."

Scarlett was soon standing on a pearly-white crystalline surface that crackled beneath her feet. A sea pooled in the distance, a vast plateau, a looking glass tendering a miraculous view. Salt flats compelled reflection, waves of distillation and an impossible bog in the distance. She couldn't distinguish the land from the sky, or where the horizon lay.

"A stunning view," Scarlett said, glancing at Nicolai to see if he thought so, too, and then at Odin. He attended to his horse and worked the leather straps, soon unhooking Sleipnir from the carriage. It was apparent the god was preparing to leave them.

"Where will I find the mage?" Scarlett asked, approaching him.

Pausing from his work, Odin perused her appearance for a lengthy period of time, but then pointed in the direction of the sea. "A league across the water. You'll find the high priestess inside her crystal palace. It's crafted with cunning and difficult to see. Employ your third sense to locate the structure as she won't permit a god of war, or any other nega-tivity, to enter her sanctuary."

"How do we arrive at this crystal palace?" Scarlett asked. "A body of water lies between here and there."

"It's purposefully difficult. I'm sorry, the light will be blinding, but you must cross the sea. It's the only way."

Scarlett worried her lip. "Is the water deep?"

She watched him working, his strong hands leading Sleipnir away from the carriage. He jumped upward, and was soon sitting astride the horse, all the while studying her. "I don't know. I've never crossed it, but a princess and those that attend a princess, will find out soon enough."

Inasmuch as the god's quick answers and stern demeanor made her feel like a lesser human being, as if she wasn't worthy to be in his company, as if she wasn't a royal princess.

"Though you can't help me any further, I am grateful for your deliverance to this place. If you had not intervened on my behalf, earlier, the witch would have…"

"Yes, I know about the queen and her ill pursuits. Let your worries go. The witch can't hurt you in the land of sea and sky. Aniron collects her energy from the earth's elements, and these forces inspire a vigorous phenomenon; destructive powers cannot exist in this place."

"I wish I didn't have to be here. I wish I could return to the kingdom. The people are facing difficult times," Scarlett said with a grimace. "I might be remiss in pursuing this question, but can you assist in ending the queen mother's rule? The people have been praying for it, you see. *Praying to you.* Eventually, I shall return to Camden Castle to reclaim what is rightfully mine. The throne has been stolen from its rightful rulers."

"I understand. Cynara is dangerous, a serious threat."

"You saved me from her, but will you save the people, too? Have you not heard their prayers? You have the power to end her reign?"

His single eye glanced away, seemingly studying the sky, his expression furrowed in thought. His silence suggested to her that he only wanted to leave.

Sleipnir pranced and Odin grasped his reins, then observed her in a dire way. "I'm not supposed to interfere in the mortal world. Godly powers can upset the balance of nature, complicating free will in humankind, thus having an undesirable effect."

"A god's act of war is required to save a kingdom from destructive forces. The queen's actions against her people are cruel and unkind. When you saved me from the queen's evil act, you altered the course of my life, for the greater good. Is that not affecting the balance?"

"I appreciate that your will is strong, but I helped you for reasons I cannot admit."

"Why did you come to my assistance if you won't advance my need?"

His expression took on a faraway look as if he considered matters more serious than a question. "I have a sensitive heart where you're concerned."

"Is that so," Scarlett said, intrigued, "why does a god have a care of me, a princess who has never made your acquaintance?"

"I have heard your petition, and I will consider it, but the hour grows late. I must return to Asgard. I take my leave," he replied, grasping Sleipnir's reins. "I have brought you safely to this land of sea and sky. Your journey is not mine. Best of wishes, Princess Scarlett. Send my regards to Aniron."

Confused by the conversation, Scarlett tried to analyze the god's excuses, while watching the warlord take flight. God and animal raced through the clouds and soon disappeared from her view. When she could see the pair no longer, she focused on a crystal mountain in the distance and the salt flats their group must pass across.

Odin's refusal to assist her in thought or deed shaped a new opinion of gods and prayer. It was clear that prayers were a useless wish, and moreover, she wouldn't abandon further trust to a god, especially, a god of war.

Chapter Twenty-Four

CAPTAIN EDWIN PERROW

"God damn it!" Edwin yelled, cursing the storm and fighting his way through the ocean waves. He wouldn't let this happen. Not on his watch. He had sworn an oath to protect Princess Rose, and he kept his promises, so he followed her into the frigid ocean and watched her sinking below its surface.

She considered him a pirate, and he had acted the part, but he refused to bequeath her to the gods of the sea. He would steal her from death if he had to.

And he was angry, angrier still that she did not fight, but let the swell suck her down. He saw the bubbles escaping from her mouth as he dove toward her.

When he grasped her arm, she appeared surprised as he fought to bring them to the surface, swimming with all his might. Encumbered, her weight felt heavy in his hands. But he kicked hard until they rose upward. Breaching the surface, each of them gasped for air.

"Swim!" Edwin yelled at her, bobbing with the waves. "Fight!"

She stared at him with unseeing eyes, sputtering seawater from her mouth.

"Let me go!" she cried out, her head dipping beneath a wave. Rising again, she choked out a sound. "Save yourself."

"I will save both of us."

Boatswain Simon threw a life preserver into the angry sea, and Edwin seized the circle, fighting against relentless waves to reach Rose again, grateful when the crew pulled them up. They landed with a splash on the deck.

"You should have let the witch go down with the sea," Hayes remarked, rebuking the boatswain. "The whitecaps calmed and the winds settled as soon as the wench fell overboard. The crew would be safer if you'd left her to find a new home with the devil."

"Who are you ordering about?" Edwin snarled, slowly rising to his feet. "I protect my men! My women, too. This man was attending to his duty."

"Are you sleeping with the wench, Captain? Your foolish desire has risked the lives of the crew by having this witch on board our ship. Look at the blue," he yelled at the rising wind. "She's coming at us again!"

Angry, Edwin dismissed the storm and approached his quartermaster, wobbling on his feet. The wind hadn't lessened much; the waves pounded against the ship, but somehow, his frightened crew kept the bow riding into the wind. *The tide had shifted.* He saw the crew scrutinizing him and he understood their concerns as the storm was wicked, but surely they didn't believe an innocent, such as Rose, could bring about such violence.

Kenneth Hayes was a stupid fool for challenging a captain in front of his crew.

"She's a pretty piece, I'll give you that, Quartermaster Hayes. But she's a guest on this ship, a ward under my protection. Princess Rose will be respected by the likes of you."

"She risks the ship. It's as simple as that."

"The storm is passing. The wind is dying away. I've no sarding idea how we've come through this, but Rose does not risk the ship. Know your place. I am your captain."

"A captain does what is best for his ship. A captain leads," Hayes said, staring at the crew. "I think a change in leadership is needed. Who will stand with me?"

A few surly crew members joined Hayes at his side, uniting with his opinion and supporting his chosen view. The wind gave rise to a distant rage and the breeze whipped their hair about their faces.

Edwin thought he heard outlandish laughter. He contemplated the red-haired princess, scrutinizing the tears sliding on her comely cheeks, remembering her dire murmurings. He shook the melancholy away that his crew might be right.

"Your position has been challenged," Hayes countered, his hands on his hips. "I'm taking command of the ship. Throw the pair overboard," he ordered. "Any hand who disobeys my orders will join the pair at sea."

"What blasphemy is this?" Edwin growled, striding forward to exert his control. But two crew members grabbed him by the arms.

"Did you not hear me? I'm taking command of the ship,

Edwin Perrow. We're throwing you overboard, but don't despair. Gulls have been sighted, so land can't be far, and I have seen your ability to swim."

Edwin glanced at Rose, seeing a goddess of the sea. He tried to ascertain what she might be thinking. To him, the princess exhibited an innocent, frozen expression, and appeared horrified at facing the bowels of the ocean again. He couldn't tell if it was tears or leftover saltwater streaming from her eyes. "I'm sorry," he offered.

"I told you," she said, sobbing, "to let me be."

Pushed roughly to the plank, he tried to brush off the hold.

"Throw the witch overboard," Hayes ordered. "I reckon the captain won't complain as much when he follows her down."

Edwin watched as Morgan, his navigator, grabbed Rose by the arms. The fear in her eyes undid him inside. The forlorn expression, a grave reality that had forgotten that hope was possible in all situations. She didn't protest; she didn't fight. But when Morgan stalled, perhaps remaining faithful to his captain, Hayes intervened and tossed her over the railing like so much garbage.

Edwin watched in disbelief. *Why in the sarding nether lands had they raised them from the sea in the first place?*

"I'll find you, Hayes, and when I do, you'll rue the day you challenged me."

"Adieu, Captain. I'll see you in the Netherworld."

Edwin broke free from his crew member's grip and dove into the water. He fought the cold sensations nipping at his flesh, and swam toward Rose, pulling her into his arms. A life preserver floated in the water nearby, and he reached for it, grateful for a lifeline, as slim as it was.

Someone had cared enough about their well-being to throw a lifesaver from the ship. *Who might that have been?*

Quartermaster Hayes saluted from the starboard side of the ship. Floating, bouncing with the waves, Edwin held tight to Rose. Together, they watched the *Sea Monster* sail away.

Chapter Twenty-Five

PRINCESS SCARLETT

The sun delivered a sweltering effect. Waves of distillation floated above the salt flats, enabling heat and obscuring their eyesight. Still they walked, trekking through a sea thick with brine, and feeling like they were crossing over a translucent mirror, while reflecting on the salt more so than the silence.

They were lost in this place. *How much time had passed?* That which was above was below and that which was below was above. Clouds and blue sky as far as the eye could see, in the sky and on the sea. One hardly knew where to walk. Fatigued, Scarlett raised her hand to her forehead, spotting a mountain in the distance. A crystal palace forged against the rock, but maybe the towering structure was a mirage, though it seemed real enough.

Eight crystal towers, forming a tetragonal shape, augmented the mountain. Constructed in a circular pattern, rosen-quartz stones caught the mid-afternoon sun, bringing about a blinding phenomenon that may have assisted in protecting the palace. Beneath the towers, numerous columns of varying colors arched diagonally, extending toward the sky. Scarlett shielded her eyesight from the brilliance.

"A circular pearl sits at the top of it all. Is this the Crystal Palace, or a pearl snatched from an oyster's shell? I have never seen a more interesting fortress."

Nicolai grasped his forehead. "It's not a castle, not really a stronghold either. There's no fortification that I can see. No outer wall, no barbican. The sunlight glints off every surface, directing light prisms and rainbow hues. It pains the eyes to look at it."

"An energy source fires from inside," Theo offered.

"An illusion protects the fortress," Bensen said, musing. "The source robs the universe of energy, borrowing capital from the world. A plundering of energy for someone's benefit."

"Ever the cynic," Scarlett replied, tiring of the journey across the salt flats. "I hope we get there soon. I'm exhausted. The light is blinding. I want to know who waits for us inside."

"No trepidation?" Nicolai asked, his brows rising. "No concern, considering we have no knowledge of this mage or what we'll find once we arrive?"

"I'm too tired to access my state of mind let alone know what awaits us, but a woman cannot guide her actions by housing a fearful heart. I'm trying to remain positive."

Nicolai squeezed her hand but said no more on the subject.

When they neared the base of the crystal palace, the group passed beneath an archway that incorporated a guard-house. Two stone knights, sculpted from salt, guarded the entrance. Scarlett led her company past them and along a narrow corridor littered with salt crystals. They crushed beneath their feet as they passed over them.

Scarlett was grateful when they entered a courtyard, leaving the daylight behind. She thought their journey was over, thought their group would be greeted and taken care of, but no one greeted them.

"Where is everyone; the guards, the palace servants? Where will I find the high priestess in a place this large?"

A voice whispered. *"Seek me and you shall find me."*

"Did you hear that?" Scarlett asked, surveying the men's faces. "I've heard a whisper, a woman's voice."

Nicolai shook his head. "I didn't hear anything."

Theo shrugged his shoulders. Bensen raised his brows in surprise.

"No one heard the voice but me? Is it possible Aniron speaks only to me?"

"It's likely," Nicolai said. "Though we can't hear the priestess, doesn't mean she hasn't spoken to you."

"I suppose that's true."

When they reached the end of the corridor, they discovered an entrance to the palace. Still, no servants greeted them. They proceeded inside and found a grand receiving room.

"Scarlett stood on a sapphire, translucent floor, staring. "I don't know what I expected, but I didn't expect this."

In a circular chamber, housing a massive staircase that circled upward, Scarlett beheld smooth columns of sapphire quartz with inlaid seams of gold. Lamp posts radiated light at each base. Farther still, wide blue steps rose skyward in a circular manner and she feared she'd have to climb them. One look at Nicolai and he grasped her hand, escorting them to the staircase. "I have never visited a palace that is as mysterious as it is grand, nor walked on such a magnificent floor. No one greets us. The silence makes me curious about who or what waits for us at the top. Do we take the climb?"

Scarlett grasped a railing leafed with gold, cold beneath her fingertips, anxiety creasing her face. "We don't have a choice. Yet, the flight of stairs seems extensive, it's an extraordinary climb," she said, despairing. "I can't see where it ends."

Nicolai stepped onto the first tread and scrutinized the staircase encircling a massive structure. "We have no choice but to climb."

"To climb a mountain, you mean?"

"Yes. To reach the sky we've just left."

Theo and Bensen retreated to the staircase and began climbing.

Bensen grunted. "If there's anything positive to be had, there's no salt and the sun won't blind us."

Scarlett wondered when the next step upward would be their last. *How much farther must they climb?* There didn't seem to be an end in sight. She rested, pausing on a stair tread, holding tight to Nicolai's arm, *afraid*, gasping for breath, her heart pounding.

The outer wall was fashioned of smooth, rosen-quartz crystal and she scrutinized it, drawing her fingers along its surface. A sunlit sky and puffy white clouds painted the other side of the façade, reminding her of the height above the receiving chamber.

The staircase was equally frightening. Huffing and puffing, she dared not glance to her left, for the inner core was no more than a slight balustrade and it disappeared into vacant space. The distance between the bottom receiving chamber and the highest point of the palace ignited her anxiety, and a fear of falling, more so here than a previous carriage ride through the sky.

"We're nearly at the top," Nicolai whispered, his voice drawn, weakened from exertion, but he had yet to complain. He held onto her hand and urged her to climb higher.

"I'm grateful for your assistance," Scarlett said, wobbling on a landing.

But, *sard it all;* she could see their journey wasn't over, yet.

A bridge extended across each quarter of a circle, four arms spanning toward a focal point, which rested in the center space of the palace. Frightened, Scarlett stared at the bridge, then peered at the extensive staircase they had just finished climbing.

Little stood between her and certain death.

"No—" she whispered. "I won't pass over it."

"We've come a long way," Nicolai said, his voice grave. "We have no choice but to cross the bridge. We can't go down again."

"You have nothing to fear. Come, join me, Princess Scarlett."

"Take my hand. I'll assist you." Nicolai held her arm beneath her elbow. "We'll walk across the bridge, together. Don't look down."

Scarlett glanced at Nicolai seeing he was as nervous as her, but he was right. They didn't have a choice.

They stepped on the walkway, ushered by Bensen and Theo. They progressed across the bridge, inching toward the center, where they came in sight of a translucent throne, placed in the middle of a circular foundation. A willowy woman lounged on the royal seat, her flesh the color of milk, her silvery hair flowing to her feet. Four guards defended the high priestess, and others, men and women equal, sat near the throne, their hands folded in their laps as if in prayer.

When they were closer to Aniron, she opened her eyes. Scarlett had never seen such an unblemished hue. A gray color, paler than the sky.

"I welcome you to the Salar, to the Crystal Palace. You have nothing to fear. You are safe in my presence." Her voice was a melody and it sang from her lips.

Scarlett bowed her head, offering her respect. "Thank you for your welcome."

"I've been waiting for you. Please, take a seat. Sit near me." She waved her hand and a large white pillow emerged on the floor. *Aniron is magical.*

Exhausted, Scarlett accepted the comfort, almost collapsing against the cushion. She rubbed aching leg muscles while Nicolai, Bensen and Theo took up a protective stance, just behind her.

Winded, she drew a quivering breath inside her lungs. "Now that I'm here, I'm not sure why I should be."

The mage's brow rose in question. "Do you not know? Have you not searched within yourself for the answer? My home is your sanctuary. My home can bring you peace. It will give you comfort in the months ahead."

"A mother I do not know has sent me to you as a witch means to do me harm, but I'm unsure how your sanctuary can assist me."

"How could you understand. You've only had time to ponder pain."

"I don't know what you mean."

"We have choices to make in this world, to do acts of good or acts of harm. A witch seeks higher power, and in her ambition, makes the wrong choices and blights the natural world. The danger she ushers in must be stopped. Madame Musadora seeks higher power. She's become dangerous. She invocates fallen angels of the underworld to do her bidding. A storm is coming; I have seen it. We must prepare for the arrival."

Scarlett fretted, fingering her ring. "I've faced the queen mother's evil ways, I've been affected by her decisions, but I've never considered the potential you describe."

"She has a powerful need. She associates with the lowly. I have sensed a change in the nether lands. A transformation that will harm the Otherworld. I have shared a vision with the gods, but they disregard my caution."

"What can I do?" Scarlett asked.

"Nothing. No one can alter the course of the future. Regana was right to send you to me. You'll be safer here. The life you carry will be safer, too."

"What life?"

The mage's brow lifted, wrinkling with curiosity. "You don't know? Have you not felt a stirring in your belly? Scarlett," Aniron said, suddenly smiling, "you're expecting a child."

"A child?" Nicolai breathed, his expression displaying one of shock.

"Yes, a child of your making, Lord Graydon. You're soon to be a father, and you must protect the child, we all must protect the child, and while sheltering in the Salar, she will be safe and well cared for."

"I'm to be a father? I will have a daughter. How did you perceive this?"

"'Tis simple. I heard the heart beating."

Scarlett touched her belly, searching for movement. "When will the child be born?"

"When a full moon waxes high in six months' time, but to keep your child safe, you must remain inside the palace."

"My mother could not have known I was with child."

"No, of course not. The former queen knew Cynara was plotting with a nemesis, one who seeks a child. 'Tis why she sent you here. Your babe could serve a fallen angel's ambition, if it is your child he seeks."

"You think the devil wants my child? Why? I have no conflict with anyone in the Netherworld."

Scarlett reached for her belly. She had only just learned of the child's existence. Now, she must mind the babe's safety.

"Your child possesses the blood of a regal line. One the devil would like to mark with his own."

"I'm a princess from a royal family. Why would he desire blood from a mortal being?"

"Your blood reigns from a higher place than a kingdom of men. You were fashioned from a god's seed."

"That's a preposterous statement. My mum was a queen. A woman with royal responsibility who would never have acted in an adulterous way."

"The news comes as a surprise, as it would," Aniron stated, rising from her throne. "You are the daughter of a god. Did you not wonder how you survived a snake's bite, or why Odin tested the balance of nature by assisting you during a combative hour? It appears the god of war has a caring heart for his daughter."

Scarlett didn't know what to believe or who to trust. Something wasn't right about this mage or her story. "If what you say is true, does my mother know the truth of my parentage? Did my father, King Rickard, know I wasn't his daughter?"

Aniron chuckled, inching forward. "Odin is known for his desire of young maidens. A queen knows the seeds she sows in her garden. King Rickard, ever unfaithful, never suspected an affair."

Scarlett stood, then staggered backward. Nicolai grasped her, and held her in his embrace. "This comes as a shock, but if what you say is true, my child's safety is foremost on my mind. How can you keep us safe?"

An echo resounded far below them.

"I have barred the palace doors. The guard tower has been enclosed inside the mountain. No one without a clean heart may enter my sanctuary. Light energy will blind intruders and protect us."

"Why do you help me?"

Aniron bridged the space that separated them and placed her hand on Scarlett's belly. "There are no children in the palace. I long for the music of a child's laughter; I'm unable to bear children of my own. In exchange for my protection, it is my hope you'll remain in the palace to share your daughter with me. In this place, she can be raised with love."

"Do you seek more than laughter? Do you mean to rob me of my daughter?"

Aniron frowned, sighing. "Your comment wounds me. I am not a thief. I have listened to your thoughts; '*that which is above is like that which is below and that which is below is like that which is above,*' but the *two* are not the same. You need to understand: That which is above is good. You don't have to fear the sky. That which is below is bad."

"I don't know what to do."

"Have no fear, Princess Scarlett. You're tired from your journey." The high priestess snapped her fingers, then ordered a guard to bring foodstuffs to her guests. "Your child won't be born for six months. Stay in the Salar de Uyuni. After I have seen your child safely delivered, you and I, we can surround your daughter with love. Two mothers, instead of one."

"And if I don't remain in the Salar?"

"The choice is yours to make. I won't force you to stay. Maybe you'll free a kingdom that doesn't belong to you, or a witch will free herself from a place she doesn't mean to upset. What's important to know is the kingdom is about to be altered. Whatever is coming, you're safer here."

Chapter Twenty-Six

PRINCESS RUBY

Since their first embrace, Garrett had assessed Ruby differently. He studied her movements while navigating the passageways inside the mountain, and it hadn't escaped her notice that he glanced at her more often, grasped her hand frequently, and kindly assisted her through limestone corridors and across rougher patches of rock. Always guiding her with a gentle pressure on her back, ensuring she wouldn't stumble or fall.

Garrett's consideration caused her awareness of him to grow with each lingering stroke and her skin became hyper-sensitive to his touch; her inner temperature warming, her cheeks coloring, too, every time he offered a protective embrace. The contact stoked her memories; licking her lips, she remembered their kisses.

But although Garrett had caressed her and kissed her passionately, he had not attempted to touch her in a sensual way again. *Maybe I disappointed him?* She hoped not, as she wanted him to caress her skin, stroke her breasts, and kiss her lips in a passionate way. When he chanced to glance in her direction, she wondered what he saw. Did he notice her desire? Did he see the light in her eyes, a light brighter than the glow above their heads?

Gratefully, the bioluminescence continued, so while the cavern shadowed darkness, a living illumination brightened the pathway they navigated. Ruby followed Garrett alongside a trickling stream that circled deeper and deeper inside the mountain. She wondered if they'd ever find a way out of the maze they circumnavigated, trekking a channel of smoothly carved limestone, always treading deeper inside the mountain.

"How are you faring?" Garrett asked, his fingers brushing against her forehand.

"I'm tired," Ruby replied, permitting their fingertip caress to linger. "Maybe we could take a break, perhaps have a sip of water."

She shifted toward him and sensed the desire in his eyes. *Did he see the wanton need in her expression, too?*

He glanced away. "We'll rest soon, but I'd like to explore the passage further before we retire for the night."

"I'd be grateful for the rest," Ruby whispered, sighing. "Have you noticed the temperature inside the cavern has increased? Sometimes I feel as if we're wandering through the devil's throat, soon to find the Underworld's stomach."

"The devil's lair resides much deeper than a complex maze hidden inside a mountain. I'm sure we're safe from that sort of evil."

No longer cold, she shivered. "Well, just in case we're not safe from evil intentions, I won't mention such names again."

Garrett reached for her hand. "Neither will I," he said,

squeezing her fingers. "The cavern is widening. We're approaching a second underground sea, a grotto. Can you hear the water dripping? Is it only my imagination, or is steam rising above the water?"

Ruby nibbled at her lip; she peered at his eyes in concern. "Do you think the water is hot? Do we travel from a cruel cold to being boiled alive?"

When he bellowed with laughter, she wasn't amused. "Aw, Amira, from one terror to another we seem to go. But if I didn't find humor in the situation, my soul would be buried along with my body."

He faced her; he pulled her into his embrace. "Maybe just this once, could we focus on the positive, that the water is warm? Shall we touch it and test your theory?"

Ruby sighed, shaking her head. "What else is there to do inside this dungeon? We might as well entertain a scientific discovery, hoping for relief from a dreary atmosphere."

"Come," Garrett whispered, kissing her forehead, enclosing her hand in his own. "Let's test the water's temperature."

At the edge of the underground sea, Garrett released her hand, knelt, and touched the liquid. "I'll be damned, the water is warm."

Ruby knelt, too, and drew her fingers through the smoothness, causing ripples. "Garrett, is it safe? Can we go in? The basin seems inviting, warm, and I can't remember the last time I had a bath. I probably smell terrible."

If he agreed with her, he didn't say. "If it's body odor you're smelling, your protector is to blame for causing the stink. I'll go in, I'll make sure it's safe."

Ruby watched Garrett retreat to the shadows. He dropped his pack on a ledge beside the cavern wall. With his back to her, he removed his surcoat, shirt, and trousers. She pondered his bare bottom, nibbling at her lip, unaware of the leather boots that followed. He turned around and challenged her awareness with his masculinity, by standing before her unabashedly naked. An Adonis, her gut wrenched with awareness while watching him streak toward the water's edge. "You're brave, Sir Garrett, treading into the sea like a soldier off to war. But what if something untoward happens to you? Who will protect me then?"

He groaned, glanced at her, then strode beneath the water.

"What is it?" Ruby asked, studying him more than the cavernous sea.

"It's amazing. A balm to my aching muscles. You should reach for your courage and join me."

"Are you certain?" She bit at her lip and her were palms sweaty while releasing the ties from her surcoat.

"I'm sure." He splashed water in her direction. "I promise I'll keep you safe, if that's what is worrying you."

"My safety doesn't concern me," she said, lifting the garment over her head and placing it on a rock.

"What concerns you then? As you can see, your soldier is safe."

My weakness—but she wouldn't make that confession.

"Some confessions a lady dared not say."

Her kirtle soon followed the surcoat. She knew she could enter the water in her bandeau and braes, but they, too, she added to her pile of clothing, and then she strode toward the water's edge.

Standing on the lip, Ruby glanced in Garrett's direction, reflecting on his eyes and the heated mien that studied her feminine figure. She blushed, aware of her nakedness; every part of her figure was exposed to his muse. His eyes perused her in an intimate manner. Despite the heated connection, shivers prickled her skin and tiny tingles threaded along her spine. A breath escaped her lips and her heart fluttered with awareness.

"You're beautiful, Amira. So beautiful…"

Ruby saw that Garrett waited for her, his hands swirling in the water, his heated gaze scrutinizing her movements. She imagined his fingers finding her and stroking her skin. One lick of his lips and butterflies would flutter inside her belly. She prepared to join him in the water, but like a nervous and unsure maiden, she stood on the bank, awaiting his invitation.

Garrett Morris

A GODDESS STOOD before him in all her naked glory, and as Garrett regarded Ruby, he knew he would never see another woman as beautiful. He had taken advantage of her simply by kissing her, and with the way their attraction was maturing, he supposed her womb could soon be thickening with his child. The thought of compromising her virginity should have filled him with regret, but he had few. The princess belonged to him and he meant to have her.

I'm sorry, Queen Regana. Coupling with your daughter is not what I promised you.

"Let me help," he said, reaching for her hand as she stepped into the water. She slipped, falling to him, landing within his embrace and the sweet warmth of the water. Ruby grasped his shoulders, her breasts nestled against his chest, and he welcomed the soft mounds.

"Fancy finding a place such as this." She giggled, her laughter a melody echoing inside the chamber, rippling across the water. "And we have it all to ourselves. A spring of water, and so pleasingly warm. It's too good to be true. I can't believe our good fortune, Garrett."

He pulled her closer, his hand discovering her waist. "I admit the hot pool is a welcome pleasure, especially after struggling through a cavernous maze. Indeed, we're fortunate, for now."

"Garrett?" she asked, turning serious, staring at his eyes. "Is it wrong, wanting to be with you?"

"Given that you're a royal?" He hesitated, sighing. "Higher men would harm me for compromising you, but lesser men wouldn't care."

She touched his chest, her fingertips circling his left nipple. "I don't care about the beliefs of other men. I do care about you and your convictions. What do you think, Garrett?"

He confessed what he didn't want to. "I'm supposed to be your protector, not your lover. But I'm also a man with masculine needs."

She stroked his cheek, drew her thumb pad across his lips. Closing his eyes, he groaned, welcoming her exploration. "Do you need me?"

Opening his eyes, he reached for her, both hands slid through her black silken strands, soon urging her lips to his mouth. "I do. You're a craving that could never be fully satisfied. I want you, desperately."

"Garrett—" Ruby sighed. "I want you, too."

He picked her up, to hold her in his arms. He carried her deeper into the water. "Are you sure? Do you know what you ask for?"

"I think so." She crooned, hugging his neck.

Garrett gently placed her on her feet, kissing her soft lips. He stroked the side of her breast and drew his fingers around the mound, filling his hand with the softness.

"Oh!" When he drew her closer, she gasped.

"You're beautiful," he whispered huskily, his heartbeat rising, picking up speed while trailing a line of kisses along her neckline. Her skin glistened in the biosphere and waxed slippery from the water.

"What do you want from me, Amira? Tell me."

"I want you—to—touch me."

He lingered just above her breasts, his tongue tasting the nape of her neck. Trailing lower, Garrett's lips lingered against her nipple, his tongue licking the bud, his mouth asserting, suckling.

"Where?" he teased, gently applying pressure to her nipple with his teeth.

"There—" She moaned. "Lower—" She begged.

Sinking further into temptation, Garrett couldn't help

himself. He caressed the side of her ribcage, his fingers quivering as he massaged her wet skin. Weakness compelled him to explore lower, his fingers massaging her hip, soon discovering the space in between her inner thighs.

"Here?" he asked, finding her sweet petal folds. "Is this the place you desire to be touched?"

"Higher," she begged, arching against his hand.

Garrett's breath quickened as her hand clenched his hair and held on tight, but her other hand nestled against his thigh, searching. He knew what she wanted. He reached for her hand and placed it on his groin. She startled and choked out a cry.

"Oh, I must not."

"You must," he replied, thrusting ever so gently against her palm, his mind thinking only of where he'd like to take her right now. But he wanted his love to be wet and ready, so he released her hand, his fingers wandering to her inner thigh, soon stroking her vaginal canal.

"Oh, Garrett—" She moaned, holding tight to his shaft with one hand, while the other clung to his neck.

Hearing his name nearly undid him. "Sweet Amira, I want you."

Slick and ready, he massaged the nub of her desire, his fingers circling the erogenous zone and gently exploring the inner warmth. New to lovemaking, she gasped, lost control and throbbed against his fingers, climaxing in his embrace.

Taking her in his arms, he carried her to the cavern's edge and laid her on the smooth, limestone surface.

"Are you certain?" he asked.

She nodded, her eyes glassy, her need expectant as her legs arched apart, giving him room.

He positioned himself between her thighs, gauging her entrance, then gently pushed inside, finding her maidenhead.

Dwelling on her confused and pained expression, he hesitated. "I won't hurt you. We can stop."

"I didn't think lying with you would cause this sort of pain, but if you stop now," she quivered, biting her lip, her hand resting on his back, "I may not have the courage to finish the task."

"Sweet Amira, this is not a task. You and I are making love."

"Pardon me, sir, if it feels like you're stabbing me instead."

"I swear to you, my love, that this discomfort will only happen once. You'll never face this sort of pain again."

She nodded, her lips curving upward into a simpering smile. "I trust you, Garrett Morris."

He saw the curiosity weep from her eyes as he pressed deeper. She grimaced, bearing the discomfort of his weight as he sheathed himself deeper inside her. He lay like that, his manhood cradled inside her heat, his body relaxed but his staff begging to move. Still, he forced himself to be patient, watching for her anxiousness to pass.

"Do you like it?" he asked, holding firm.

"I'm trying to," she said, thrusting her hips cautiously upward, reaching for his back, her arms around his waist.

He gazed at the desire in her eyes; he kissed her mouth, believing he'd never again love a woman as beautiful.

I'm a lucky man, he considered, withdrawing and then entering again.

"I want you desperately."

"Take me then," Ruby blurted. "What are you waiting for?"

He responded to her earnest invitation and thrust inside her, withdrawing and entering again. He wanted to race, to rush in and out, but for her sake, he must have patience.

"I've never wanted a woman more in my life," he exclaimed. He breathed raggedly, his heart keeping pace to his breath. He pushed inside her again, touching her womb. A slow sheath of emotion quickened to desire, soon rushing toward release.

"I want you. I want to lay with you for the rest of my life."

The princess clung to him, her nails raking his shoulders as he planted his seeds. Breathing hard, he surrendered to weakness and relaxed against her, his head nestling against her forehead. He couldn't leave her warmth; he remained inside. Emotion built; a tear slipped from his eye.

She clutched him close to her breast, having heard his grief. "Why are you emotional, Garrett? Did I do something wrong?"

"You've done nothing to be ashamed of, my love. It is I who must answer for this sin."

"But surely it's not a sin if two people desire it so."

"You don't understand," he said, shedding tears. "I promised to protect you."

She pulled him closer, unconcerned. "And you have, my love. You have ushered me into womanhood gently. I'm grateful. Quiet your fears and bestow your love on me."

"You're a princess, and I am but a simple man with even

simpler needs. I have not kept you safe and I have shamed you."

"If it concerns you so, we will cast aside my royal name. Cast away my birthright, too. A kingdom of riches has only brought me pain. I'll be your Amira, now and always."

He gazed at the love, at the sudden hope shining in her eyes. She cooed softly to him, her hands playing with his hair. Soon enough, they lay on the bank together, embraced in the afterglow of their lovemaking.

After a while, he heard her sigh.

"Garrett, would you like to take another swim?"

He lifted himself up on his elbows, smirking, searching her expression. Already excitement twitched and pulsated within his shaft.

"Is that an invitation?"

She kissed him quickly, pushed him off of her and then fled into the water, daring him to give chase. "You promised a second coupling wouldn't hurt, and it's cold lounging on the bank. Surely you want to enter the spring?"

He rose; he waltzed toward the naked desire shining in her eyes. "I want to enter a place, but it's not the warmth of a spring I seek. May the gods help me, Amira, I want to enter you."

She giggled, splashed water in his direction, then sauntered into a welcoming heat. Weak like a lamb, he pursued.

KING LOWELL

The conduct of Lowell's privy councillors frustrated him. They didn't have the answers he expected and their ignorance in relation to his goals only irritated him further. He might be young, even so, youth didn't make him incapable of engaging in an intelligent discussion. Education didn't make a learned man smarter than a king. He wasn't stupid. They manipulated him with wit and insensitivity. Their behavior was appalling. It was his responsibility to manage his affairs and their guidance would not overrule his right to choose a suitable partner. He threw the papers on the table.

"Your Grace, I know the difference between diplomacy and fear mongering. I won't submit to such tactics. If the rulers of Perun and Neeyce won't offer up their daughters, I have no issue in finding a suitable bride from my own kingdom."

"But a royal pairing is of the utmost importance, Your

Majesty," Lord Chancellor Mikkel Daniel offered. "A marital match with a commoner gains Velez and her people nothing."

"It could gain me a son," Lowell replied, stating the fact. "Your argument does not earn my confidence, as to date you've had little success contracting a royal wife from across the channel. I understand that His Majesty Carloman won't bargain his daughter, Princess Iola, and King Reynes holds Princess Phaedra equally tight, unless the kingdom succumbs to an exorbitant fee. I won't squander the treasury. You seek to form protective alliances of prestige and wealth. I don't care about titles. My goal is to find a wife."

"Maybe the council should consider the real problem, which the men around the table fear to mention," stated Sir Arden Wyborn, his judicial position apparent. "A situation gives other rulers cause to distrust the possibilities of matrimony. This truth threatens our alliances. Your Majesty, you deserve to know the truth."

Lowell leaned against the padded armchair, his fingers drumming on the fabric rest. Sighing, he considered the secret that might slip from someone's lips. Silence filled the drawing room while he waited. Brave souls with their advice before, now the king's men regarded one another with wary expressions, waiting for a weaker soul, a weasel, to unleash the truth. Enjoying the struggle, he watched them squirm.

Evil lingered in the distance, already present in the privy council chambers. He could feel his mother's influence. Finally, the silence angered him. "Say it," Lowell barked. "Who has the courage to say the name?"

Nevin Islip coughed, then cleared his throat. "The queen mother is the difficulty, Sire. I mean no disrespect against your mother, but her reputation has grown. She has come to be known as The Ebony Queen. The commoners believe her spirit has turned to blackness. Seeds of rumor have traveled across the channel and reached our royal partners."

Lowell observed Nevin, the intendant of the civil list. A small man, he bowed his head, his demeanor earnest.

"You need not feel shame or fear on my accord, Nevin. I am aware of the whisperings. I know my mother well. Better than you. Better than the gossips who spread dark chatter."

"Despite what the people say," Nevin replied, "I have a fondness for Her Majesty, the queen mother."

"Is that so? I didn't know anyone had a fondness for my mum. Please explain."

"We share a common interest."

"And what exactly could that be?"

Nevin sat up, his expression coming alive. "Your Majesty, the queen mother has taken an avid interest in my resource portfolio of energy and science. She has come seeking my advice."

Lowell leaned forward and placed his elbows on the table. "Could her interest have anything to do with *angelica* or *prunus spinosa?*"

The intendant's brows creased, confused. "Not on such substances as botany, herbs, or branches, but on planetary alignments and the like."

"Planetary alignments?" Sir Arden chuckled. "Have you been spreading your dire predictions of disaster with the queen mother?"

"I assure you," Nevin said, sitting taller in his seat, "when a man understands the science of things, predictions are not necessary. The planets will align—the sun, the moon, and the Earth—and when they do, the moon will turn red."

"Blasphemy," Mikkel Daniel bellowed, shaking his head.

The change in conversation concerned Lowell. He raised his hand for quiet, while contemplating what a planetary alignment could possibly mean to his mother. He knew her far better than these men. "Why is this the first I've heard of an alignment?"

"Your Majesty," Mikkel said, clearing his throat. "We didn't believe the information was prudent or pertinent to our conversation."

"Be honest, Lord Chancellor. You had no faith in Nevin Islip or his science."

"I won't deny it. I am a religious man, after all."

Lowell focused his attention on Nevin. "When do you expect the alignment to begin?"

"In the course of the next few days. Twenty-seven days have already passed since the last full moon."

"The man's a fool," Arden grumbled. "Surely you don't believe him?"

"Sir Arden Wyborn, must I remind you, you're the hand of the king. It's your business to be suspicious. Where the queen mother seeks information, truth is waiting to be found."

"We must prepare the kingdom," Nevin stated, rising. "All manner of horrible events could come to pass."

"We will not worry the kingdom or the people. I will take care of this."

"Of course," the Lord Chancellor agreed. "But what about the other matter?"

"The matter of my marriage?"

"Yes."

"Your Grace, I instruct you to prepare a list, a document that should encompass all noble families in the kingdom. Once you've seen to this work, present the potential candidates to me."

"The time-frame?"

"Yesterday. I expect you to attend me during the dinner hour. We will discuss the options, after which, you may invite potential brides to court."

"Your Majesty, you do not give me much leeway."

"I give you everything. Remember that, Mikkel." He eyed the chancellor meaningfully.

"As you wish, Your Majesty."

"That's enough for one day," Lowell stated. "Consider this meeting adjourned."

The king's men rose from their chairs, preparing to leave the chamber. Keldan Ashburn, master of the horse, rose, too.

"Keldan, will you do me the favor of remaining. I need to speak with you."

"It would be my pleasure, Your Majesty."

When they were alone, Lowell looked fixedly at Keldan.

"The conversation about my mother concerns me. Tell me about her. I know you have an association."

"I assure you, Your Majesty, our relationship is not personal. She comes to the stable and collects her mare. There is no more."

"I'm aware the queen mother travels into the king's forest late at night. Do you follow her? Do you know where she goes?"

Keldan glanced away, then met his observation again. The action gave Lowell cause to wonder. "I have offered to assist the queen mother on several occasions. Though I don't know where she goes when she rides into the forest, I have been concerned for her safety, as it's often late at night when she collects her mare. I've offered to assist her, but she refuses my help."

Lowell almost laughed. His mother didn't need anyone's help. She was capable of contriving her own schemes, to suit her purposes, she was also able to guard her own well-being.

"You need not concern yourself. My mother can take care of herself. But you must assure me that you don't know her exact destination in the king's forest, or the actions she pursues once she gets there."

"I'm sorry, Sire. I respect the queen mother's privacy; I cannot answer your questions. I do not know the answers."

"Are you certain?"

"I am."

"Thank you for your confidence, Keldan. Do not speak with anyone regarding this conversation. Not even the queen mother."

"As you wish."

"You may leave now."

After Keldan Ashburn left his company, Lowell contemplated his mother's behavior. *The Ebony Queen.* Why had the people given her this name and what was the reasoning behind the moniker? What was her purpose in spending significant periods of time in the king's forest? And now a concern over a planetary alignment? He was more suspicious of her than ever and wondered about the implements she had kept hidden from him inside a basket in her bedchamber.

She was plotting a new scheme. He knew it. He felt it. If the planets did align, what would happen then?

Rising from the armchair, Lowell retreated to his bedchamber inside the tower. While the sun was setting in the sky, he stood near the window, staring beyond the moorlands at the king's forest. He didn't want to venture into an enchanted woodland again, but it seemed he had no other choice. He had to discover his mother's secrets.

If Lady Regana's admissions were true, he could be personally affected by the truth, and one uncertainty bothered him more than any other question. Had his mother murdered King Rickard, his father?

Chapter Twenty-Eight

QUEEN MOTHER CYNARA

The evening of the eclipse waxed ominously in the night sky, a period of darkness that the people of Velez were afraid of, but Cynara held no such fear. Her emotions were fired with enthusiasm and promise. The hunter's moon illuminated a supernatural plan and a place in the forest where she had toiled to achieve her greatest victory.

Cynara watched the moon from a vantage point in the king's tower, knowing the full bulbous shape lit the promise of her heart's ambition. Power.

She celebrated the impending conjuration and weeks of hard work by way of a fruity tasting blood-red claret. If Daemonis kept his promise, her victory was certain, and reasoning that her strategic plan would be successful, self-satisfied thoughts twisted her lips into a winsome smile. She took a final sip of her wine and then placed the goblet on the side table. The time had come to act, and to leave.

Cynara took a final inventory of minor details; items and ingredients, names and methods, then did a thorough perusal of her bedchamber to ensure items of interest were not left behind. When ready, she fetched a large saddlebag, confident in her preparation.

The situation would be different when she returned. *For the better,* she told herself, refusing to indulge in negative thoughts that her plans might miss the mark.

Heady with excitement, she left the bedchamber, and strode along a corridor of the inner ward. An iridescent black feathered collar was fastened tightly to her neck, embellishing an ermine cloak that lay on her shoulders. A long ebony surcoat trailed behind her slippered feet.

She walked stealthily through the stone passageways of the castle, mindful of sleeping souls. No one traipsed at this hour who might question why the queen had left her bedchamber. Lady Eliza, her lady in waiting, had left her private apartment hours ago, and she didn't require a guard, inside or outside her room, to keep her safe.

No one was a threat as everyone feared the queen. She appreciated their submissive regard.

"Worry away," she cackled in the darkness, rushing down a stone staircase in her hurry to reach the stables. "I will feed off your plight and change the course of tomorrow."

When she passed from the relative warmth of the corridor to the outer courtyard, fall winds gusted against her pale skin, ruffling her skirts. *Just the wind.*

Approaching the stable, she passed beneath the large beams of a wooden entry, seeking the master of the horse.

"Master Keldan?"

She paused at the archway, listening for his response. When a reply was not forthcoming, she entered the stable and walked along a narrow aisle-way that passed between the horse stalls, searching for him, but silence greeted her here, too, so she advanced to his private chambers.

She didn't knock at the doorway, having little thought or respect for anyone's privacy. She grasped the handle, opened the door and went inside.

Keldan Ashburn was reclining against his bed. "Good evening to you, Master Keldan."

Although her visit might be unexpected, he didn't seem surprised to see her. Lying comfortably on his bed, his chest naked; his hand remained at his side and he made no attempt to conceal his masculinity, or shield himself from her attention. The boy was bold.

"Your Majesty," he said, chewing on a length of straw. "I'm surprised to see you. What brings you to my bedchamber at this hour?"

Almost too calm; she couldn't ignore the intrigue in his emerald eyes. "I'm in need of my horse this evening."

"I can saddle Maisie for you, but before I act on your request, there's information you should be aware of," Keldan said, pausing. "Your son, the king, he's been asking questions about you."

Master Keldan unnerved her. Distracted her. She scrutinized well-defined pectoral muscles, seeing the pubic hair lying below his naval. She swallowed, considering the guttural ache beneath her own pelvic mound, but one's sexual needs required control. This was a busy night, and she couldn't dwell on sexual frustration or afford to be late.

"Has he?" Cynara ventured, sidling closer to him. "What subjects concern my son?"

"Your late-night adventures, traveling into the king's forest. Alone."

Cynara smiled slimly and sauntered cat-like toward him. As she neared, he edged closer to the wall and boldly patted the counterpane beside him, giving her a space to sit on the bed.

"My actions do not concern the king, but your conversation with him troubles me. What did you tell him?"

He had the audacity to smirk. "What could I say? I don't accompany you; I don't know where you go, I have no idea how you pass the time or what you do in the forest. Even so, I can well imagine, and I am curious about your purpose."

"You are a daring young man, Keldan Ashburn. In my presence, most people would be more cautious about their choice of language."

The warning didn't deter him. He reached for her hand, and she accepted his overture, placing her fingers on his palm and soon sitting beside him on the bed. "You don't want me to be cautious. You want a frank and honest conversation from your subject. A woman like you doesn't tolerate deceit."

"Young man, you are wading into a dangerous subject."

"I'm unconcerned. You won't hurt me."

"Why are you so comfortable? Other men have been in your place, quivering with fear, behaving poorly."

He massaged her fingers. "I am more secure in my behavior as I care for your horse, and she's important to you."

Cynara's brows rose. "Maisie is important to me, but she's a horse, an instrument, an animal that must be fed."

"That's what I'm trying to say, that you take care of her, so maybe you're not as bad as *the people* think."

"Keldan, you're just trying to earn my sympathy."

"Look, I respect your secrets, but are you certain you should ride tonight?" he asked. "The wind has begun to howl; peasants have taken to their beds for fear of what the night winds bring. Mayhap you would be safer in your bedchamber, abed."

Cynara dropped her saddlebag on the floor. "Is there a reason, a motive that you deter me from my ride? A situation other than Lowell's questioning mind. You seem to make a space for me here."

Perusing his emerald eyes, she reached for his handsome face with her free hand and cupped his chin where dark whiskers lay. She caressed the side of his rugged jaw, lingering and twining in the short, chocolate strands of hair. He was but a boy, a young person dressed as a man. As scarce as she could tell, he was about the same age as Lowell, but a widow couldn't concern herself with something as insignificant as age.

"The only goal I hope to thwart is rising from a warm bed to prepare a mount for my queen, unless you'd rather stay the night. It's warm here. I care for your safety. And you shouldn't ride into the forest alone, especially with the promise of a storm. I'm sure this is what concerns your son the most. That you enter the forest without a guard."

"My activities do not concern my son, or you," she said with a grimace. "The guards are afraid of me, and you—you're too calm in my presence."

It would be an easy divergence to satisfy her need with his charm. She considered his desirous expression while leaning toward his lips, assessing a hunger that lingered beneath the surface. *A secret unseen.* She stole her hand away from his handsome face to slip along the well-haired path between his nipples, where his heart beat a quick and irregular rhythm. He seemed to stop breathing. *He was afraid.* Twining her fingertips in his chest hair, she traced the ridges of his chest, teasing the hair while on a quest to his throat.

He visibly swallowed.

"I assure you," Cynara said smoothly, her voice not betraying her desire for this young man, "I'm not afraid of what the night brings. I live for the night. The man holding my hand, tempting his fate, you're the one who should be afraid. I see the game you're playing. Fortunate for you, I don't have time to fetter out the truth."

He chuckled, nervously. "I'm curious by nature."

"It's not your curiosity I'm assessing. I wish my needs could be satisfied, since you seem eager to comply."

She dallied further, lowering her hand beneath the blankets to grasp his swollen shaft, which rose to life beneath her fingers. *Surprising.* Maybe she was wrong about him given his arousal. "Most men would not be easily aroused in my presence."

He closed his eyes. "Are you hungry, Your Majesty?" he moaned, seeming to enjoy her hold of him. "It would be my pleasure to satisfy you. A ride in my chambers prior to the journey into the night forest?"

Cynara removed her hand and covered his nakedness. "You should be careful of your desires. I am the queen mother. I am..."

"Beautiful—"

"Please, I'm not easily impressed by lies. You're trying my patience."

Undeterred by her warning, he reached for the hand that rested near his shaft, soon clutching her fingers to his manhood. "I stand in wait of you, as I have on other occasions. I do your bidding. I see the way you look at me, as a woman looks at a man when she's been denied passion for too long. Would you deny your womanly pleasure?"

Sighing, Queen Cynara removed her hand, shaking her head. "Who suggested you test a queen's patience? I have restraint, Master Keldan. I don't play with opportunity if it conflicts with my efforts. While I appreciate your attention, I am old enough to be your mother."

"And young enough," he whispered, his voice breathy with excitement, "to lead me into your dark arts."

The request compelled her to smile. Lowell had never shown an inclination to follow her artistry. Maybe after tonight, she could force his hand. "You would be my student, my sapling? Your blood isn't royal. I have a son to be my apprentice."

"Your son shows little interest in your magic. I could learn your art and color the world with the light."

Cynara snickered, his statement amused her, but she didn't have time for distractions. She rose from the bed, staring at the master of the horse.

"The only service I require of you waits in the stable to be saddled."

"I could accompany you. I could guard your way."

"Be careful what you ask for, Master Keldan. Penalties have already been earned, and I'd hate to lose you before I could consider your worth. Prepare my horse. Maybe on another evening I will give you the pleasure you seek. But tonight, I have work to do and the king's forest awaits me."

"As you wish," he grumbled, rising from the bed. The woolen blanket slipped from his figure, revealing loose fitting breeches that nearly fell away.

Cynara sighed, but didn't turn away, choosing to watch him dress, attempting composure while studying his perfectly sculpted attributes. A pity she had no time to play. This young man reminded her of King Rickard and for the life of her, she couldn't understand why.

THE WIND INCREASED, howling and blowing as Keldan accepted Queen Cynara's hand, assisting her to mount her mare. Maisie was a sedate little filly that wouldn't frighten from strong elements, despite the chants or magic needing to be performed. She was perfect for the ride into the woodlands.

"Your Majesty, are you certain about taking this journey on your own? It's my duty to serve you; I should accompany you. If your life were to be placed at risk…"

Cynara laughed, a wicked noise that probably grated his ears, but Keldan held tight to the reins and led the mare from the stable into the brisk night air of the courtyard.

"My life is mine to risk. Enough discussion. Escort me to the gate, Master Keldan, but do not follow me where I go."

He passed up her saddlebag, eyeing it briefly, perhaps

considering the weight, or the ingredients hidden inside the leather, but then he offered her the reins.

"I am curious—"

Cynara grasped the reins. "Do your job," she said, flicking the reins against the filly's neck. "You know who I am."

He nodded, then patted Maisie on her rump. "As you will," he murmured, bowing from the head in an apparent show of respect and then gestured toward the portcullis with an outstretched hand before backing away. "Be safe."

Queen Cynara pressed her heels into the mare's flanks and urged the horse into a canter. The filly complied, carrying her across the courtyard and underneath the portcullis, taking them into a cloudless darkened night, lit only by a bright silver moon.

Cynara led the mare across the drawbridge, pushing the girl into a full gallop, soon running across a field of sun dew, sweet sedge, and soft rushes with errant reeds of emerald grass, where the crickets' chirps amended to silence, alarming the peasants who equated the foul bog with eerie happenings. Cynara grinned while listening to their legs twitching and then relished the wind that replaced their song, a draught that guided her toward the break in the forest. She longed to be inside the woodland. Opportunity waited for her there.

She urged Maisie toward the gap in the trees. They were soon passing beneath towering oak, trotting along a dirt-packed trail. The breeze lessened, the power of spirit demons rose; magical pleas beckoned in the night air that she breathed, and she loved the dewy, earthen smell, but something else lingered in the air, too.

The traces of a life and death struggle loitered on the

forest path. A life had been dragged along this ground; she could tell a portion of the victim's spirit still lingered here and would likely follow her to the vale, even in death.

She had passed this way so many times before, crossing this trail repeatedly in preparation for one night's work, that the mare hoofed easily forward, unafraid.

You are a good horse, Maisie, Cynara whispered, patting the side of her neck. Useful and loyal—welcome traits as compared to men, who could be deceptive and inconsistent. Unfaithful, too. In her estimation, men and their masculine gods were equally fickle.

"We need not fear their wrath. Don't be afraid, Maisie. We will prevail in this quest."

Cynara urged the mare forward, soon crossing a stream to take a narrow path, a path less obvious to the naked eye. She followed the trail for some time, curving left and right among tall timbers, wandering deeper and deeper into the woodlands until Maisie carried her to the hollow glen.

It appeared as if a fire had ravaged the land. The bark had been stripped from the trees, their trunks weathered until they'd bleached white, naked in their glory, gouging the sky with treetops that were as sharp as talons.

"Not much farther until we reach the valley."

She had nicknamed the vale Woden's Destiny. In this brief expanse of reworked land, her magic would light up the night.

Chapter Twenty-Nine

KING LOWELL

Hiding in the shadows, Lowell watched his mother leaving the courtyard. She passed beneath the portcullis and stole away into the night, soon disappearing from his view. Feeling immobile and helpless to prevent her ride, fear not only made it impossible for him to think clearly, but also prevented him from pursuing her across the moors.

Why was his mother strong of will and mind, while her son, at least in terms of his actions in her regard, was weak?

His incapacity to face up to her behavior had permitted his mother to leave the castle, with no one, not even the guards, preventing her escape. His inability to influence or prevent her actions from harming others, permitted trouble to ride toward the king's forest, undeterred by moral responsibility or judicial regard.

Though he was the king, a queen who induced an all-encompassing desire held too much power. *How could he change her?* Was it too late to change her, and did he have the will to try?

He focused on the interaction he had witnessed between his mother and Keldan Ashburn. He should have interrupted their discussion, should have prevented the queen mother from taking her midnight ride. *What held him paralyzed?* Even now, he was afraid of answers and how they might impact him. He stepped from the shadows and approached the master of the horse, uncertain if he could trust the man.

"Master Keldan, we need to have a conversation. Why are you assisting my mother at this unseemly hour, and where does she go?"

Appearing surprised, Keldan jumped at the sound of his voice. "Your Majesty, you gave me a fright. What brings you to the stable at this hour?"

"I asked you a question. Why have you risen from your bed, to assist my mother in leaving the castle in the dead of night? She's the queen. She should be accompanied by a guard."

"As you so aptly stated, your mother is the queen. No one questions her, even the guards turn a blind eye to her ambition."

"But you, more than most, have had discussions with my mother. Be honest with me. Do you know of specific facts, or pieces of information that I should be made aware of?"

"What gives you the idea that I, or anyone else, knows the reason that the queen rides into the forest, on this night or any other night?"

Lowell gauged his haughty demeanor. "You care for her horse. You frequently assist her in the late-night hours. You know her movements more than any other person inside the castle. What has she said to you? Where has she gone?"

"Where do you think?" The master of the horse threw his hands in the air. "I mean no disrespect, but you beg your questions having never listened to your subjects. Surely you know by now, *the Ebony Queen* urges her horse toward the place where she always rides late at night—into the king's forest."

"Do you follow her? Do you know the reason for her late-night adventures? Were you truthful with your disclosure?"

"Your Majesty," Keldan said, pleading with him, "you wound me with your lack of trust in my regard. A wise man does not follow the queen. After all, a man could end up on the wrong side of a midnight adventure, and not one to his liking."

Lowell remembered the spy in the forest; he heard the yowling and the yapping. He swallowed his fear, never wanting to place another arrow in a victim's chest, and he knew a king must change if the man were to permit a new mindset.

"I didn't say I didn't trust you. Please, I beg of you to help me. I promise, our conversation will go no further."

"Look," Keldan said, shaking his head. "I don't know what activities the queen mother entertains after leaving the stable. Your mother doesn't appreciate spying. Her privacy is important to her, so it's important to me, too. Sire, my life would be in danger if her wishes were not respected, more so than the answers you seek."

Lowell stepped closer, hoping his resolve was clearly expressed. "Master Keldan, saddle Drakones, and be quick about it."

He refused to obey a king's command and bridged the gap

between them. "I cannot have two royals traipsing about the forest. If harm should come to either of you, it is I who shall face the blame. Sire, you cannot take an unchaperoned midnight ride."

"Where I go, I must go alone."

The master of the horse separated himself from further scrutiny and strode toward the stable. "She'll be angry," he replied, his brows rising in question.

"Concern yourself with my horse. Our discussion is over and time is wasting."

Chapter Thirty

QUEEN MOTHER CYNARA

The magic hour approached, in a place beyond the hollow glen, in a vale a witch had named Woden's Destiny. Cynara stood beneath the glow of a bulbous moon, *soon to turn red,* preparing for the arrival of the planetary alignment.

Cynara examined every last detail of the reworked land. Pleased with her labors, she stepped toward a massive three-ringed circle; realizing the next few hours would reveal if her scheme could prove successful. Although, come what may, she was ready to ply her art and invocate her spells, as she was determined to steal supernatural power from Princess Scarlett's pagan god. She usually achieved her purpose—success was certain in this quest.

She contemplated the incantation and considered each step, while pondering a black velvet sky, peppered with diamond ambition, while she rested in a meadowland with the forest touching every side but one. This open edge commanded a sweeping view, which spawned across the lower hills to an eastern vista, a black ocean and a midnight sky. She required this open view to bring the god of war into the open reach of the supernatural. They would meet tonight on this reconstructed field: angels, demons, the antichrist—*and one god*, in and around these circles.

Cynara appraised her handiwork on the forest floor. It had been a grueling feat to rework the earth; removing bracken, wood litter, and unruly grasses from the earth. She had carved a massive three-ringed circle in the dirt, and had surrounded the outer curve in four quadrants with pentagrams, four in total. Inside the innermost circle, four stars, *hexagrams*, were situated in the shape of a diamond.

The work had been exhausting; even so, she knew her handiwork relied on perfection. The preparation had taken many days, with the most time spent completing the triangular art: the black *Triangle of Solomon*. She would test its limits.

Magnificent! Superbly done! She grinned, appreciating her work.

Cynara tittered with delight, joy wailing from her lips, clapping her hands with glee and mischief, stepping carefully around the perimeter of three circular bands inscribed with the names and sigils of fallen angels, who were in truth, proper demons. She smirked, considering the new powers that one spell could gain her person. Gazing at the moon, she saw the alignment had begun. The time had come to light the candles.

Cynara approached her horse, Maisie, and removed a ceremonial cloak from the saddlebag. She draped herself from the top of her head to the tip of her leather slippers, cloaking herself in black. Then gathering her saddlebag, she placed it at the ready in the center of the enclosed circles, next to a large black cauldron, where she would stand and go about her craft. *Later.* Opening the bag, she retrieved two leather pouches and slung them over her shoulders.

It was time to begin.

She walked clockwise to the northwestern edge of the circle where a black candle rested in a star-shaped pentagram. Raising her hands above the candle, she embarked on her invocation.

"By earth, by sun, and by unholy moon, I command your wick to ignite! Let your dance of fire give watch to forces great and small, and stand in wait of the one I soon will call."

"Comprehendo!"

A quick flash of silver flew from her fingertips, igniting the wick to flame.

Devoid of expression, Cynara moved with a slow measured gait to the northeastern edge of the outer circle. She raised her hands again.

"By earth, by sun, and by changeling moon, I command your wick to burn! Let your dance of fire keep watch over forces, above as below, below as above, and stand in wait of the one I beg to call."

"Comprehendo, fervere!"

A second flash of silver flew from her fingertips, igniting the wick to flame.

Cynara paced to the southeastern quadrant and regarded the black ceremonial triangle, sitting separate from the circular rings, ensuring that each black edge had been executed perfectly, before positioning herself near the third candle.

"By earth, by sun, and by a moon that will soon disperse blood red, I command your wick to flicker. Let your dance of widowed flame attract fallen angels and demons to the circle, where I stand in wait of the one I soon will call."

"Comprehendo, fervere, ardeo!"

Cynara raised her hands to the Otherworld; sparks flew from her fingertips, lighting the third candle. She finally paced to the southwestern edge.

"By earth, by sun, and by a moon whose glow will bleed red tonight, I command your flame to spark and stand tall, standing watch over this southern perimeter. Let your dance of fire flash true, and stand in wait of the one I must yet call."

"Comprehendo, fervere, ardeo, scintilla!"

The fourth candle was lit.

Cynara walked to the western edge of the circle where the outer band included an opening door. She stepped inside the first ring of the three. Once inside, she turned to the entrance and knelt on the ground, pulling salted sand from one of the pouches hanging at her waist, and released the salt to close the circle. Once there was no retreat, either outside or inside the first ring, she rose from the ground and extended her right hand to the western skies.

"Fallen angels, demons from the underworld," she said, extolling their glory. "I command your spirits into my presence. I invoke and conjure thee to appear before me as decreed and promised by Daemonis."

"Consequor mea, consequor mea, consequor mea," Cynara chanted. *"Diopetes! Angelus! Daemonis!"*

Although the wind gusted, the candles' flames were not extinguished. Cynara swept her arm around the circular arc, her midnight gown wafting with the wind, while she called on the demons of the seven deadly sins to approach the circle.

"Lucifer, Mammon, Asmodeus, Leviathan, Beelzebub, Satan, and Belphegor," she intoned in a slow, insipid, murmur. "Fallen angels, the first demons, from your place in the microsphere, I call on you for your protection. By the power of the most unholy, *Daemonis*, I do conjure thee, to protect all that surrounds me and to aid in my revenge."

"Consequor mea, septum, ater, vitium, antichristus!"

Cynara reached inside the second pouch for a dash of fine dust, garnered from the grinding of human bones that had been soaked in blood, the embodiment of lost human hope. She threw this to the western sky, raining brownish-red particles on the circle. She then stepped backward to the second circular ring and knelt against the ground. She massaged the salted sand between her fingertips, letting it fall once more, and enclosed the second band inside the circle.

Cynara reached to the northern sky, screaming names in earnest. "Amy, Beleth, Carnivean, Carreau, Crocell, Gaap, Lehahiah, and Uvall; by the light of a changeling moon, I command thee to appear near this circle. I call on thee, requesting your powerful aid, inviting you into the circle to add strength to my revenge and prevent harm against my person."

"Consequor mea, robus roboris, antichristus!"

Cynara reached for a dash of blood-red dust, throwing the lost hope of the dead to the northern sky.

Inching to the third sphere and enacting the same process,

she closed the final circle with salted sand. She was not afraid; she was prepared for whatever dangers and risks that might arise. Reaching for a knife, she drew the blade across her wrist, wincing momentarily, while considering the red droplets of her lifeblood dripping to the salted sand. Slowly, she walked around the circle, moving clockwise, dribbling her life fluid on the final circle. She paused to consider her words, knowing she must be careful, for the spirit she called upon next would exact a high price, a price she would be forced to pay. Even so, she must not fail, and the hour grew late to change course.

"Seraphim!" she screamed at the night, observing a candle's wavering flame. *Uneven*, the southwestern portal sparked a warning. "By the light of the full moon, I call to thee. By the power of Solomon, I sacrifice my blood, my life; the witch's price we agreed on for the invocation spell. Belial, Leviathan, Satan..." Cynara paused, lowering her head. "I command you to appear, I call on you to keep your promises. I conjure and invoke you to come before me now, to assist me in my hour of need."

"Consequor mea!"

Cynara moved counterclockwise, eagerly lighting four blue candles, each one nestled inside the center of four hexagrams; one each facing north, south, east and west.

She lit the northern candle first.

"Northern gateway, I invoke the element of earth."

She lit the western candle.

"Western gateway, I invoke the element of water, mist and vapors."

She lit the southern candle.

"Southern gateway, I invoke the elements of fire, to trap Odin inside my triangle."

After lighting the southern candle, Cynara crouched against the reworked ground and reclined to her knees. She held her hands in an upright position, her palms facing upward, her fingers tipped to the sky, even as she bowed her head in homage to the earth.

"Eastern gateway, I invoke the element of wind."

Cynara moved to the center of the circle and rummaged in her saddlebag for four large stones, which she placed carefully at each quadrant.

To the east and west, she placed septarian dragon stones, olive green rocks with crevices of dark brown. "With these two stones, open the door wide to my third eye and aid my psychic abilities."

To the north and the south quadrants, she placed black onyx. "With these two stones, protect me from gods and angels, supreme beings who would threaten my quest and cause me harm."

Now, Cynara paused, and surveyed her work thus far. She saw that it was good.

She proceeded to the cauldron standing in the middle of it all and lit the wood beneath the large black pot with a flash of lightning from her fingertips. It didn't take long for the water inside to boil, sending streams of vapor erupting into the night.

Cynara chanted: "*Attend me! Consequor mea!*" Repeatedly whispering the Latin words, but Daemonis, Antichristus, did not appear before her Solomonic triangle.

She angered, seething with indignation. If he chose to

defy her, she could not stop him. He was as powerful as the god she sought to steal from, but she couldn't give up on her ambitions, not yet. *She'd worked so hard…*

"*Consequor mea—*"

Anger grew into frustration. Tears released from her minty eyes, and her voice grew hoarse from her wailing.

"*Consequor mea, consequor mea, consequor mea! Daemonis, Antichristus,*" Cynara bawled, "*attend me!*"

Against all reason, she chose to begin the spell without him. Standing before the black cauldron, Cynara opened the bag of ingredients hanging at her waist, preparing to begin. Reaching for her first ingredient, she took a deep breath. What if the only one who could satisfy her revenge spell didn't attend her? *Had she not signed a pact?* She shook her head, reaching for the magical ingredients, and threw one after the other inside the cauldron.

> *A root of angelica to control you,*
> *A thrush of blackthorn to banish your*
>   *powers,*
> *Bright red blood, several drops,*
> *taken from my wrist to command*
>   *your attention,*
> *A dash of cinnamon, an offering,*
> *to steal your magical powers,*
> *A devil's shoestring,*
> *to overcome unseen obstacles,*
> *A shovel of graveyard dirt,*
> *in payment to prevent a price*
>   *afterward,*

A lock of Scarlett's hair,
to garner your sensitivity,
A lock of my hair,
to curse your ending,
A clipping of my nails,
to bind the invocation,
And saliva,
that will oblige you to do my bidding!

Cynara spat into the mix.

As the fire beneath the cauldron rose higher, she threw one cubit of wormwood into the mix. Cynara watched, delighted, as the brew emitted a noxious smell. A foul mist erupted from the cauldron, pouring forth to flow across the land.

The planetary alignment had begun, and a quarter of the moon glowed a brilliant blood red.

"I command you into my presence, oh great god Odin, God of War. I call on you to enter the Triangle of Solomon, where I bring to you the prophesied Ragnarök. I force you into my circle, to face me, the one you have wronged with your wrath. Come to me, you shape-shifting warlord, Odin!"

"Consequor mea—Oh great All-Father—God Odin."

She only had to call his name once!

A crack of thunder sounded on the eastern horizon. The rumble rippled across the sky and the sound of galloping hooves pounded across the ether. Cynara scrutinized the night sky in amazement as Odin made his appearance in the image of a man, sitting astride his eight-legged horse, the phantom animal, Sleipnir. She watched him crossing the eastern sky, galloping above a black ocean, rising from the sea to tower above the land. Soon, man and animal landed on the ground just beyond the triangle.

"Cynara Musadora," he growled, sitting comfortably on his horse, holding his long spear in his right hand. "Why have you forced me to your circle? What do you want, enchantress? What spell do you think to conjure now?" He gazed at the circles, at the triangle and her work, as if in contempt. As if he didn't believe she could hold him here. "Your work in the vale, and nothing else, compels my curiosity to meet you here."

"All-Father Odin," Cynara said. "I invoked you because you assisted my enemy. I invoked you to right wrongs and wrong rights through your powerful magic, a power I desire for myself. God Odin, those who do me harm pay for their crimes."

"I have committed no crime. How could I have wronged you, Mistress Cynara?"

She took her time responding while studying her enemy. Composed, he drew thick meaty fingers through a long gray beard, his pale blue eye contemplating the nightmarish scene.

"We have no debts to pay, you and I." His deep voice rumbled. "You condemn yourself by forcing me here."

"You assisted Scarlett. You caused these scars," Cynara replied, pointing at her covered neck, "the scars on my neck and body."

He leaned backward on Sleipnir, fueling her anger further by guffawing. "The princess is the rightful queen. I know what you've done, and I aim to set the mark in her rightful place. Maybe see a few wrongs righted, too."

Cynara tried not to anger; anger could weaken the spell. Instead, she shouted: "Daemonis! Wherefore art thou, evil spirit?"

A sinister voice grated: "Beside you." Unsettled by the joining, more so than his voice, Cynara stumbled backward.

"How are you with me inside the circle?" she cried out in alarm, realizing she could not leave the inner sanctum of the circle.

He seemed to press closer. "When you beg the damned into your circle, surely you know that no salted sand, nor any other rule, could keep a fallen angel out. And since you chose not to protect yourself with a true god, YHWH, you are helpless unto me."

Daemonis was a handsome man when his lips curved upward, but when he waved his hand in a circular motion, changing the wind's direction, Cynara realized he not only cast evil intentions, but also put forth phantom shadows beneath his eyes, revealing his true nature. The changeling mien, at the edges of his transforming face, frightened her. All the blue candles snuffed out.

"We made a pact," Cynara said, sneering, worried, trying to appear in control. "I signed your contract with my own blood."

Odin shook his head. "Queen Cynara, surely you understand that mortals, witches or otherwise, should never make a pact with the devil. The devil has his own agenda."

Daemonis snickered, gazing at the old warlord. "Maybe it would be in your best interests to consider a deal with your old friend, Odin. It may not be too late for you to manage your fate."

Cynara quaked with anger at the thought he'd strike a new bargain. Men! She stared at both the fallen angel and the god of war, wishing she could harm them both. They were men, and despite her needs, she didn't like for masculine images. She glanced at the skies and saw the moon was half covered in red. She had to enact the final step of her spell.

"Daemonis," she bellowed, "I command you to stand true to your word."

He gazed at her with longing. "Are you certain, Queen Musadora, of the path you take? For if you fail in your quest, the price of your spell is great."

"I won't fail."

He snickered again. "Cynara, you have failed before."

He swung his hand and the elements responded to his energy, ripping the feathered collar from around her neck.

"How dare you!" Cynara screamed, her fingers rushing to her flesh where swollen red welts had been revealed. "You will keep your promises, or I will—"

All-Father Odin gazed at her in dismay. "I've heard enough. Come on, Sleipnir," he said, urging the beast to leave the vale, slapping the reins on the animal's neck. "Away with us."

But with one wave of the devil's hand, Odin was compelled against his will to remain in the forest, and when Cynara next contemplated the circle, the fallen angels she had summoned stood around the circular perimeter of salted sand, each of them cloaked in black, all staring at her with inky seriousness. When Daemonis shifted closer, he placed his hand on her shoulder, and a chilling pain knifed through her heart. She cringed, collapsing into herself.

"It was foretold a day would come when the sun would turn to darkness and the moon would bleed. On this great and terrible day, I want you to feel the pain you have inflicted on others. Queenie, can you feel it?"

"Yes," she cried. The light from a full, blood red moon, hurt her eyes. The earth rumbled beneath her feet, but it could have been her own body shuddering as the evil contact gripped her throat.

"It was foretold a night would come when *that which is below would be like that which is above*, and *that which is above would be like that which is below*. Father Odin, the Ragnarök prophesy has arrived at your door. I command you," he bellowed, "to enter the Triangle of Solomon."

"Take flight!" Odin screamed at Sleipnir, but his command was useless. Cynara watched Odin fighting, struggling to escape the pull of the triangle, his feet digging into his horse's flanks, his large meaty hands urging Sleipnir to run, but the horse couldn't move. Still, he fought the devil holding him, gripping his spear tightly. The fallen angels surrounding the circle chanted. Daemonis openly crowed with laughter.

"Introitus, circumscriptus!"

Repeatedly, the sinful chanted the words. Odin struggled, doing all in his power to overcome the evil prodding him toward the triangle. Cynara covered her ears as the chanting grew louder, *stronger,* piercing her inner eardrum when it became shrill.

Cynara watched in amazement, liquid trickling from her eardrums. The circles on the ground lifted into the air and swirled around her. She became dizzy, unbalanced by the motion.

Daemonis howled with glee when Odin fell from his horse. The devil then beckoned her to approach the cauldron. She suffered a moment of pleasure when she saw the god had landed on his knees and was held captive inside the black triangle. She loved it even more when the triangle climbed upward, and his angry expression altered to one of abject fear. His brows furrowed and his facial expression twisted with fright, diminishing his blue gaze. The triangle enveloped his body and trapped him inside a churning black prism. Confounded, he held tight to his spear, but was unable to defend himself through the act of throwing the weapon at his enemies.

This was her work, her art, and she was glad of it.

"Let me out of here!" Odin bellowed, searching for a way out, his fists pounding against the ground.

Daemonis ignored Odin, beholding Cynara instead. "We enact the final steps of the invocation. But before we do, Queenie, invocation spells have a price, and you must deliver the payment."

It was too late to do anything else but agree. Cynara merely stared at Daemonis, nodding her head.

"You require three more objects to make your spell complete. Objects that only I can provide. Close your eyes, Queenie. Tightly!"

Cynara did as requested.

When he placed a solar flare from the sun inside the cauldron, she heard a sharp bang. This was followed, she knew, by a drop of blood from the moon and volcanic ash and molten lava from the nether fires of earth. Opening her eyes, she watched as the brew toiled and bubbled, spinning light as if a magician stirred the contents. When she observed Daemonis, his eyes glowed red with power, similar to the blood, red moon.

"Gather the brew, Cynara. Odin must drink while the circle inflicts a dizzying spell."

Cynara complied, seeking a cup from beneath the cauldron and spooning one ladle of the wicked brew inside. It was no easy task with the circle spinning around her.

She walked to Odin, holding the cup in her hands.

"Take the cup," Daemonis commanded, "and drink."

Odin refused. "You'll not get your evil liquid anywhere near my mouth!"

In response, Daemonis split into four people, and each shadow rushed forward to hold Odin, wedging his mouth open with eight hands and many more fingers.

"Come forward, Queen Mother Cynara. Give this god his quarter. You need only one drop in his mouth to steal what you desire."

Cynara did as he instructed, smirking hatefully, revenge making her ugly. She pressed the cup to Odin's mouth, forcing him to swallow. He screamed as he did so, the matter hot by many degrees, burning his mouth. He doubled over, crying in pain, then releasing his useless spear. Cynara watched his face change, the light diminishing from his eyes, his body slumping to the ground.

"You have only moments," Daemonis said, laughing and staring at her, "to drink your fate."

Cynara wasn't amused by the nastiness. The situation wasn't funny. "You didn't tell me I had to drink the brew."

He motioned toward the cup. "I told you a price must be paid. Drink up."

"But the brew will burn my mouth."

"Will you see your art, all this work on the ground, wasted? Drink up, or your godly powers return to Odin."

Cynara contemplated her fate, but seeing she had no other choice, she drank. One sip of the brew burned her throat. She collapsed to the ground, writhing, her innards on fire. Forever changed—forever new.

A boom of thunder rippled across the sky, sounding in the ether. The rings of the circle exploded, sending salt and sand flying toward the horizon. The demons quieted their song and evaporated into the shadows. Odin lay limp on the earthen ground, glaring at her in confusion and anger.

"You'll pay for this crime," he said weakly.

Celebrating, Cynara ignored his warning, her hand shaping into a fist. Though blood suffused her mouth and oozed across her lips, she leered at him, sensing a new awareness rising within herself, a godly strength she had stolen.

In gratitude, she pivoted toward Daemonis. "Thank you, for agreeing to let me have this power."

"It was time to upset the Otherworld's balance and change my circumstances, and with Odin's rule of the Otherworld compromised, the lesser gods will be in chaos. Like you, some are greedier than others for power. I live for chaos, but more importantly, you will give me our agreed upon price."

Confused, Cynara considered his smug expression. "A child. Yes, I know."

"You've been preparing for this occasion for weeks, but still, you do not understand. I don't seek a lowly child. I seek my son." He shouted at her, and the evil grated at her conscience. "You've had him long enough, you wicked, revenging witch. You stole him to gain your place in society. I've provided your heart's desire, now you'll provide me with my only son."

Chapter Thirty-One

KING LOWELL

Once Lowell reached the land bordering the king's forest, his stallion refused to move farther along the trail. A spirited horse, the equine seemed to sense the energy force that he himself could neither see nor hear, but he needed the animal to get past its fears, so he prodded the horse in the flank. It did no good. Drakones whinnied in alarm, prancing, and then reared upward, to paint the night with his hooves.

Lowell attempted to reassure his horse, but gentle coaxing failed and a firm whipping against his neck failed to quiet the panic flaring from its nostrils, only making the situation worse.

Frustrated, Lowell leapt to the ground and tied the frightened horse to a tall oak. Angry, he clenched his hand into a fist. A part of him wanted to strike the equine for disobeying his commands, but the situation couldn't be blamed on a horse. He took pity on the equine, surrendered to the will of the beast, and patted Drakones' neck in reassurance.

"I'm sorry, boy," Lowell murmured. "This is a dark place. I understand. Perhaps you know better than I what lies ahead?"

A disconcerting awareness came over him while peering at the pathway. The temperature diminished, causing him to shiver, and sounds, eerily quiet, made him wonder if he should untie his horse, climb on his back, and return to the castle. Yet, he disregarded his fear and set off on foot. He trudged along the hard-packed earth, his chest suffused with panic, his breathing stilted. Yet, determined to learn his mother's secrets, he trekked deeper and deeper into the forest, following a well-trodden trail. As he meandered through the tall oaks, passing alongside scattered grasses, he reflected on the silence and the negative space that spiced the woodland area, permeating the air he breathed. No wonder his horse had cried of fright.

"What are you up to, Mum?"

No reply.

Whatever mischief she attempted, her escapades boded an ill will. He surmised an evil plot, but could not imagine what the scheme might be.

Alert, he reflected on the silence. The owls were quiet tonight and not one cricket clicked its legs in song. Evil airs wafted around him, a reeking stench of rotting bog that infiltrated his breathing. A cold air brushed across his flesh, dispersing his black hair. Embraced by a sudden chill, he shivered. He shook it off, hoping the touch didn't elicit some sort of warning.

"I won't succumb to the fear you inspire in others, Mum."

I do not fear what I cannot see!

I'm a king, and kings should not succumb to terror, but

though he attempted to dismiss the tremors that lodged like a lump in the pit of his gut, something wasn't right, and he did fear what he couldn't see.

A rustle of wind swept along the pathway, stirring up the grasses and causing dead leaves to flutter with the breeze. The full moon, glowing red, just as suddenly illuminated a pathway the leaves had exposed, one he had not noticed before. The chill night air slapped his face, stung his eyes, and caused fluid to ooze from his tear ducts; he felt as if an evil force greeted him, walked past him. He paused, searching behind, then faced the way the wind had whooshed, wondering if he should return to the castle. But he'd come so far already.

Cautiously, he strolled onward, somehow certain he had discovered the right path. A strange light illuminated the clearing ahead. Creeping closer, he heard voices raised in anger. *Who was fighting?* Pausing, *uncomfortable*, he wondered if he dared to progress farther.

Every instinct compelled him to leave this place, to find his horse and retreat to the castle, but a power greater than himself spurred him onward, compelling him to face the answers waiting to be found.

Chapter Thirty-Two

QUEEN MOTHER CYNARA

The wind screamed, connecting to the queen's anger. Her hair streamed wildly about her face and her cape swirled around her legs, but she stood strong and tall. She brought the storm.

"You can't have him!" she spat cruelly. "Nothing in this world would *ever* give me cause to forfeit my son."

"It's too late for fiery words of conscience," Daemonis replied, boldly stepping toward her ripping tide. Presenting the original contract, he unrolled the parchment in his hands. Stalking forward like a wolf on the prowl, he presented it, his index finger aligning with the blood signature.

"Is this not your handwriting?"

Cynara examined the line, witnessing her own handiwork. "The blood is mine, but I didn't agree to this."

He assumed a winsome expression with her admission. "The deed is done, Cynara. You will give me back what is mine. My son!"

She seized the contract from his hands, and then furiously

reading, she found her name scrawled on the bottom edge of the parchment. Anger caused her cheeks to flame red when she realized the devil had deceived her.

Raising her eyesight, she confronted him, anxiety causing her hand to quiver. "You asked for a child. This contract does not mention my son."

"I told you the price for your power was to give me a child. I was not specific in the regard of *my child*, but I did caution that my abilities and influence in this world come with a price; I don't give power away without a fee."

"Daemonis," she pleaded. "You cannot take my son. I'll never agree to this demand."

Cynara ripped up the contract, and watched the pieces fluttering to the ground, but her reckless action didn't make a bit of difference. The shreds of paper flew upward and formed back together, taking shape again, the contract returning to his hand.

"What choice do you have? The contract is binding and not severable by either party. I have helped you, and you have agreed to my demands." He chuckled, scanning the reformed document. "I will take what is due."

A tree branch snapped. They quieted, shocked to see the man who intruded on their conversation. Lowell passed through the burnt trees, leaving the shadows and slowly walking toward them. *Why had he come?*

"Mum, who are you talking to?"

Cynara studied Lowell's perplexed expression. Quiet, he studied the disturbed ground: an irregular circle, candles extinguished, a cauldron, and all her magical implements strewn on the forest ground. Surprise registered in her son's expression as he pondered the black triangle, its shape still holding the god Odin. He shook his head, clearly upset, gaping at the fallen angel, Daemonis. Confusion caused him to anger. She felt this powerful emotion building inside of him.

"Who are these men?" he asked.

Daemonis snickered, grinning. "I'll gladly tell him, Cynara."

"What will you tell me?" Lowell demanded. "Who are you? What evil takes place here?"

"Lowell?" Cynara began, inching toward her son, but she couldn't respond to his question, so she eyed the ground instead.

"For all the power you seek," Daemonis said, "you're a weak woman. Tell His Majesty the king the truth."

"What business do you discuss? Who is this man? Why is he here with you?" Lowell asked, stepping toward her.

"Lowell," Cynara attempted, swallowing, having no option but to reveal a partial truth. "This is the fallen angel, Daemonis. He has helped me achieve a goal."

Lowell was too curious. Her son shouldn't be here. His brow pinched as he studied Daemonis. "This man is helping you achieve a goal— What goal have you achieved, Mum? It looks ugly to me."

"Power," Cynara murmured, glancing at Odin, and wondering herself if the reward was worth the price.

"Power." Lowell repeated. "And this man on the ground, what of him? It seems like he's trapped in some sort of triangle. Did you place him there? Have you stolen your power from him, too?"

Daemonis looked at his nails, massaging his fingers. "She has taken his enchantments for her own."

"Who is he?"

The soul on the ground moaned. "Odin."

"What did you say?" Lowell asked, stepping closer to the god. "Who did you say you were?"

"Odin, the god of war."

"No longer," Cynara said, snickering, smiling triumphantly. "Now I am the god, or rather a goddess, with all the godly powers you once held. You are no more than a mortal man."

"You don't know what you've stolen. I will always be the god of war. You can take what you think is supernatural power, but you can never rob me of my identity."

"And you, Daemonis," Lowell barked, scrutinizing the dark one. "Since you're not the one trapped by my mother's magic, would you mind telling me what's going on?"

"Lowell, unlike your mother, I see no reason to lie to you. There's a simple reason that I am here, and I don't have a problem answering you honestly."

"I'm waiting."

"I'm your father, and you're my son."

Cynara watched the changing expression on Lowell's face. The color drained from him as the shocking truth took hold. He staggered backward. "You jest. You lie. My father is the former King Rickard."

Daemonis approached Lowell calmly, shaking his head in acknowledgement of the truth. He placed his hand on Lowell's shoulder, but her son shrugged off his contact. "King Rickard is not your father. Search your soul, you know it's true. Your mother has never gained anything by honest means. Her hunger for power has always been excessive, even before you were born. I assure you, I do not lie."

"Is it true?" Lowell begged of his mother, the pain evident, the words rasping from his throat. He searched her expression for answers. "Did you lay with this man when you should have lain with my father? What have you agreed to this time?" Lowell barked, glaring at her. "What price have you paid to steal this god's power and harm him in your sarding scheme?"

She saw his face darken, like his true father's. "I'm sorry, Lowell." Tears sprang to her eyes. The liquid slipped to the ground, tainting the earth.

"Mum, answer my question. What have you done?"

"You will come with me now," Daemonis whispered. "I have a new kingdom for you to rule. Bid your mother goodbye."

"Was this your plan for power, Mum, to gamble away your only son? To root me toward a kingdom I do not want?"

"Lowell," Cynara cried out, racing to him, attempting to hold him in her arms. "I did not know."

He shoved her away, his action rejecting her in the cruelest manner. He glowered at her with disgust. "I won't go with you," Lowell growled, turning away from the devil. "My kingdom is here. My home is here. Take this woman and her evil ways instead."

"You will go. You have no choice but to go with me."

Lowell gawked at his father and scrutinized his mother one final time. In that moment, she felt his acute pain, a pain so wretched it squeezed her decrepit heart. And then she watched Daemonis gloat at her with a winning, knowing expression. He touched Lowell's back, and together, they vanished.

She collapsed to her knees. She pelted the earth with her hands. A scream of anguish tore from her lungs, thundering in the ether.

One power reached; but a powerful legacy stolen away.

"I'll save you, Lowell," she cried, tears slipping down her face. "Do not fear. I'll find you!"

When Odin moaned on the ground, Cynara refocused her attention, realizing she had to complete her work. She gathered the orb from the saddlebag and held it in the palms of her hands, mindless of tears bleeding from her eyes. She didn't consider Father Clement's warning, not to open the orb. Even with the loss of her son, she didn't mitigate the trial that might come to pass *if* the orb was opened.

"Light," she whispered, and a brilliant silver hue illuminated the orb.

"Open to my desire," she commanded, and the orb broke apart into two halves.

She considered Odin while walking toward him. The man appeared pitiful, dejected and downtrodden. She dismissed his sorrow, holding the two halves to the night sky.

"Prepare a new path for a mortal soul, a god no more. *Transform!*"

A flash of light, a breath of wind, and Odin was delivered inside the crystal orb. Cynara stared at his trapped essence, uncaring, unfeeling as she placed both sides of the orb back together.

Sleipnir tore into the sky, dashing away.

Sighing, she retrieved the saddlebag and placed the orb inside its folds. Seeing Odin's magical spear, Gungnir, lying on the ground, she recovered the weapon and reflected on the power pulsating in her hands, and how she might use it. Climbing onto Maisie's back, she scrutinized the forest, soon waving her hand over the land. With her new powers, she returned the vale to its former foliage, erasing most, but not all, of the evidence of her night's work. A single drop of blood clung to a flower's petal.

As Cynara rode back to the castle, it didn't take long for her tears to cease. Her sadness was replaced with anger; and a stony expression emerged. Her son was gone. His father had stolen him, but no one need know the truth.

She exited the glen, brooding over the loss while traveling the well-trodden pathway inside the king's forest. Nearing the forest's edge, she noticed a length of rope tied to a tall oak tree. It had not been there when she had passed this way before. She paused, considering. *Lowell,* she cried, her voice breaking.

King Lowell was gone.

In light of this certainty, she had no idea what she'd reveal to the Privy Council. Maybe, she mused, the time had come for *the Ebony Queen* to take her rightful place as ruler.

A swish of wind swirled above her head. In her grief and infuriation, she didn't notice the raven flying high above her, its wings flapping soundlessly, stalking her path. The attack happened without mercy. The black bird flew in front of her, jabbing at her face, the hard, black beak diving into the socket of her left eye.

Cynara screamed, a blood-curdling misery that pierced

the quiet of the forest lair. And although she fought with her hands, trying to fend off the attack, the bird plucked out her eye and then flew away, stealthily returning to the night.

"Aah!" Cynara bawled, moaning, tumbling from the horse to the ground, writhing in pain, her hands covering her eyes.

She didn't know how long she lay on the woodland floor with her mind wandering and the blood seeping between her fingers. If not for the vibration pounding along the trail, she might have succumbed to unconsciousness. Squinting, she tried to see who came this way, but with her sight swimming with red, she couldn't tell who approached.

"Who goes there?" she sniveled, weeping. "Who dares to come this way?"

"Your Majesty," a man beckoned, jumping down from his horse, hurrying to where she lay. He knelt beside her before too long. "What has happened to you?"

"Keldan," Cynara moaned, recognizing his voice. "Why have you come? I gave you strict orders."

"Aye," he replied, his hands grasping her head. "You're hurt. You're bleeding. What's happened, Ma'am? Did a branch catch your face? Let me see the wound. Let me see if I can help."

"He took it," she cried, permitting Keldan to remove her shaking hands from her face.

"Oh no," Keldan said, his tone serious. "Your eye is gone."

"I know that, you fool!" she bellowed, raging.

"Don't worry, Your Majesty, I'll help you."

Cynara heard the sound of cloth rending. She didn't resist his assistance as he wrapped soft fabric around her head, binding it tight to her temples. Strong, he soon grasped her arms and pulled her nearer to his chest. She rested there, slumping against him, weeping.

"I'm taking you to the castle."

"Keldan," she murmured, gaining a new awareness of the ages. It weakened her. "Why did you come here? I warned you not to…"

"I heard your cries. They were fierce. I knew no one else would enter the king's forest to see what ailed thee. I am here for that reason."

Assuming he spoke the truth, she reclined to his chest while he carried her to his horse. "Master Keldan," Cynara wailed, "I don't know what to say."

"Your Majesty," Keldan said with a grimace, "a queen's appreciation of her subject acting against your wishes to offer my aid will suffice."

Chapter Thirty-Three

PRINCESS ROSE

The waves rolled to shore, lapping against the rocks and streaming across the shoreline. Exhausted, Rose waded through the surf, suffering water higher than her waist. She progressed closer to the shoreline, struggling to reach safety. Her kirtle, or what was left of it, trailed behind. The surf wrenched at her equilibrium and she fell, collapsing against sand and seawater.

She rose upward onto her knees and saw the tree line in the distance. There was little time to reflect on the connective feeling of joy as a wave breached the shoreline and crashed against her, tackling her strength. The backward motion of the wave streamed against her back and rolled her back into the ocean. Determined, she got back on her feet and strode through the current, suffering the ocean's ripping tide, but soon crawling across the shoreline to collapse on a sandy beach.

"I'm alive—" she whispered, panting, dragging for a

breath, emotion lodged at the base of her throat. The realization that she had survived the worst, minded her attention.

The storm had passed, and she didn't know why or how it had ended, though she had been grateful when the seas had calmed. The swimming effort, to survive, had left her weak. She had no strength, no energy to lift her head. Thirsty, she lay on the sand, her fingers swollen, touching tiny granules, while cold ocean water lapped against her toes.

Grateful for her life, she sobbed with relief. Wisps of air and saltwater choked from her lungs.

Where was Edwin?

Rose attempted to rise. She tried to lift her head from the embankment, but slumped against the sand. Pivoting onto her buttocks, she raised her hand, shielding her eyesight from the sun's oppressive glare. She lay there against the sand, unseeing, studying diamonds radiating above oceanic water, gathering her strength.

After a time, she rose upward to a sitting position and scanned the shoreline, searching for the captain. True to his word, Edwin had fought rough seas bravely, and in doing so, he had saved her life.

When she saw him lying near, she stifled a cry, realizing she wasn't alone. He opened his eyes and gazed at her in a meaningfully way, but said not a word. Perhaps he was as weak as she.

"Edwin," she said, crawling toward him, soon grasping his hand. "I'm not a witch, Edwin Perrow," she said, her voice breaking, "I'm not a witch."

He embraced her cheek. "I know."

"After all I have caused you to suffer, how can you trust me?"

"No visions as of late, *Bella Rosa*? Maybe you buried them at sea."

"You saved my life."

"You gave me a reason to save my own."

Edwin's burnt face and chalky countenance communicated a vital message. Rose was grateful for his sacrifice, happier still for a nickname. Yet, his honest expression filled her with wonder, more so than relief. Though it seemed her visions were at an end, this moment she shared with Edwin Perrow? She'd recall it for the rest of her life.

Thank you for reading *The Ebony Queen*.

IF YOU ENJOYED book two of A Reign of Blood and Magic, your honest opinion of this fantasy novel matters to this author. Please review this book on your favorite book site, review site, blog, or your own social media properties, and share your opinion with other readers.

A sincere *thank you* for taking the time to write a review!

Afterword

I knew the royal title of Her Majesty would not be enough for Cynara from the initial imagineering of the novel, *The Ebony Queen.* A queen mother may have felt a little lost when her son took the throne, which inspired a greater ambition. A queen desired more than royal life. To assist her ardent desires through magic and conjuring spells, I researched how a supernatural event could assist her goals.

And bam! The image of a triangle, which incorporated a three-ringed circle, came to my mind.

When I began researching spells; especially revenge spells, my research led me to *The Triangle of Solomon*, a triangle of conjuration. I was astonished to find an image in keeping with my imagination, and even a video, of people practicing this form of magic. I struggled with exploring the theory of invocation further, as if this medium is a form of evil, I don't welcome such practices into my life, nor do I wish to deliver such ideas into the minds of my readers.

Although this novel is a work of fiction, characters have a

will of their own. I found myself imagining how Cynara might achieve her goals. The conjuring scene was the first chapter I wrote, but other true to life events during the writing of this book inspired the narrative, too.

Cecil the Lion was murdered for sport in Zimbabwe. This impacted my story in the form of a human hunt. We are all Cecil the Lion; we should be careful with our strength, or future generations of majestic animals could be compromised, perhaps becoming extinct.

The lunar eclipse or blood moon of September 27, 2015, was an interest as well. In medieval times, the people feared such happenings and believed the world might come to an end. In *The Ebony Queen*, I thought it would be fun on such a night to play with magic! And so I did, giving the queen mother the perfect evening to practice her sorcery.

What comes next? The Immortal Blood is nearing completion. The next volume is dark, twisty, and perhaps creepy, too. I can't wait to share it with you!

Contact Abby Lane

If you would like to learn more about Abby or her novels, visit her website at abby-lane.com. Here you can read excerpts from her books, linked reviews, blog posts, as well as discovering her professional affiliations and accreditation.

Abby enjoys hearing from her readers. If you'd like to contact the author, send her a message at: abby@abby-lane.com.

FOLLOW ABBY ON SOCIAL MEDIA

facebook.com/abbylane.author

instagram.com/authorabbylane

amazon.com/author/abbylane

bookbub.com/profile/abby-lane

goodreads.com/abbylane

A Reign of Blood and Magic
A Medieval Romantasy
The Immortal Blood, Book 3

**An Orb opened after an act of sorcery.
A Kingdom impregnated by a single drop of blood.
The Art of War is the only grand strategy.**

When an orb opens after an act of sorcery, an immortal infiltrates the kingdom of Velez through a single drop of blood. The blood impregnates the animal yolk, the cocoon of an undead king and a crippled queen, seeding new life and new worries.

The kingdom is threatened, but as lords' scheme and privy councillors take power for their own; *unknowingly*, the king's forest yields new life while an undead king escapes the mortar that has held him, giving rise to a mind that isn't his own. The immortal desires retribution from the god who stole his former life, and he'll use a woman, *the Ebony Queen*, to exact his revenge.

How might the birth of a new age affect the kingdom, the royal family, or a former queen who has kept a prince's life secret from everyone? With the assistance of a witch's sorcery, will the Art of War seed the ultimate strategy, permitting an immortal god to live again.

About the Author

The author of several novels in genre fiction, ABBY LANE admires the many ways myths, fairy tales, and fantasy connect us to our inner child. She credits Disney's *Sleeping Beauty* and George R.R. Martin's *Song of Ice and Fire*, with inspiring her love of storytelling. She appreciates the corridors of medieval history and in particular the Tudor period. She has visited the United Kingdom, touring many castles in her pursuit of story, having a special affinity for Anne Boleyn and King Henry's court. Abby shares her life with her husband and adores her adult children, including two special grand pups named Bella and Arya. When she isn't at her home in Calgary, she's admiring the ocean at her cottage in Maple Bay.